Universally Screwed

Thrown across the Universe,
deeply confused,
looking for the bathroom.

By Mike Alread

www.MikeAlread.com

Dedicated to the memories of
Douglas Adams and Terry Pratchet,
and written with the hope that it will
brighten someone's day.

Line 1: NO AI TRAINING.

The Author believes that the utilization of AI to generate literary works is like finding that someone has jammed a giant cockroach covered in flesh-eating bacteria into a tub of ice cream, and then offered the ice cream for public consumption. Thus, I must state the following:

The Author reserves all rights. No permission is implied or given for this Work, or any part thereof, to be utilized in the training of any artificial intelligence technologies. Without limitation, any technologies, electronic, software related or otherwise, that have, or could reasonably be expected to gain, the capacity to generate works in any style or genre, in any way related to, or not related to, this style and genre of this Work, are included within this, unless express permission is provided by the Author. This will not be given. This is my ice cream, devoid of literary necrotic foulness and associated insect.

No publishers, platforms or companies or people called Gerald, Susan or Bertie or in fact any persons, publishers, platforms, companies or others, including, but not limited to, those whose naming or identification contain any letters, numbers or, in fact, any written or spoken characters whatsoever, may sublicense to any others to, in any manner, train artificial intelligence technologies to generate text or do anything else with the artificial intelligence that the Author has the capacity to withhold permission for, without first gaining the express and specific permission of the Author, which you are unlikely to get anyway. So, take your giant cockroach infested, flesh-eating ice cream and bugger off.

If, however, you believe that your artificial intelligence company is so much of a nameless faceless corporation that it avoids the above definition, rest assured that I have a name for it, thus subjecting it once more to the constraints outlined. You may or may not agree with the name.

Line 2: GOTO line 1

Main Characters

Sebastian - A pizza delivery driver from the South of England.

Melissa - Sebastian's neighbor when he was a child.

Artun - Sub-Commander of the Callaxian Guard.

Ertic - Head of Security for the Veltrid Sector base.

Triven - First in Command of the Veltrid Sector base.

Sardok - Second in Command of the Veltrid Sector base.

Sh'ockley - Veltrid Sector Communications Officer.

Garrat - Chief Engineer and advisor to the Emperor.

The Emperor - Chief Commander of the Empire and the Military Union of Planets.

Selim - Doctor stationed on the Veltrid Sector base.

Fludge - A General on the home planet Callaxia.

The Pyramid - A paperweight with an unusual backstory.

The Commanders of the Union - A group of seven Commanders who control the seven different branches of the Military Union.

Bernice and Paul - who appear but briefly before leaving to chase their dreams.

The ranking badges on the Callaxian uniform sash

Badge	Rank		Badge	Rank
|	Private		▭	Second Officer
||	Corporal		▭ over o	First Officer
|||	Sergeant		▭ over oo	General
o	Third Lieutenant		▭ over ooo	Chief General
oo	Second Lieutenant		▭ over oooo	Vice Commander
ooo	Lieutenant		▤	Commander
oooo	Sub-Commander			

Identification colors used in the Union:

Intelligence - Purple

Science and Research - Blue

Security - Black

Logistics and Communications - Yellow

Transportation - Horrific Puce. This is the color worn by the Chief Commander of Transportation. Non-pilots within Transportation are the only others who would wear it, the rest of Transportation choosing to wear the Pilot green color instead. The non-pilots that wear this diabolical color tend to have a genetic mutation that means they can only see in shades of Frank. Frank is a color not unlike the odd brown colour in an old photograph, although, to be fair, it is not particularly like it either. Horrific puce was 'suggested' by the Chief Commander of Troops and Strategy after he caught the Chief Commander of Transportation attempting to pass suggestive notes to his niece. It was either that or he promised to burn the Empire to the ground, starting with Transportation. The color itself had taken five years to develop. It was created for use in prisoner interrogation at a cost that would shame the GDP of a small planet. It was effective too. Prisoners were made to sit in front of a large, horrific puce colored square and the ones who didn't want to go mad quickly parted with their secrets, just to escape being bathed in its horror.

Pilots - Green. Pilots are officially a part of the Transportation arm but are able to escape the designated horrific puce color. This is essential as prolonged exposure may damage the eyes that they normally use when flying.

Engineering - Orange

Troops and Strategy - Red

On an interesting note, members of the Transportation group, with the exception of pilots, are the least likely of the service members of the Union to be asked on a date. This is because of how they choose to dress, as they only see things in shades of Frank. The last time someone from Transportation tried to go on a date, they were misidentified as a lesser quilted mimic, promptly shot in the buttocks with a tranquilizing dart and then left in a box at the city zoo. The Effermian milk cargo that they were meant to deliver, went rancid, mutated and eventually ate its way through the transport ship. The Transportation Officer was finally located when officials held a ceremony to put a rancid Effermian milk creature into a zoo enclosure and found it was already occupied by a lesser quilted mimic with low-level security clearance

Prelude

The Universe is full of wonder. It's not its fault. It's just so big that it has trouble getting rid of all that wonder before more wonder appears.

It had been toying with the idea of giving up entirely, turning out the lights and going on holiday, possibly visiting another dimension, or taking a cruise.

Then irony came along, and the Universe thought it might just give it another go.

The Universe is notably happier these days, but those within it seem a tad more confused than they had previously been. Some of the inhabitants had started to notice that any and all progress only seemed to further increase their confusion.

This also made the Universe happy, as it was able to both crush wonder and generally confuse its inhabitants with impunity while allowing its coherence to gradually dwindle.

Excerpt from: The History of the Universe by renowned philosopher Stragnamarus Garbtin.

Chapter 1

Bernice fell backward into the bush. Spider webs and leaves covered her hair and summer dress, as somehow a small twig ended up hooking her by the nose. Paul, for his part, fell rather more sideways into a softer bush, with an en–suite puddle and some snails, while mud squelched up between his fingers.

This was not how either of them had imagined their first kiss.

They sat for a while, each momentarily lost in their thoughts, separated only by a bench. Paul wiped some of the dank, wet fur from his lips, which left him with a thin mud mustache.

Ever the optimist, he offered Bernice a mint after taking one himself, but it seemed as though the moment had passed.

This is not the story of Paul and Bernice, their first kiss, or their future life together. This is not the story of Paul's meteoric rise in the cut–throat world of mattress protection, or of Bernice and her boutique business selling birthday cards for cats.

This is a story of a set of events, of which this is one, that had been set in motion some forty-two minutes earlier in a military outpost on a distant moon, somewhere in the vicinity of Rigel B.

Humans know nothing of Rigel B, let alone the rest of the galaxy. They have, over time, created stories to help them make sense of their place in the Universe, using these as techniques for handing down what passes for wisdom on this planet from one generation to the next.

The people on Earth who study the development of intelligent life believe that the human species is unique in this.

The aliens in the Universe who study the development of intelligent life and have even heard of Earth believe that humans are unique for being so isolated that they actually believe that they are unique in this.

But they would rather not give the humans any credit.

Those same aliens generally view humans as a group of people who stand facing a corner in a crowded room, with their eyes shut and their fingers in their ears, while maintaining that the room is empty because they can't see anybody.

That is not to say that the Universe is otherwise full of wisdom or enlightened life forms.

'It has been said that if you could gather up all the wisdom in the Universe and share it equally between all its inhabitants, then you would have a Universe populated by uniform stupidity. To show how dangerous that could be, if you were to do the same not with wisdom, but with kindness, then the Universe would be populated solely by politicians, and I am currently unable to locate an exit.'

Excerpt from: *Musings of the Mad: Erklefingen Flrat.*

On Earth, no mention is made of the tens of thousands of inhabited worlds within its home galaxy. The glorious marketplaces, the bizarre bazaars, the towering monuments to the hopes and dreams of a million different races and empires.

From the Duckpeople of Ventroth, who went extinct after the most irresponsible ceasefire in history was negotiated, to the Snakepeople of Ventroth 2, with whom the ceasefire had been negotiated and who had become rather fatter as a result of it, to the politicians who negotiated the ceasefire and then claimed they needed to be more involved with the running of the Universe, so that they could help to avoid the type of situations that they themselves are likely to create.

The Universe is indeed ripe with wonder.

Plump, juicy, wonder.

For the most part, of course, people in the Universe choose to leave Earth alone. This isn't the result of some prime directive, but rather because, if they wanted to, aliens could download all the television shows from space.

But nobody does.

Forty-two minutes ago.

In a far and distant corner of the galaxy, in the vicinity of Rigel B, a large rocky moon the size of a planet was just minding its own business as it quietly orbited the outermost gas giant of a majestic binary system. This moon is home to a massive military response bunker that is also minding its own business. Those within the bunker, however, had been on high alert for the past five years and were thus not minding their own business at all.

Sardok, the Second Officer of the Veltrid Sector Command, often referred to as Number Two, sat in the command room of the bunker. He was a small–ish, green–ish sort–of–a fellow. Slightly larger around the middle than he would have chosen to be, but always a pleasant chap. He had grey hair, green skin, and a pair of magnificent grey eyebrows that looked like sophisticated caterpillars sitting above intelligent blue eyes.

His uniform was regulation dark trousers and a light-yellow shirt with a red band that went from the rear center of his shirt up and over his right shoulder and back down to the center of the shirt at the front. It looked a little like a sash that could be draped across an award–winning tractor or a supermodel. A five-inch-thick red band wrapped around his waist.

The sash had the effect of hiding the slight bulge where he

kept his non regulation snacks, which he ate while pretending to look thoughtful. Across his chest, on the sash, was a horizontal bar that was half yellow, reflecting his time in logistics and half red from his experience with the troops.

On the table next to him, atop a couple of papers, was a small, cobalt blue, metallic pyramid, about one inch tall, that was being used as a paperweight.

Nobody had ever thought to ask when, or how, it arrived there, or why it just sat on the table being carefully overlooked. Instead, people just went about their business, carefully overlooking it.

This was unfortunate as it was exactly the sort of thing that a base full of people on high alert, and in a heightened, agitated state, should have noticed.

It was the type of thing that they should have been looking for.

The pyramid is an entropy engine, a living intelligence of almost unimaginable power and the only one of its kind ever created. It was all that remained of a civilization so old that nobody remembers their name. Their planet long ago laid waste through the passage of time.

A few hundred years ago, the pyramid was found by the Flingewatts. The Flingewatts were an isolationist culture, happily staying on their home planet, avoiding others, and just taking up space in the Universe. Then the pyramid arrived, and, about a month later, their civilization ceased to exist.

Their sudden disappearance created confusion and fear that rippled outwards among the nearby species and cultures.

It wasn't as though the Flingewatts had left a note saying: 'going out for a quick drink,' or 'popped off to Sirius for a few months.'

The rest of the Universe woke up one morning, and the whole planet on which the civilization had lived, the civilization, all its dinner plates, and space stations had all vanished.

The planet wasn't hiding behind the sun or a nearby nebula cluster.

It wasn't in the bath or putting on a cup of tea.

It had vanished with no forwarding address.

The absence of the Flingewatt home planet, Regelmass 9, was particularly confusing for the millions of sentient attack robots intent on conquering and destroying the Flingewatts. They turned up just in time to find the party canceled and the punch bowl empty.

To avoid any more fear and panic, the galactic council eventually put down some traffic cones and left a note saying that the work would be finished in a few hundred years, and the robots went on their way.

The pyramid drifted through space for centuries before finally arriving at the base. And now it was being used as a paperweight.

It had been watching the events unfold. It was waiting.

The officers of the Veltrid Sector Command Post moved busily about the large room, each wearing the regulation light-yellow uniform adorned with a red sash and thick red band around their waist. They had markings on their sash showing rank and expertise.

Near the rear of the room, full of workstations and people, was the seating for the First Officer and the Second Officer of the Veltrid Sector Command, on two very comfortable looking chairs. Stretched out in front of them, on six levels of a descending gradient were rows of desks, twenty across, finishing at a gently curved wall at the front of the room. The surface of each desk doubled as a small viewscreen that could input and display information and a stool sat in front of each desk. Sitting on the large, curved wall, at the front of the room, was a large viewscreen, forty feet across and ten feet high.

Sardok sat in his comfortable chair, a small table extended from the right arm of the chair that held the pyramid. He tilted his head slightly as he looked at it. As the lights bounced off the surface, they created an iridescence that always seemed to cheer him up.

The little pyramid tilted its head back. As it was a pyramid though, nobody noticed.

It liked its place in the room. It had a nice view and a beautiful breeze at all times of the day. It almost felt sad that it was due to destroy the base at any time now.

It just had to wait a little longer.

Triven was the First Officer in Command of the Veltrid Sector, often referred to as Number One. He sat in his comfortable chair to the left side of the Second Officer and a little farther back. Like many Callaxians, Triven had grey hair and green skin. His uniform was identical to the Second Officer's, except on his sash was a solid green horizontal line with a small round green circle beneath it, the color hinting that he had been a pilot. Triven ran the base and the sector like a tight ship, if the ship was wrapped in duct tape, dressed in a corset, and set in concrete.

He was subtle and adaptable in much the same way as an industry standard house brick and was liked by the crew in the way a dose of the clap would be enjoyed by a sailor.

Comparing Triven and Sardok was like comparing an attack dog and a gerbil.

In management styles, the difference between the two was like the difference between that which is possessed of and that which is possessed by.

Sardok seemed possessed of a convivial and jovial disposition and was generally well-liked by the crew.

Triven was more possessed by the spirit of an emotionally disturbed, aggressive, hyperactive weasel.

One that held a grudge and unpaid student debt.

In fact, the First Officer of the Veltrid Sector Command was only really tolerated, as he was very good at his job.

Sardok sat back and smiled at the pyramid.

The pyramid smiled back.

But, being a pyramid, nobody noticed.

The Second Officer rested his hand on it.

"You know," he muttered quietly to himself, "this just might work."

At this, the pyramid grinned and let out a sigh. It was finally time. It willed a few minor changes into existence, and, very briefly, the entropy of the entire Universe dipped. All the lights of a trillion galaxies flickered, and three things happened at different points in the Universe.

In a small line of code, in possibly the most complicated software ever to exist, a qubit changed its setting to become self-referencing.

In a tiny hyper–advanced supercomputer in a dog's collar, a homing circuit spontaneously repaired when a deactivated nanite fell across the gap that it had itself created.

In a small pizzeria in a university town, in the South of England, a coffee machine exploded.

And as suddenly as it happened, the lights came back on, and nobody noticed except a small sentient pyramid.

A surprised–looking officer briefly worried his paperweight may have sighed, but then dismissed the notion entirely.

Of course, the Universe also noticed, but just thought it had a mild case of irony.

Triven glared over at Sardok, who was too busy looking thoughtful to notice.

He glared at the pyramid instead.

This time, the pyramid grinned back.

But, being a pyramid, nobody noticed.

The Communications Officer, Second Lieutenant Sh'ockley, sat at her station. She was a tall–ish, blue–ish woman with an air of sophistication. Her hair was tied back in a way that made her look like she was ready for a board meeting. The two dots of a Second Lieutenant adorned her sash.

A little red light started to flash on her desk.

She looked at it.

It had not flashed before.

She tapped it.

It kept flashing.

She tapped it again.

It started beeping.

She quickly checked the screen in front of her, poked the light once more, rather tentatively, and turned to Triven. "Number One, we've located Sub-Commander Ertic." she said urgently.

Triven stood up quickly from his rather large and comfortable chair, and rushed over to the console, carefully observing the screen.

"Should we open a transport corridor, Sir?" the Second Officer asked, leaning forward in his chair.

"It'll take a lot of reserve power. We'll be working under minimal reserves. The base will be vulnerable." Triven responded, weighing his options. If he could get the Sub-Commander back, he'd be the only person who'd retrieved anybody from the Diplomatic Gateway program. He paused and looked around the room at the expectant faces, set his jaw, and decided.

"Have you found a suitable location?" he asked.

He looked to the Transport Officer, Trom, who was intently studying the readouts on his viewscreen. He was a blue individual, five and a half feet tall, with the optimism of a morning DJ and the haircut of a camel.

Trom turned to him and nodded, his camel-fringe flouncing gently. "Yes, Sir."

"Prepare to generate a transport corridor. Transmit the coordinates to the Sub-Commander's tracker and begin the opening procedure immediately."

"Will he have enough time?" Second Lieutenant Sh'ockley asked, her keen eyes watching him.

"It's all we can give him." Triven said grimly, a little irritated that his directive had been questioned, "If the circuit goes down again, we lose him for good."

Chapter 2

There's a muddy, wet planet out there in the galaxy. A backward place. It is home to a race of creatures who are absolutely convinced that they are enlightened, despite all evidence to the contrary.

In fact, denial of any evidence that doesn't agree with them seems to be a staple of their existence.

They believe that one day, they will spread throughout the galaxy, colonizing it, and elevating their enlightenment further. They hope to help other worlds to reach their same height of culture. However, having invented the internet and AI, those in charge have now managed to turn their entire population into addicts of short videos, opinion pieces, and games that allow them to match pieces of fruit while simultaneously monetizing them.

The people in charge have little incentive to let them leave the planet to spread anything, at least until they've found a way to monetize it.

Those in the Universe who are aware of them suspect the entire species will be lucky to survive past next Tuesday and deeply, deeply hope that they will not expand, spreading whatever it is they have to the rest of the Universe.

At least not until there's a cure for it.

The Sub-Commander of the Callaxian Guard was on this planet at this very time, and he was running for all his life was worth. He was running as fast as his little legs could carry him.

Ertic had not always been a dog. He had chosen the disguise to help him blend in and observe people after he had endured a variety of difficulties with social interactions. It was to be a vantage point from which he could better observe and study humans to understand their capabilities.

He had initially tried to disguise himself as a human, as the Callaxians were so similar in shape, but felt he didn't look quite right. The idea of being almost himself, but just not green, seemed a little too alien.

He found there were no food printers, clothes printers, or general things you would expect in any civilized environment. However, Ertic had a trick up his sleeve. Literally, in this case, he had a morphing circuit on his tracker. Rather than just altering perception, it was able to alter the physiology of its wearer, enabling him to take on the disguise of any life form he chose and being as motivated as he was, this was a trick he was ready to use, despite the obvious dangers.

Shortly after arriving on Earth, he made his first miscalculation.

He had quickly learned that he would need money to survive on Earth. Ertic then overheard a media broadcast that declared people could make money as drug mules and that they were being identified by customs agents.

He thus reasoned that a good way to make money would be to hide out at the customs counter of a local airport and disguise himself as a mule.

Ertic had carefully approached a busy local airport and slipped past the guards. After some maneuvering, he positioned himself in the customs checking area, standing behind a team of five customs agents who were having their morning coffee.

It was then, and with a great deal of optimism and self-confidence, that he turned himself into a mule. After all, he was a motivated member of the Callaxian Guard, ready to work hard and make the money needed to survive on this fledgling planet.

He stood behind the customs guards for a little while, waiting to be noticed. Sadly, they seemed blissfully unaware of his existence, merely choosing to infer that 'someone,' whom they chose not to identify, was smelling a little dungy today.

After a short period, Ertic grew impatient.

He maneuvered himself until he was just behind the two closest to him. They were standing together, so Ertic placed his muzzle within inches of their ears and brayed as loud as he could.

This was a shock to the customs officers, whose main expertise was lacking in the equine department and who had been eyeing some of their favorite Wednesday donuts on the table.

They were quite unprepared for a six–foot–tall braying mule fully equipped with mule breath and very convincing fleas.

One officer collapsed on the floor, one threw his coffee across the room, and two others screamed. The last one, who was a far more experienced customs official, was also as deaf as a post and didn't hear the mule behind him. When he reached for a donut, he was genuinely pleased by the variety still available.

Ertic the mule sat there, awaiting his financial reward.

Thankfully, they had an x–ray machine to check for contraband, and thus, both the customs agents and Ertic remained unaffected by the town's great shoulder length rubber glove shortage.

The customs staff were often referred to by the other airport staff as the suppository superheroes or the colorectal avengers due to the nature of their curiosity. However, in this case, they were able to use their x–ray machine to ensure that the mule was not concealing anything within its person.

They knew there was no need, as the mule had clearly not come in on a plane, they didn't even think that it was concealing anything, but they wanted to check it anyway. They may never have a chance to do something like this again.

They had purchased an extra-large x-ray machine the previous year and they wanted to see if it could actually handle a mule. This was their first chance to truly test its capabilities. This job was a passion for many of them and they had to struggle to contain their excitement as they loaded the mule onto the machine that they had nicknamed Fat-Mantucket.

Even though the x-ray came up empty, there were many cheers heard and many high fives were passed around as the images came onto the screen.

Once the head office got wind of it, they equipped Ertic, that same afternoon, with a cute little hat and financed a professional photographer to get some photos for the in–house customs magazine edition titled 'smuggle, snuggle and struggle.'

Eventually, after much photography and a newspaper article, which included the x-ray images, they sent him to the city zoo.

The zoo was comfortable, and he enjoyed the food and attention. It also afforded him some time to study humans, but he could feel a chill in the air, and he was concerned that it would begin to turn colder.

Ertic decided to move on from the zoo, to increase his exposure to Earth's culture and technology, but first he needed the timing to be right.

At the end of the week, he heard a weather report from a phone as someone passed by his enclosure. He had been resting comfortably on his straw bunk, gently scratching his back on the floor. He heard the news that a storm was coming, and it was going to be unusual and nice, it seemed like the timing was perfect. According to the report, it was going to be eerily similar to the ones that they sometimes had in North America.

That evening, he gathered the clothing that he had been carefully amassing from unsuspecting visitors in the days since he had arrived.

The visitors to the zoo would look in his stall, and, as they did so, he would present his back to be rubbed. As they rubbed his back, he would carefully thrust his snout through a small gap in the fence to grab any clothing that was hanging out of their bags. The zoo was quite close to a swimming pool, so this was often a swimming costume or some sunglasses. He had managed to do this for the most part without being noticed. In fact, it had only gone wrong once when he had grabbed someone's shorts as they were wearing them. But after a few hard tugs and a scream, he had those too.

This was when the staff came over to block up the hole, but it didn't matter. He was ready.

Later in the evening, after the zoo had closed and the staff and visitors had gone home, he transformed into a human form once more. He equipped himself with clothing, jumped over the fence, and left, taking with him a full-size hammock that he had grabbed from the chinchilla enclosure.

It was over the next day that he realized that he was not as attuned to human subtleties as he believed.

Ertic had experienced quite a lot of nice weather on his travels about the sector and was quite excited by the prospect of finally having some nice weather on Earth to compare his experience to, especially as he could feel the temperature starting to drop.

In fact, according to the report, the coming storm was going to be so nice that there were likely to be some power outages. The emergency crews would also be on standby, although he wasn't entirely sure why. He had thought that they might be sunbathing, and that was why they could be on standby.

He set up the hammock between two trees in a park. It had started to feel pretty chilly, but, having faith that the Earthers had at least mastered basic weather control, he stripped to his bathing costume, jumped on his hammock and waited for the nice weather to hit. He even put on a summer hat that he had found that he thought made him look authoritative, yet friendly.

Over the next seven hours, he grew far more aware of the limitations of his translation circuitry and human linguistic structure. Although, to be fair, people on Earth could really communicate more clearly.

Ertic discovered that there really is no storm that is 'particularly nice'. In fact, there are very few that are even remotely 'nice'.

On that day, there was no nice storm at all, and he spent a great deal of time wondering why the nice storm was canceled for an ice storm instead. The entire episode came as somewhat of a surprise to an alien in a bathing suit, stretched out on a hammock in a park.

After seven hours, so much ice caked everything, including himself, that the weight of it had bent over the surrounding trees. This effect was so complete that he was now shielded from the very sun that he needed to melt it.

It took three days for the ice to melt enough so that he could free himself from the hammock, and another four hours to fully extricate his thong.

That was also the last time he had worn his summer hat.

As he finished the process of defrosting in the sun, he sat himself on a rock with a good view of the park and studied the humans' behavior. He watched in the distance as many of them arrived with small, furry, four-legged creatures. He watched the care with which they treated them and the way in which those little creatures seemed able to disarm the humans of their suspicion.

Thus, it was after that debacle that Ertic used the morphing circuit to turn himself into a dog. A fluffy one that looked as though a poodle had been cross bred with a duster. He travelled about the area to see how humans interacted and it gave him a chance to study them up close. He discovered, quite happily, that dogs often got free food, the good stuff, as well as a scratching of hard–to–reach areas. The fact that they enjoyed their own fur coat was an added bonus.

After the ice storm, it was perfect.

This disguise had been invaluable in his work, although living in a university town meant that drunk students were always giving him their food.

He was so preoccupied with studying the humans, their technologies and interactions that it took him three weeks to notice the morphing circuit had stopped working, as had the rest of his electronics. He was stuck as a dog.

Now, five months later, with the amount of free food he had been receiving, he was a little embarrassed by how much more challenging it had become to run.

For some reason, his circuit was working again, and he was getting directions for a transport corridor. He ran as fast as he could with the body type of an overweight hamster. There was an urgency to the rate at which the device on his collar vibrated that meant there was little time left.

He had to get to the corridor before his window of opportunity was gone.

Ertic ran as though his life depended on it. Because, if he didn't want to be stuck as a dog for the rest of his life, it did.

Chapter 3

Sebastian tossed the book down on the gray cloth of the passenger seat. The map light from above gave a gentle white glow over everything in the front of the car as the dark of the night contended with the yellow of the parking lot streetlamp outside. It had taken him a week to make it through the first ten pages. It was terrible. Lots of quantum mysticism. He'd even flipped ahead to see if the book improved–it didn't.

It seemed to get worse; imagine the goal, and the Universe will make it happen. If it doesn't happen, then you're not believing it enough; try harder and concentrate more. Garbage masquerading as a plan. The book itself was small, but sadly, so was the writing. It was as though he was being tormented by Lilliputians.

Sebastian was a clean-shaven man in his early twenties. He looked as much as you would imagine a successful artist or retired entrepreneur might look. This was unfortunate as he worked delivering pizzas. He was five foot eight inches tall, with scraggly hair and a friendly face. His near-neon green polo shirt advertised Alonzo's Pizza and generally failed to contrast favorably with anything else.

He sat back in the chair, his seat reclined and pushed as far back on its tracks as it would go. Sebastian stretched himself out and pulled out his phone to play his favorite game. It started up, and his fingers began to dance across the screen as he took control of a dog piloting a biplane. As his fingers glided rapidly, the plane rose, dove, dashed, and looped about the screen to avoid the enemy fire, oncoming birds, and, at random points, flying fish.

He glanced up at the clock on the dashboard; it was almost

midnight. There were five minutes left on his shift, and all he needed to do was run out the clock.

He glanced back at the game as a flying fish appeared and slapped the plane with its tail. The words 'Fatal Damage' appeared across the screen and then slowly faded out.

"Dammit," he sighed, sitting up and reaching over to take a sip of soda. He glared at the book again as it sat on the chair, mocking him. Alonso, the owner of the pizzeria, had made it essential reading for anyone to get a wage increase. He said it was good for motivation, but it was so bad he had no motivation to read it, and, at this rate, he'd have a wife, kids, and a different job before he got the wage rise.

He now wondered if that was the point.

Sebastian hit the start button on the game again. There were now four minutes left on his shift.

Four small, hopeful minutes.

Sebastian's phone rang. The number from the pizzeria lit up the screen and forced the game into the background as it crashed.

"Aw, man," he sighed and hung his head. He reached over, picked up the book, and put it back into his jacket pocket. Sebastian slowly got out of the car with a level of enthusiasm more often reserved for a free course of medicinal leeches as the phone continued to ring. He moved with reluctance towards the backdoor. The yellow streetlights filled the parking lot full of shadows. They concealed the rodents that were slowly making the area infamous. He continued forward at a snail's pace.

If he could wait out the next few minutes, he was home free.

The back door of the pizzeria was thrown open, and a short, stout figure with short black hair and a pinstriped apron, aggressively waved at him before disappearing back in.

"Three minutes," he muttered under his breath as he continued across the car park, picking up his pace.

Sebastian opened the staff door and entered the pizzeria. He stepped over the various traps that Alonso had left out to ensure that no rodents or bugs could ever enter and get through to the kitchen. It was like a trial by fire.

The traps were all empty.

Alonso thought that some of the local rodents had taken it upon themselves to work together, searching for weaknesses in the system. He even started to check identifiable marks on their fur to see if they returned after he had caught and released them. He believed that they did and that they had formed some sort of social hierarchy to beat his traps.

Alonso had toyed with the idea of killing the rats but had decided that it was much more humane to release them next to the upmarket restaurants in town.

Sebastian was beginning to become troubled by Alonso's sanity, or possible absence thereof.

He looked about for Alonso but couldn't see him.

"Last one done, I'm heading out," he called loudly.

A gruff-looking face popped up from behind the counter.

"Need you to do me a favor," he said, his pudgy cheeks lit up his demeanor like a tax inspector chewing a rock.

This made Sebastian a little nervous. Some months back, when he had just started, Alonso invited him over for a beer with that same look. When he got there, Alonso gave him a beer, a screwdriver, the instructions for an IKEA wardrobe, and a flat-pack wardrobe still in a box. Then Alonso had left for a walk.

The tools and instructions would have been helpful if the flat pack wardrobe in the box had actually been an IKEA wardrobe, and the beer would have been appreciated had it not already been drunk.

It would also have been helpful had it been Alonso's house or his beer.

"What do you need?" Sebastian asked with some reluctance.

"Last few to go out." He nodded towards a pile of four pizzas that were sitting at the end of the counter.

Sebastian looked at it and weighed up his options.

"Coffee machine exploded," Alonso said. "Pick one."

Sebastian was toying with the 'illness in the family' routine, but Alonso knew he didn't have that much family left, and he didn't know how many more times he could use it before Alonso would catch on.

"Where to?" he sighed.

Alonso nodded. "There's a big party over by the university. It's opposite that big building off the main road, on the right, the ugly one. It's the psychology department this time. Take some two–for–one vouchers with you when you go."

This cheered Sebastian up. He'd delivered to most of the buildings near the university campus, but this one had eluded him. It was where the members of the psychology department held their meetings. With this, he could have a full set, and more importantly, he might even get into the party.

"All right," he replied, quickly diving into a small room to change from his work uniform to the clothing he had arrived in. After a few minutes, he was done and emerged wearing a smart dark blue shirt and jeans, holding the book in his hand once more.

He grabbed a handful of vouchers and placed them in the book. Then he reached over and picked up his beige canvas jacket that was hanging on the wall, and put it on. He had bought the coat in a secondhand store, and it looked perfect. The angular but small collar and the mysterious epaulets that seemed to do nothing just made him happy. He slid the book with the vouchers into his inside coat pocket. There was no way he would give them out, but he didn't want Alonso to know that. It didn't seem realistic that a set of discount pizza coupons would enhance his image.

He walked over to the counter and scooped up the pizzas. He knew from experience that he had to leave soon before Alonso came up with any other tasks for him.

"See you tomorrow," he said as he headed towards the rear door.

"Count on it," came the reply.

As he left the building, he saw what appeared to be a couple of rats watching him.

He held the pizzas in his hands as he headed out towards the party with a spring in his step. It was late now, pushing past midnight, and this was his chance to finish the evening off with a party.

He came out from the rear of the pizzeria, back into the car park, and followed the exterior of the buildings round, through the alley onto the high street. He walked with purpose and optimism towards the university. There was no point taking the pizza–mobile. If things went well, there would be free beer and no way to drive.

Chapter 4

As he neared the university, he passed some revelers who had left the party to end the evening and return home early. Unfortunately, by their gait, it was clear that they had failed to consider the extra distance they would have to walk if they were heavily inebriated, moderately confused, and slightly lost.

They also traveled as the crow flies, when the crow has a serious head injury.

Those who noticed him as he passed by watched his pizzas like zombies seeing brains for the first time.

He retraced the path of the undead into a side street, the streetlamps lighting him and the departing zombies as he continued toward the psychology building.

There it stood in all its glory. Students and some of the locals referred to it as the White House. This was an ironic name, in part because it was pale blue.

The house itself was more than a little odd. It was recessed from the road by a concrete path that was sixteen feet long and held eight steps. Next to the path leading to the house, the grass was sparse but neat. There were pillars by the front door, at the end of the steps. They were originally intended to invoke images of Atlas holding the heavens on his shoulders, but now made it appear that Atlas had a sore back and might, in fact, require some smaller pillars to help.

The architect had been going through a psychedelic phase in his life and had decided that he should share this with the world. However, as he wanted to get paid for his work, he also had to hide this from the world.

The first thing he did was to take the golden ratio and throw it out of the nearest ill-shaped window. He decided he wanted to build the house in the same ratio as a pile of lumber he had seen that inspired him. It was forty feet high and twenty feet across, linking to the terraced houses on the right. It looked a lot like a shoebox on its side with a visor tacked on.

In ancient Greece, they carved columns to bulge a little in the middle so that they looked straight when viewed from a distance. The architect had taken a different approach with his columns. He believed that they should represent discordant music. So rather than slightly bulging in the center, they just gave you a feeling of impending disappointment.

Although the architect didn't realize it at the time, much of the reason for his inspiration could be traced back to some powerful hallucinogenic fungi growing on a wood pile in a hardware store, that he had come into contact with.

The effect it had on the store clerks was the reason the hardware store released an official statement saying family pets and grandparents would no longer be accepted as a down-payment on a new kitchen.

The overall effect of the house was one that you couldn't quite put your finger on. There was just something about it that was wrong. The effect pleased the architect immensely.

It was, however, known as one of the better buildings when it held a party, given the proximity to the arts department. Unfortunately, they were very selective about who they let in. They limited the list to anybody who walked by from the same university and people who were already students of the department. Not even free beer could guarantee entry, although it helped.

Sebastian walked up the concrete stairs towards the building with his pizzas held aloft, anticipating victory.

Previously, he had got into the other departments with a mixture of luck and cunning. Mostly, however, they had just let him in because he had pizza.

He smiled to himself.

Two pillars awkwardly framed the large red door at the end of the short run of stairs. Neither was quite standing straight, as though they were losing a fight with old Father Time and an octopus. The door opened, and a couple more revelers spilled out, accompanied by the doorman, a very large man stuffed into a large man's suit jacket.

Sebastian recognized him as he had ejected him from the pizzeria for taking his shirt off and dancing on a table while singing 'La Traviata' just before closing time.

He was large, gruff, and more than a little annoying, not least because he appeared not to know either the words or the tune, and his dancing lacked luster.

"Dammit," Sebastian muttered under his breath. There was still hope. He kept moving forward, desperate not to be recognized.

The doorman, which was not an inappropriate name for him, given his physical size and apparent lack of wit, looked at Sebastian. He squinted, reached into his pocket, and pulled out his wallet. Sebastian stood there for a while as the doorman counted out the exact change.

"No tip?" Sebastian suggested.

"Here's a tip. Don't throw me out of a pizzeria," the doorman muttered, looming above him.

He dropped the money in Sebastian's hand and snatched the pizzas, glaring at him. He turned, went back through the door, and indelicately shut it behind himself.

Through the closed curtains and the meandering students, it was clear that the party inside continued.

Sebastian looked to the side of the building and saw an unguarded gate with some students leaving through it. He quickly walked towards it, and they held it open for him. One of the benefits of delivering pizza in a university town.

He thanked them and gingerly made his way through.

Chapter 5

Sebastian continued up the darkened path along the side of the house. He could hear people talking in the garden ahead. Reaching the rear of the house, he could see that the garden had a few groups of people in it who had arranged themselves into circles and appeared to be reading poetry. He looked at them with suspicion. This was not what he had been hoping for.

The backdoor of the house had been propped open with a small wooden wedge. From within came the sounds of the party he had been expecting.

Sebastian smiled. "The evening can start," he said quietly to himself.

As he stood there looking from the corner of the house, two more students staggered out of the party. They were more worn by their sweaters than the other way around. As they left, one of them kicked the door jamb out and stumbled as they drunkenly attempted to exit before they both continued unsteadily on their way.

Sebastian walked towards the door, trying not to draw attention as the door slowly closed. He had to cover about ten feet as the door continued on its inevitable path. He carefully looked around as he walked. Nobody was watching. The door was almost closed now.

Sebastian rushed forward to grab the edge of the door, but by the time he got there, there was only enough space to fit the end of his fingers in the gap.

He muffled a shout from the pain and shook his hand about vigorously.

Pushing the door back open, he looked at the others still in

the garden, put the wooden wedge back under the door to hold
it open, and made his way inside.

The house was thick with people.

Inside, the loud music pumped through the building, almost
in step with him as he walked along the hallway. Curious, he
paused at one of several doorways and looked in. In the melee,
he saw a group of people gathered about a sofa, talking, while
others played some form of drinking game that involved
throwing something he couldn't see at a massively oversized
dartboard on the wall.

He wandered farther along the hall, looking in various
rooms to get the lay of the land before settling in to enjoy the
party. As he wandered, moving between the revelers, he
caught the looming sight of the doorman heading to answer
the front door, and he slipped sideways from the hallway into
the kitchen.

He found himself in the middle of a small group of six well–
dressed people whose cotton jackets, linen shirts, and
meticulous goatee beards spoke volumes.

It looked as though someone had called an emergency
meeting of second–hand bookshop owners, boutique start-ups,
and high school history teachers.

They were holding themselves slightly separate from the
rest of the party and had gathered about the breakfast
counter, forming an island in a sea of people, arguing about
whether a vegetarian would kill a chicken to save a cow.

There were a couple of untouched beers and a collection of
innocent-looking bottles of red wine nearby that looked like
they didn't stand a chance.

"Oh God," he muttered, "philosophy students."

"What do you think?" one of them asked as they turned their
heads toward him.

Sebastian looked at him and reasoned that he was the
leader of the group. He was about an inch taller than the
others; his goatee was slightly more angular, his hair
exhibited more oomph, as though advertising shampoo, and

his history teacher vibes were off the charts.

"What about?" Sebastian replied.

"Right," he said, taking a breath and looking far too comfortable. "Rabbits eat carrots, okay?"

"Okay," Sebastian replied.

"And foxes eat rabbits."

"Mmmm…?"

"Because they are higher than them on the food chain."

Sebastian looked around and couldn't see a way out of the conversation.

"Absolutely agree," he said, reaching for a bottle of beer. If this was going to happen, then there was no way he wouldn't ease the pain. Thankfully, they were already open.

The philosophy student looked suspiciously at one of the bottles of wine. The air of disdain made the wine feel particularly nervous. Suddenly, he descended upon it with a fluidity that belied his goatee and linen disguise. His eyes shone with the voracious focus of a Naiad descending upon Hylas or a civil servant descending upon a buffet, and his true nature was betrayed. He was an apex predator stalking his prey in the savanna lands of Bordeaux and Burgundy, a ruthless connoisseur of the bargain basement, an air of sophistication compounded by a draft of literature.

"Now, vegetarians eat carrots," he continued, balancing the wineglass in his hand as he elegantly filled it.

Sebastian watched him cautiously. 'Oh no,' he thought, 'I think I can see where this is going'.

The student continued mercilessly. "Can I eat vegetarians because I'm higher than them on the food chain?"

He paused, evidently not finished,

"And theoretically, can a vegetarian eat a vegan because they are higher than the vegan on the food chain?"

He waited dramatically for a moment before continuing.

"You know," he said quietly, "that they're full of natural goodness and moral fiber." He finished with a flourish of his now half-empty wine glass.

Sebastian pretended to think about it for a while.

"No," he said.

"Ah, but why not?" the student responded.

"It's illegal."

The student seemed confused by the answer.

Sebastian toyed with the idea of feigning a migraine and making a break for it.

"But what is illegal…?" the student began.

"Eating people," Sebastian said as he took a large sip of his beer, "pretty sure about that."

"But what is a law…?" he tried again.

"One of those things that says you can't eat people," Sebastian said helpfully.

"Society is based upon made-up rules…"

He was clearly not about to give up. Sebastian was wondering if he needed to feign the headache after all.

"There you are," said a soft voice as a hand grabbed him by the arm, pulling him firmly away.

"I was wondering where you went to," said the voice that must have been attached to the hand that kept pulling him in the opposite direction to the philosophy students. Sebastian kept hold of the beer tightly and mouthed his apologies as he allowed the hand to save him as he reentered the crowded hallway.

In the hall, he turned and, looking down, saw a smiling, freckled face looking back at him.

"You looked like you needed a hand." She was smiling, her voice pleasant, like honey.

"A lovely hand it is too, very effective," he replied, pleasantly surprised.

"You don't remember me," she said sweetly.

He looked at her closely. She stood about five foot four, shoulder-length chestnut hair, wearing a red top with a wide neck and jeans. She was small, attractive, and very familiar.

"You have me at a disadvantage," he said, choosing his words carefully.

"I do," she replied, her eyes twinkling.

He looked into her eyes and smiled.

"That's nice," he said.

She raised an eyebrow. "We'll see," she said, still smiling back.

There was something incredibly familiar about her. He knew her from somewhere, and he was deeply suspicious that he knew her well.

He glanced up the hallway and saw the doorman still standing by the door, talking with someone outside.

"Bugger," he said and dodged rapidly back into the kitchen.

The philosophy student's eyes lit up as he gently removed the glass from his lips and parted them, preparing to talk once more.

"Oh, hell no," she muttered, glanced at the door, and, seeing that the doorman was still facing outside, pulled Sebastian's arm hard.

They quickly moved through the crowd and along the corridor toward the front door. Then, they reversed their direction and quickly and quietly ascended the stairs behind the doorman.

Chapter 6

Sebastian looked carefully at the woman in front of him. There were far fewer people milling about upstairs, affording him the time to look at her closely.

She stood there, looking back.

"Figured it out yet?"

"Not yet," he replied, desperately trying to find an answer that seemed to say something to him from the darkest reaches of his brain.

"How about I start?" she said sweetly. "Your name is Sebastian."

She looked at him and waited, smiling.

The little voice in his head was now shouting as loudly as it could.

"You're enjoying this," he said.

"You have no idea," she smiled.

There was something about that smile that seemed to remind him of his childhood.

"Melissa!" he sputtered.

She grinned.

Melissa had lived in the house next door to him for a few years when he was growing up. They had moved when he was fourteen. Her dad imported fireworks, and one day, when she was babysitting him (she was a whole year older), they built a fort out of all the boxes of fireworks in the garden.

One of the neighbors saw them playing in the firework fort and called the fire brigade, but the boxes were empty, which the fire brigade was oddly disappointed about.

Unfortunately for her father, the numerous bottles of propane gas he used for cooking in the basement were full. He had been working on developing a side business making and delivering food as a prelude to starting a restaurant. As he did it without the proper permissions, they were forced to move out of the rental, and before he knew it, she was gone.

"Now I'm pretty sure that you don't go to this college, or I would have taken it upon myself to harass you sooner," she said, watching him with large eyes. "I always wondered where you ended up."

"Pizza restaurant down the road," he said.

"Had I known that I might have put on some weight," she replied.

"You mean you didn't?" he grinned.

She punched him lightly on the arm. "You ass," she retorted, grinning back.

"How did you end up here?" Sebastian asked, gesticulating to the party.

"I helped arrange it; it's just a way to raise the department morale."

"Ah, so you're not a party animal," Sebastian mused.

"Limited parties and no philosophy discussions. They're the only rules so far," she said. "What's the deal between you and Derek?"

"Who's Derek?" Sebastian replied, feeling a little lost.

"The guy manning the door downstairs."

"Ah, apparently, he didn't like being asked to keep his shirt on, or to stop singing opera," Sebastian said.

"Oh, dear God," she muttered, "I'm not sure that would be a good look."

"Yeah, it didn't seem to work for the other customers. I think they were feeling bad about possibly having some of his relatives on their pizza."

She giggled.

Sebastian's heart soared.

He took a large sip of his beer and looked happily at Melissa.

"Come this way," she said, pulling him towards a quieter

room, "I want to hear what you've been up to."

"I want to hear about you, too," he replied, following her, "but first, I just got off shift and could really use the bathroom."

"This way then," she said, steering him towards a light blue door labeled with what must have been an artistic attempt to show a symbol for a unisex toilet. It looked like a silhouette of an unhappy tree.

She opened it and walked inside. "As you can see, we have a sink, as well as some fine facilities located for your pleasure," she said grandiosely.

"Any privacy?" he asked.

"Spoilsport," she retorted.

"Well, if you really want to stay…"

"Interesting, but…" she said, smiling at him.

"Yes, I do have an interesting butt. Thank you for noticing. Everyone's very proud," Sebastian replied, tongue in cheek.

This time, she outright laughed and put her hand on his chest.

Sebastian took a large swig of his beer.

"Could you hold this for a few seconds?" he asked, handing her the bottle.

"Is that all it takes?" she said, grinning.

"Only if I add extra time for optimism," he replied.

She thought about it for a moment.

"And would you say that your optimism is large?" she asked slyly.

"Tiny," he replied, "you wouldn't notice it unless someone pointed it out."

She snorted and blushed, and they both fell about laughing.

Chapter 7

Ertic ran and ran through the cool night air until he felt his lungs would burst. He was a dog, and he was loving this.

The wind flowed through his hair as he ran between the parked cars at the edge of the park, dashing across the darkened pavement and onto the grass of the park itself. The ground felt soft between the pads of his paws as the cold ground and the cool breeze worked to keep him from overheating.

His ears bounced up and down, looking like he might, at some point, take off and fly to his destination.

He had to admit that, with his heart pumping and the wind rushing past, he felt like he had purpose. He hadn't enjoyed running in the same way before he was a dog, but now, with the cold air and the smell of spring grass, he felt alive.

He stopped suddenly, conflicted as much as he was with his immediate need to follow the signal.

Dammit, he couldn't help himself. The draw of the kebab shop was too strong. Ertic had often found himself in conflict with his instincts as a dog, and, too often, the dog side would win. He changed direction and dove towards the restaurant, dashing across the road and stopping at the base of one of the outside benches. Nick, the owner, noticed him as he was cleaning. He took a few scraps of meat that he was clearing away from the previous customers and passed them down to Ertic.

He wolfed them down as Nick gently stroked his head.

Damn, when he changed back, he would miss this, he thought.

Nick rubbed him behind the ear, and Ertic tapped his back

paw to the rhythm of it, closing his eyes in joy at the situation.

"You're in a rush tonight, aren't you?" Nick said. He stood up and went inside, returning quickly with a small tray of water.

Ertic thrust his face into the water, lapping it up with great licks from his tongue as Nick continued to rub his back and neck.

He really liked this place, but there was no time to lose, and here he was, getting distracted. Ertic looked at Nick and nuzzled his hand, hoping for a little more meat.

"Go on then," Nick said, as he pulled some more meat down off the table and passed it to Ertic, who took it, and with one last look at his friend, he was gone, across the road and running into the dark of the park once more.

He ran across the grass, through the unlit flower beds, and past the duck pond while fighting an urge to sniff the sleeping ducks. He made his way across the amphitheater seating that the council had decided would look wonderful surrounding the location of the old fairy tree.

The tree had looked lovely in the 1950s but had lost some of its luster after being struck and destroyed by lightning. A set of pictures taken of two tourists had even made national headlines when it showed how the event unfolded.

The first picture showed them initially posed, happy, and in love without a care in the world, the fairies suspended to look like they were flying about them.

The second image showed a massive bolt of lightning crashing down from the sky, rendering the tree into a giant illumination.

This led seamlessly to the final picture.

It was the last picture that had really made the main event, possibly because of the absence of the previous romance and mostly because the council hadn't wanted to spend the money upgrading the old gas lighting.

It was an image of the tourists running whilst screaming

from a flaming Tinkerbell that had been suspended by a string. The gnomes that flanked Tinkerbell were either exploding like firecrackers or giving out impressive bursts of flame from the tops of their tiny hats while a twenty-foot-high fire tornado leaped from the remnants of the tree.

Near the edge of the image, a small Bakelite Pegasus seemed to exude what looked like a stream of lava from both ends, covering an innocent–looking troll in glowing hot liquid.

The image had gained so much national coverage that the local theater had removed the showings of Peter Pan and swapped it for a horror instead, hoping to gain from the town's newfound tourist industry.

Ertic, though, couldn't stop for anything else. He couldn't even stop to smell the bushes on the side of the seating, although his canine instincts were urging him. This was the culmination of his mission. He chewed and swallowed the last piece of meat as he felt himself gaining his second wind.

Ertic ran under the swing arm for the closed parking. He raced down the promenade at full speed, and as the blood pounded in his fluffy ears, he felt alive.

He howled; however, being a small dog, it was very similar to his singing.

The tarmac beneath his feet was firmer than the grass as the vibrations from the collar increased in intensity. He was near, but the window of opportunity was closing.

He was Ertic, Sub-Commander of the 5th Fleet Infantry of the Callaxian Guard and hero of the Battle of Banakar, strong and motivated. He was clear about who he was and what was needed of him. Determined and ready, he would complete his mission.

Ertic continued along the promenade as fast as his furry little feet could carry him while trying to use his tongue to get to what remained of the meat between his teeth.

Running past the statues and the trees he saved time by jumping through the fountain. It helped to cool him down and he continued onward with spray now flying from his wet fur coat, covering everything he passed in a dog-scented mist.

Ertic could feel he was close now.

Clearing the park, he crossed London Road, and headed onward. His collar was vibrating urgently. He needed to get there fast, and it couldn't be more than a hundred meters. Ertic took what he hoped was a shortcut running through the front garden of a large, old house towards an alley that ran beside it.

Music was coming from somewhere in front of him. He continued down the little alley that separated this house from the one next to it, towards the rear garden. The sounds were louder now. They seemed to emanate from the house directly behind the one whose garden he was running through.

The rear garden opened as he left the alley. He ran through the marigolds and the roses at full speed. In front of him lay a fishpond, visible in the moonlight, and at the end of the garden, a hedge made of large-leafed bushes. He jumped across the fishpond and almost made it, landing in some foul–smelling mud at its edge, covering his small paws and underbelly. He dragged himself out quickly, squelching as he did so, and aimed himself at a small gap in the hedge. He leaped as high as he could and howled in triumph as he flew between the tops of the bushes.

Bernice sat on the bench, at the rear of the garden, next to Paul. She was holding his hand. She had come to the party just to see him. Bernice was surprised by how well they hit it off, they had been talking all night, and now, were about to kiss.

Paul slowly closed his eyes and moved carefully towards her, ready for this moment.

Bernice slowly closed her eyes and was almost as surprised as Paul when a small, fat, wet dog that smelled of fishpond and kebab meat came flying through the bushes and landed on Paul's shoulder. Its damp head collided with his cheek as one of its muddy paws somehow ended up in Bernice's mouth while the remaining paws covered them both in grimy, muddy, foul–smelling water.

Its sodden fur was matted with leaves and twigs, and it appeared to be howling the first part of "She'll be coming around the mountain."

The dog scrambled onto Paul's head as Bernice fell off the bench into a bush. It leaped through the air towards the house with the grace normally reserved for blancmange, leaving nothing but wet dog smell and foliage covering Paul's shirt and hair, and Bernice's blouse.

A few leaves and a twig from Ertic remained in Paul's hair, giving him the appearance of a police suspect who had been dragged through the undergrowth as Paul completed his descent, almost silently, sliding sideways into a bush of his own.

Bernice sat in her bush for a moment. The wet dog smell filled the air in the same way that an aphrodisiac wouldn't.

Ever the optimist, Paul offered Bernice another breath mint, his mud mustache giving him a slightly debonair look.

Bernice, however, declined.

Ertic ran through the rear door of the house, tearing past the students in the hall. He bolted up the hall towards the doorman, turned 180 degrees at the base of the stairs, and then started running up them.

The doorman turned and saw him. "Get that dog out before it ruins the carpet," he yelled.

He was too late; Ertic was already heading up the stairs, his chubby little body giving the impression of a gravity-defying slinky, leaving a trail of damp, leaves, and mud behind him as he dragged his belly all over the carpet.

"He's gone upstairs," shouted the doorman, going after him

Chapter 8

"Prepare to deploy the transport corridor," Triven ordered.

"Ready to engage," came the reply from Trom at the transport desk. Trom was particularly excited, sitting at his station, proud of the two green dots on his sash. This was to be one of the largest transport corridors that they had ever made. To be fair, they had made a few others of this scale, one of which had been used to send the Sub-Commander out in the first place, but this was a matter of pride. This was the largest that he had ever created.

He had taken over the position four months ago after it had proven impossible to contact any of the soldiers sent out.

There was still some uncertainty with the workings of the transport corridors, but he felt that he was making good strides in developing protocols to help it stabilize effectively. One end of the corridor would finish in the command room, as close as possible to the computer monitoring circuits. This would allow the computer to respond near–instantly to fluctuations in the transport corridor.

Now, all he had to do was ensure that the other end of the corridor opened successfully and was stable.

The previous Transport Officer had taken to starting the transport corridor and then adding extra energy directly into it before finishing the connection to the other side. He did this by firing a thermal lance through the opening to force the extra energy in. Once the light built up inside the corridor, he knew it was time to finalize the connection.

Trom's technique was different; he pumped the energy in by flipping the switch to open and close the corridor rapidly eight times. He reasoned that the extra energy would build up internally, creating a more stable connection to its ultimate destination.

Finally, he would connect through, giving enough time for a location that allowed resonance to occur between its boundaries to be identified. That would minimize energy expenditure while forcing the corridor into a superposition of stability.

His current theory was that the transport corridor was initially weakly spread over a wide area, and then it would begin to materialize more strongly in multiple workable resonance areas closer to the transmitter.

The Sub-Commander's communications equipment could then be located, the closest workable resonance identified, and the Sub-Commander informed of its location.

Once he got close enough to the potential transport corridor, the signal from his return beacon would force the collapse of all alternative transport corridors, creating a burst of feedback energy that would solidify the corridor closest to him.

The Sub-Commander already had the location. He had been broadcasting the signal to the Sub-Commander since his tracker had opened a communications corridor. Now, it was Trom's time to shine.

He took a deep breath, giving a moment of silence for the enormity of the task about to be undertaken. He was preparing himself mentally to push the button.

Triven walked over to the transport desk and pushed Trom's button to finish opening the transport corridor.

Trom was crestfallen.

As he watched, the corridor began to form It was difficult to see, as light tended to avoid it unless it traveled directly towards it. It could look like a mirror or a minor blur if you stood off-axis.

Trom angled his head to view the scene better. He could feel a mild pressure in his head as the portal was being created, telling him that that he was on axis with it.

He watched as a strange–looking creature honed into view. It seemed to be bipedal and looked remarkably like everybody else, but its skin was pinkish and not blue or green.

Trom stared at it.

Chapter 9

Sebastian took another drink of his beer.

"Alright," he said after they had taken a slight break from laughing. Their cheeks were flushed, and it felt good to see Melissa again. From what he was seeing, she felt the same way.

"I really need to 'use the facilities,' so to speak. Could you hold this for a minute?" he gave her his beer, and she happily took it.

There seemed to be some sort of commotion coming from the garden outside.

His head throbbed. "That feels a little odd," he said.

Looking towards the toilet, he saw something happen. Small sparks seemed to appear in front of him as the air started to shimmer between him and his target. He quickly did a mental calculation. Six steps, that was the distance to the toilet.

"Alright," he said, "I'm not entirely convinced that the beer is devoid of hallucinogens."

Melissa looked concerned.

"What do you mean?"

"Well, it was out on the counter downstairs. It was already open, and now I think I'm seeing things," He responded.

"What are you seeing?" She asked, concern evident in her voice.

"Just flashes and spots. Nothing too bad." He replied.

"Are you okay?" she asked urgently, touching his elbow.

"Not a problem. I'm more than happy to ride it out with you. But I still need to use the bathroom. Tell you what, don't look, or you can pop outside. I'm going to give it my best shot, and if it ends up in the sink, that's on them." He smiled at her, but she still looked worried. "It is good to see you again."

"Alright, I'm not looking, and I'll wait outside, but I'm leaving the door open," she replied.

In front of him, the sparks seemed to intensify. With a gentle whoosh, a large opening appeared. Staring at him was a room full of people, some with green skin and some with blue.

"God, I hope they don't start dancing," he said.

Sebastian heard a voice that sounded familiar.

"He's gone upstairs."

"Dammit, Derek," Sebastian muttered. "Right, this is happening." He felt his resolve grow stronger. He was going to use this toilet if it killed Derek.

He started on his path, counting the steps to the toilet.

"One," he muttered, stepping forward.

"Two," he counted aloud, taking another step forward.

Suddenly, a small dog covered in water, mud, and leaves, brushed past his legs, as it ran through the portal.

"Sure, why not?" Sebastian said.

"Three." Every step was moving him closer to his destination.

Sebastian focused on a flashing light in front of him as the vision of the room seemed to encompass his entire view. Behind him, he could hear Melissa squaring off against Derek.

"If you go in there, Derek, so help me, I'll take your …" her voice seemed to fade into the distance.

"Four." There was a sudden bright flash as he continued to move forward. Just as quickly as the flash appeared, it was gone, and he was standing on an alien base on an alien moon.

"The computer says he's here," Trom said.

"I'm pretty sure that's not him."

"Someone ask him."

"Close the corridor."

"Five," Sebastian said, still stepping forward.

"Sub-Commander, is that you?"

"Six."

Sebastian reasoned that he should be next to the toilet. Given the circumstances, he was going to use the 'close enough is good enough' rule.

He unzipped himself and began to urinate, finally relieved of the burden that he might do something embarrassing.

Sh'ockley stared in disbelief as Sebastian started to urinate on her flashing light.

"I really hope that's not him," said Trom.

"Scan them," said the Head of Security, a large bipedal humanoid creature standing six feet tall. He was covered in thick black–and–white striped fur with a horizontal black line on his red sash.

The Science Officer, who was about the size of a human and the color of a gummy bear, with three small blue circles horizontally arranged on his sash, jumped to it. His fluffy white hair bounced about as he quickly tapped on the screen at his station.

"It's the other creature," he said quickly, pointing at the dog.

"Why hasn't he changed back?" someone asked.

By now, Ertic was sitting on the floor, scratching his ear with his hind leg while trying to decide whether he should scoot his behind across the carpet.

"His circuit's not responding."

"Use the base computer. Force the restore," came a voice from someone distinctly blue sitting in the center of the room.

"His transformation won't be reversed completely. Only the parts of him that are recognizable to the database."

Ertic made a decision on his 'to scoot or not to scoot' dilemma.

Triven watched him with shock as Ertic the dog started scooting his behind about the room.

"Transform him now," he demanded, unwilling to tolerate this type of behavior under his command.

"Transformation underway," the Science Officer said.

Over the course of a few seconds, the dog scooting on the

floor was replaced by Sub-Commander Ertic, sitting naked, his legs lifted in mid–scoot.

"Is it weird that you're watching?" Sebastian asked his hallucination, who was staring at him wide-eyed in horror as he continued to urinate on her flashing light.

For a moment, the room seemed to stand still amidst the madness. A strange zen-like calm almost descended before realizing it was in the wrong place.

It made a break for another room somewhere in a different civilization.

Sh'ockley's blood was slowly moving from overheating to boiling as she gripped the edges of her desk in a rage.

"He's still urinating!" she screeched.

"Right, he's trying to take ownership or assert dominance," the Head of Security moved fast across the room; his black-and-white striped fur seemed to bounce in slow motion as he rapidly traveled the eight feet that separated them. His uniform held tight on his muscular frame.

In one deft motion, he pulled out a stout baton and changed the setting to what would best translate as 'stun and regret.' He raised his hand and swatted at Sebastian. A small halo of light appeared around the end of the baton as it hit Sebastian in the back.

Sebastian collapsed semi-conscious on the floor, a little stunned and feeling full of regret, although he wasn't exactly sure what for, before he finally passed out.

Ertic stood up and looked at Sebastian, now unconscious, on the floor.

"Not either of those. Not a human's style," Ertic said, fondly remembering his own recent excursions to take ownership of an entire city block from some feral cats. All the while the humans had been lazily marking the same three doorways.

Ertic looked about the room, feeling a powerful urge to mark it as his own. It appeared that some of the canine instincts had imprinted.

A medic that had been on hand for their arrival quickly

passed him a blanket. He covered himself over, glad of the warmth now he was devoid of his fur.

"I think he's on drugs," the Head of Security said.

"System is reading clean, at least as much as we can tell. His species isn't on the database," the Science Officer said.

"Really?"

"He could be. He was at a party, but he may just be confused. They don't even know how to control the weather on their planet," said Ertic.

"Does confusion cause them to urinate on things?" the Head of Security asked.

"Not normally," he replied hesitantly.

"Get the Sub-Commander some clothes," Triven said, "and take that creature to the medical bay."

The Head of Security leaned towards Ertic, "You should probably know, you have a tail," he said quietly.

Ertic's tail stopped wagging and froze.

"What?"

"Good to see you again," he said with a smile.

Chapter 10

Sebastian stirred on the bed and pulled the surrounding sheets about him.

He reached out and felt a hand reaching back. He held it.

"Thanks for looking out for me," he mumbled, "that was a strange experience."

He slowly opened his eyes and was rather surprised to see someone who looked a lot like a five–foot–tall lizard looking back at him. "You're very welcome," it replied in a calm, feminine, soothing voice. It seemed to be wearing a fitted white suit.

"I don't think it's worn off yet," he said. "You don't look like yourself."

"Well, that's an interesting idea–who do I look like then?" the creature replied.

"You sort of look like…" Sebastian began slowly.

"Go on," she urged.

"A large lizard person," he finished.

"Well, that's understandable then," she replied.

"Really, why?" he asked.

"Because I am a lizard person, but, if I might add, I look rather good. I wouldn't say large. I'd say just right." She responded.

Sebastian was concerned that he was having auditory and visual hallucinations. He glanced about.

It didn't help.

He seemed to be surrounded by hospital beds. Each of the beds seemed to be accompanied by equipment and panels. There were a few people wandering about, but they were green or blue. They could easily pass as human, were it not for their particular color scheme not being found on any human in history.

There were two guards standing near the end of his bed wearing light-yellow uniforms with a fat red sash coming down from the left shoulder and a red waistband. Both had two small black circles arranged horizontally on their sash. One had bright green skin and white hair while the other appeared eerily similar, but his skin was bright blue. Such was their complexion they could easily have been advertising chewable gummy sweets. They looked how you would expect soldiers to look, if any two major candy manufacturers went to war.

"Where do you think you are?" she asked.

"Probably at a university party with a friend," he replied. "Maybe on the bathroom floor."

"I see," she said.

"Problematic really, as I may have peed all over it." Sebastian paused for a moment. "Why do you ask?" he inquired of his new imaginary lizard friend.

"Because I'm trying to find out if you're on drugs," she replied honestly.

Sebastian paused and thought for a second.

"So am I," he said.

"A curious quandary," she looked at him, smiling. "Do your people get off planet much?"

"No, never," Sebastian replied. These hallucinations were far more lifelike and talkative than they had any right to be, although having never hallucinated before, he was utterly devoid of a frame of reference.

"Much contact with other species?"

"None," said Sebastian.

"First time on an alien moon?"

"On any moon," he replied.

"Then it will probably take longer for you to find out if you're on drugs than it will take me," she said, still smiling.

"Hang on," Sebastian said, "if this isn't a hallucination, then why can I understand you when you talk?"

"A few thousand years ago we were all becoming connected to a vast interrelated store of knowledge," she began, "But not everyone wanted to be connected. One company had the idea to infect everyone with a tiny computer chip. That way they could get paid money showing people who didn't want to see, products they didn't want to buy and charging desperate companies, large amounts of money to do it."

"Hmm…" she said thoughtfully, "Don't move. One of the chips has already attached itself to you and I need to check the install."

She prodded his cheek several times, staring into his eyes, and each time there was a beep.

"What are you doing?" he asked.

"Checking the ad–blocker, it should activate automatically but as you're a new species, it's worth ensuring that it'll behave properly," she replied. "In the end, several worlds were dominated by a single communications provider, but when one of the mandated updates went wrong, people's heads started exploding because of an overload of adverts." She continued.

"Wait, what ad–blocker?" he asked, confused.

"This will hurt a bit," she said and slapped him, hard.

Sebastian's head spun.

"What was that for?" he said, pulling back.

"Just checking the settings. The slap opens them up. Before the company was pressured to automate it, they tried to get as few people as possible to install it. The manual install was triggered by a good solid slap. It was pretty effective at stopping people using it until heads started exploding."

Sebastian's head reeled. "Wait, couldn't people just demand they took the chips out of their heads?"

"Not really. Once installed, you became part of the company's intellectual property and you had to pay them subscription money for your continued existence. Not much, but it was their business model. They owned everything that anybody created, as well as all the ideas that anybody had. So, people could ask to have them removed, but as the people already belonged to the company, they just argued that it was an internal matter and that it wasn't in the company's best interest."

"It also meant that as long as you were using their chip then you were 'on the clock'. This meant that they could legally take ownership of your intellectual property. Imagine a world where someone else stole every original idea that you had, because you were always using a chip that you never asked for and couldn't turn off."

"That's madness," Sebastian said.

"Yep, however, all the chips come with a multi–language auto translate feature that's automatically switched on. It allowed everyone to understand each other, despite the language barriers. Can't tell you the number of problems that's caused," she muttered. "Still, it seems you get to benefit from it at this point. The ad–blocker is compatible with your species."

"What happened to the company?"

"Well, once people finally discovered the company had taken over the government, the judiciary, the PR firms, and the press, it was too late, they didn't care. They'd been propagandized for so long, without even realizing it, that they just perceived everything as being how it was always supposed to be. They didn't understand that things could be different, better." She sighed. "It seems universal that people will do anything to avoid facing unpleasant truths, especially if nobody else wants to face them either. The tiny chips still fill the air waiting for someone without an uplink to show up. Nobody ever bothered to get rid of them."

"So, the company's still around?"

"No," she said, "the company was making a huge amount of money, but they decided that they needed to make more from as many people as they could. They created a small and extremely addictive game that they gave out for free. It hooked up directly to the reward and pleasure centers of the brain. There were stories of people playing until they starved to death, but still dying happy. After that they tried to implement the second part of their plan–to use some kind of exclusive subscription model for it, or people would no longer have access."

"What happened?" Sebastian asked.

"People of all nations and ideologies banded together and burnt the company down before the update went out. It was the only time everyone agreed on anything. Luckily, with the company out of existence, they were no longer paying the exorbitant subscription fees to their sister company for bandwidth usage as a tax dodge, and eventually the game was shut down."

Sebastian's head was spinning.

"I tried to uninstall an ad–blocker once," he said, "ended up having to phone a call center in India. Never uninstalled the ad–blocker, but I got offered a good deal on a Bollywood streaming service. Turns out the person on the other end of the phone was working two jobs."

She gave him a more serious look. "Never uninstall the ad–blocker," she said sternly. "I'm not sure that your synapses could take it."

Sebastian felt more than a little uneasy about that statement.

He sat up to see more clearly and looked around. He was sitting in a vast room about the size of a large aircraft hangar. The bed, along with hundreds of others, seemed to be in the rear corner of it. All the beds were empty, except his.

"What is this place?" he asked.

"Triage center," she responded, looking over her shoulder at the room. "We're set up to take in up to one hundred casualties, if required, with room for evacuation craft."

"Why?" he asked.

"Do you feel like a little walk?"

Sebastian nodded, and she helped him to his feet. They

walked towards the main doors and the two guards followed. He wondered if they had some kind of jingle and dance number planned.

Chapter 11

Ertic sat at the table as did Triven, Sardok, and the Head of Security, although with his stature the Head of Security seemed a little too large for the small chair. In the corner a junior officer sat taking notes on the discussion.

"Has the monitoring of the room been suspended?" Triven asked.

"All recording of the chamber has been turned off," Sardok replied.

"Command?" Triven called.

"Yes, Number One," came a pleasant–sounding voice.

"Turn off all active communications devices in this room. Turn off the remote monitoring systems covering this location."

He paused.

"Command?" he called again. This time, there was no response. Triven looked hard at Sub-Commander Ertic.

"Report," he said.

Ertic sat upright and began his answer.

"I was transported to the planet six months ago and have spent that time examining the planet for any weapons that could help us defend against the creature," he began.

"We know that." Triven snapped. "We sent you. Tell us about any strategic value or alliance the planet could provide. Anything we can use against the creature that doesn't break our armament treaties. Even if it could break the treaties, we need to know about it."

Ertic paused for a moment and took a breath.

"None," he said flatly.

"None?" Triven replied incredulously.

"Really?" Sardok seemed genuinely surprised.

"They don't even control the weather on the planet," Ertic responded.

"How can they not control the weather? How would they ever be able to guarantee a nice summer in winter?" Sardok asked.

"They can't even guarantee a nice summer in summer."

"Astonishing," Sardok said, "We normally avoid contacting species that underdeveloped."

"I left no stone unturned in my analysis of the planet," Ertic replied.

This was not untrue. In fact, Ertic had spent much of the time, since becoming a dog, relaxing with a nice young couple in the suburbs watching TV. He had learned how to use the remote, despite having paws. He had watched the history channel and the news and was normally feeling somewhere between optimistic and pessimistic depending on the time of day.

He even figured out how to input the pass code to allow him to study human courtship rituals. However, he stopped after the couple started arguing about it. Also, he thought the documentaries were unrealistic, given that, in his experience, the washing machine rarely broke, and the plumber they hired was a fat man from Croydon.

The couple he'd been staying with were very impressed with him and even entered him for an animal intelligence contest. In the end he lost to a lemur after he got distracted sniffing a hamster as they moved some boxes about the room. That and an absence of the general knowledge round. That was where he had been really hoping to shine.

Triven looked pensive.

Then he stopped looking pensive and went back to looking annoyed.

"What about other species in the vicinity?" he demanded.

"The humans don't have contact with any other species."

"I didn't even think that was possible," Sardok said.

"They've only made it to their own moon," Ertic responded.

"Don't the other species nearby want to assimilate them into some sort of collective?" Sardok queried.

"They're in a bit of a void," Ertic said. "Normally you wouldn't go that far unless there was really something that made it worthwhile."

It annoyed Triven that he wasn't in control of the conversation anymore.

"What about previous civilizations?" he asked.

"There have been many previous civilizations on the planet, but none of them could maintain structure," Ertic responded.

"Did they have contact with any aliens?" Sardok asked.

Ertic took a deep breath. "There are some humans who believe that they did."

"Finally, something useful," Triven said sharply. "What do you believe?"

"I did not find the arguments convincing," he replied.

"Why not? What were they?" Triven was getting quite annoyed by this apparently colossal waste of time.

Ertic took a deep breath.

"Well, on Earth," he started, "there are some large structures made of rock."

"Piles of rock, structural columns, large obelisks, shaped mountains?" Sardok queried.

"Geometric piles of rock, huge and pyramid shaped. They have nice angles and some little tunneling holes and a nice entrance area. They're quite well constructed," Ertic replied.

"And are they perfect pyramids?" Sardok asked.

"No," Ertic replied, "they're sort of lumpy."

"Do they float in the air?"

"No but some humans believe that because these piles of rock are quite large, aliens must have done it."

He paused.

Everybody else paused as well.

"So," Triven began, "Some humans don't believe that other historical humans could have made an enormous pile of lumpy rock, on the ground, with pleasant corners and a door."

"and some little holes," Ertic added, "that is correct."

Triven began massaging his head.

"Was there anything else?" Sardok asked.

"Yes," Ertic continued, "there are also some very large pictorial structures that depict creatures on Earth," he said.

"Are they in the sky? Do they float?" Sardok asked.

"No," said Ertic, "they're also on the ground."

"Enormous pictures on the ground," Triven repeated incredulously, "of Earth creatures," he continued, more than a little bemused.

"Yes," said Ertic. "Some humans believe that because in some parts they form straight lines and they're big, aliens must have been involved."

"But they show creatures on Earth, not alien species," Sardok said, a little confused.

"That's correct," Ertic responded.

Triven was massaging his head hard now.

"Anything else?" He demanded impatiently.

"There are some walls..." Ertic began.

"Let me guess," Triven said, fuming. "They form straight lines?"

"Some of them curve," Ertic responded, "but the bricks differ in size and fit together very well."

"They built walls?" Triven raised his voice.

"And the humans of today are a bit confused how they could have done it." Ertic finished.

"How can they think walls are evidence of aliens?" Triven's voice was most definitely getting louder. "How stupid are these people?"

He took a moment to calm himself.

"That is the single least impressive evidence for an advanced alien civilization I've ever come across, and to these people I am from an advanced alien civilization. At this point even I don't think I exist," he muttered.

Triven supported his head with both of his hands, stroking

his temples.

"How are they confused about building walls?" Triven demanded, talking to himself, still unable to process the information as he shook his head.

"What about their weaponry?" he demanded. "Do they have anything that we can use?"

"They have only gotten as far as fission and fusion weapons. Their range is limited to a few miles of direct destruction, although fusion weapons are easily expanded, but nothing that we don't already have easy access to."

"We already tried some large fusion weapons. The creature didn't seem to mind," Sardok said.

"They have nothing more powerful?" Triven asked.

"Nothing," Ertic responded.

"It's probably for the best," Sardok said, thinking about the walls.

Triven shot him a look. "Well, that doesn't help us now, does it?"

"How many others have returned?" Ertic asked.

"Just you," said the Head of Security. "None of the others have been contactable. I need to discuss this with you further, although we are quite busy at the moment," he motioned his hand slightly to indicate the general surroundings, "so we have to prioritize and frankly, you can wait." He finished.

He paused and looked at Ertic.

"I want to know about the creature that came through the portal with you."

Ertic nodded.

Triven raised himself up from his chair.

"This was a waste of time," he stated loudly. "Number Two, you're needed in the command room." Triven turned and stormed out.

"It's good to have you back," Sardok said as he stood and followed Triven out.

The Head of Security sat back and watched Ertic carefully.

"So, tell me about the creature," he said.

Ertic paused and thought for a moment.

"He's a human male, not particularly dangerous, although they are prone to making poor decisions."

"And the female of the species?"

"They're prone to making poor decisions as well. It's a species thing. Also, humans express themselves unclearly. Their language is odd, too ambiguous, hard to translate," he said thoughtfully. "The circuitry struggles with it and has, on occasion, been unpredictable."

"What are his strengths?"

"Optimism," Ertic said, "and if he's on side, humans can be quite loyal."

The Head of Security nodded. He appeared to like this answer.

"What are his weaknesses?"

"Optimism," Ertic replied.

He thought a little longer.

"Optimism and testicles," Ertic finished.

"Where are they located?"

"Between his legs," Ertic responded, starting to smile, "they're external," he added and chuckled.

"They're external?"

"Sometimes," Ertic began laughing, "sometimes," he repeated mid chuckle, "the shear act of sitting down means that they actually squash them." He finished his sentence laughing quite hard. "Then they either roll about on the floor or sit there with their eyes watering trying to pretend that they didn't just crush their own gonads."

The Head of Security chuckled as well.

"And," Ertic began, "you won't believe this bit." He breathed deeply between chuckles. "They look just like..." he took a deep breath in and finished "...like a little Kevoran punching bag."

They both fell about laughing.

The Head of Security brought himself back under control.

A beeping noise came from the ranking patch on his chest.

He tapped it. "Here," he said.

"The visitor has woken up," a voice from the badge said.

"I'm on my way," he said over the intercom, and then tapped the badge again to switch it off. "How do I assess our visitor?" he asked.

"Bring him to me and I'll talk with him," Ertic said. "I'll go down to the hangar bay to check on the squadron in case they need me. You can bring him there." Ertic replied, still breathing hard.

"We should have the results in from his screening. We'll be able to see just how many drugs he was taking when he arrived." The Head of Security stood up and paused. "It's good to have you back."

"It's good to be back, Artun," Ertic replied, relieved to be returning to his old life.

Chapter 12

"Have a look up there," she suggested pointing upwards, now that they were out of the hangar.

Sebastian looked upwards. Lit up like a streak against the stars there was a comet. Its tail was clearly visible in the twilight, as it stretched out in the sky. Over the horizon of the moon, it seemed that a sun was attempting to rise.

"What is it?" Sebastian asked.

"It's a comet," she said, looking at him strangely. "Do you not have comets where you come from?" She was wondering if she had interacted at too high a level.

"Do you know what space is?" she asked seriously.

Sebastian suspected he had made an error. "I think I meant to ask if there was a problem with the comet being there."

She nodded, reassured. "The comet returns on its route every two hundred and forty years. On each occasion, it has brought us luck. In fact, the first recorded details of it discuss how it brought an end to the great sector plague of accountants."

Sebastian looked at her quizzically.

"It's a long story," she replied.

The accountants had been amassing and increasing their concentration in the sector. They planned to consolidate themselves to a single part of the galaxy. In order to maximize efficiency, they loaded most of their number on a single starship to travel to their new headquarters.

For efficiency reasons they also decided to pilot it, as no pilots in the Universe were accurate enough for the crew.

The results were swift and almost entirely predictable.

Rumors of a misplaced decimal sent the chief pilot and all the people on the bridge into a frenzy, attempting to correct a rounding error. Fifty bridge officers frantically focused on their calculators. Nobody noticed the enormous comet in the sky. It took three hours to hit them, but such was their quest for perfect balance that it could have taken a year, and they would have remained focused on their task.

When it finally did hit them, it sent them off course to an undeveloped planet and what happened next was the greatest leap forward of any civilization in the galaxy. Within weeks they were starting to industrialize, and everything was being maximized for efficiency. They outlawed marketing and politicians were banned. Universities were formed and new mathematics created. Even the sciences flowered under the umbrella of mathematics and categorization. It was a golden age.

Sadly, what followed this meteoric rise was also just as inevitable.

As with any society focused on accountancy, a secret sect of actuaries formed. They used funny handshakes and robes as they practiced their dark arts making tables and predictions. As the society developed, so their tables increased in accuracy and precision. In the end the society collapsed, not because of mismanagement or the quest for excessive precision, but rather because the actuaries said it was about time and made a convincing mathematical argument.

The accountants then wrapped everything up and responsibly scheduled their societal divestment.

A few weeks after the scheduled collapse, managerial courses, marketing courses and economics sprung up across the universities as enrollment in math and science dwindled. Within three years they were inviting guest speakers. Ten years after the collapse had begun it was over. A few horrific advertising campaigns to encourage tourism and some terrible marketing research surveys and it was done. Everyone was back to living in the mud.'

She paused and shuddered at the thought of an excess of accountants, "What's a little more concerning sits some way behind the comet. There is an enormous creature, its skin is a thick layer of neutron armor, impervious to attack. The creature itself is completely non-communicative. We've been monitoring it for the past five years as it's approached, trying to initiate communication or illicit some type of response. We're not even sure that it's conscious. It certainly appears to have levels of biological sophistication that should represent a greater higher–level functioning, but it may just be some type of giant space slug acting purely on instinct..."

She seemed to mull over the idea.

"...and it's currently on a collision course to destroy the home planet of the Callaxians."

"Who are the Callaxians?" Sebastian asked.

"They are the people whose forward moon base you are currently standing on. This is the edge of their solar system."

"That doesn't sound good," Sebastian said.

"It's not ideal."

"So," Sebastian paused, picking his words carefully, "is there a benefit to the comet and the giant creature being in the same area?" he asked hopefully.

"Only that the comet always brings luck. Now, as it seems unlikely to be the creature that's lucky, it also seems to have brought us you," she said curiously. "Do you consider yourself lucky?"

Sebastian thought about it, "Well I think I'm on drugs, on a toilet floor, at a party with a girl I haven't seen for ten years and it's possible that I'm lying in a puddle of my own urine, so the jury's out on that one," he said. "You know, it's been a pretty interesting night so far."

He looked up at the sky.

"What will they do to the creature?"

"As all attempts to communicate with the creature have failed, we're stuck in the unfortunate position of having to destroy it."

She seemed sad.

"How do you destroy something that could destroy a planet?" Sebastian asked.

"With something else that could destroy a planet," she replied grimly. "They appealed to the General Council of Planets to retrieve and deploy the Decimator." She shuddered at its mention.

"What's that?"

"From what I've been told it's a bomb large enough to destroy almost anything, even a planet. Nobody had even heard of it before the creature appeared." She sighed. "I imagine there are more than a few parties out there who would give anything to get one. They're too dangerous. Imagine if one fell into the wrong hands," she paused. "Not that there are any right hands for a weapon like that."

"Where are you getting one?" Sebastian asked.

"A few years ago, after the creature was discovered, the Emperor confirmed he had one and, since then, about five other species have claimed the same. This one was stored away under top security in the Callaxian capital, in the Emperor's own vault."

"Will that keep everything safe?" he asked.

"If all goes to plan, it should. At this point it's being placed on board a starship, personally, by the Emperor. After it's loaded they'll send it here. Once it arrives, we'll do a final check and send it on its way. We're ready to take in casualties caused by any tectonic movement generated by the explosion. But it makes you think," she said looking up. "What wonders has a creature like that seen, and over how many millennia or tens of millennia, maybe even longer."

"What if it doesn't work?"

She looked at him.

"You can remove the ad–blocker," she said dryly.

She saw he looked taken aback. "Most of this place has already evacuated as a precaution. For the past few years its sole purpose has been to mount a response to the creature. Everyone had the opportunity to leave, but the soldiers who stayed are here by choice," she paused. "Everyone's very motivated to make sure the planet survives but there are multiple contingency plans already in place. Multiple planets stand ready to help."

"Is that why you're here?" Sebastian asked.

She smiled, "No, this isn't my home planet. This is a small moon base, on the edge of a system of planets, that orbit that binary star." She pointed up at two bright stars in the heavens sitting very close together. They were starting to dim slightly in the morning light. "I'm from much farther away."

Sebastian was confused "Why does it look like the sun's about to rise if those are the binary stars?" He asked. It was starting to look like the morning sun was threatening to expose itself over the horizon.

"There's an artificial star orbiting the moon, that's what's giving the daybreak. This moon is so large that the Callaxian's have been working on planet-forming it. If they're careful, then it could be used in the same way as the home planet, to grow crops and house people, helping to spread the civilization. They've been transforming it over the past ninety years."

Sebastian looked thoughtful for a moment, "So why are you here?"

"A long time ago there was an immense war. Everyone got sucked into it, my own people included. The Callaxian home world, my planet and countless others were all reduced to rubble. Once the conflict ended, peace was always being strained. There's too much money and opportunity in war. Politicians don't make much money from peace."

She shook her head. "To enhance the ties between the different peoples, and against the wishes of the politicians, medical staff from opposing sides volunteered to fully staff the facilities of the other sides. It's more difficult to depersonalize someone when they're helping you. Better to build bridges than bombs. We've been doing it for a long time now. Because of this, peace has had the chance to preside, despite the financial incentives."

She paused, watching the Head of Security as he strode around the corner.

"There are always other reasons to hang around as well," she said meaningfully.

Artun stood about six feet tall and stalky. He walked with purpose and was the most physically dangerous person on the base. A pristine matting of thick black and white fur, striped like a tiger, covered his thickly muscled body. A black horizontal line adorned the red sash on his uniform.

"Artun, it's good to see you," the doctor said.

His eyes lit up as he approached her.

"Selim," he said, with what appeared to be a smile. The smile faded a little as he turned to Sebastian.

"What's the news with our guest?" he asked, sizing Sebastian up carefully.

"He's clean," she said, "there are no drugs in his system."

"Surprising," Artun said, a little taken aback. He turned to Sebastian. "I incapacitated you because I thought you were taking drugs," he said matter–of–factly.

"I probably am," Sebastian replied.

Artun paused. "He's not on drugs, is he?" he asked of Selim, as he carefully watched Sebastian.

"No."

"Good, good," he nodded, reassured.

"But he thinks he's on drugs," she continued.

"Really?" Artun was feeling like something wasn't making complete sense. "He's not on drugs, but he thinks he is?"

"That's right."

This was not the answer Artun had been hoping for.

"Seems wrong," he muttered.

He turned to Sebastian.

"Are you on drugs?" he asked in a loud, clear voice.

"I think so," Sebastian replied.

"But he's not on drugs?"

"No," she replied. Her scaled skin had taken on a distinctly pinker hue since Artun's arrival.

Artun turned to Sebastian. "Why do you think you're on drugs?"

"Because I'm here."

"Right," Artun continued, thinking that this was not going how he had hoped. When he got out of bed this morning, there were only a few things on his mind: Giant space slug, see Selim, update security logs. Now things seemed to be getting a little more complex. Here in front of him he had a creature that thought it was on drugs. Unless it was delusional, this meant that it had to have taken drugs. Thus, drugs should be in its system. However, Selim, whom he trusted implicitly claimed that there were no drugs in the creature's system. This led to a multitude of questions not least of all - what did the creature actually take? Why did it take it? What did it think would happen? Where were the drugs? And should he be worried?

He thought about it for a moment and turned to Selim.

"Am I on drugs?" Artun asked Selim, hoping that something would start making sense soon.

"No," she replied.

"And you're sure about that?" Artun asked carefully.

"Yes."

"Pity," Artun responded, "and you're sure he's clean."

"Absolutely."

Artun watched as Sebastian looked about the room.

"If we put him on drugs, will he make more sense?"

"I doubt it," she said, smiling.

"If we put me on drugs, will that help him make more sense?" Artun asked hopefully.

"Absolutely not," Selim replied firmly. "He asked what a

comet was a moment ago."

"Damn," Artun said, thoughtfully. "I need to take him to the Sub-Commander. He's interested in speaking with him."

Artun turned to Sebastian. "Walk with me. I need you to answer some questions on the way."

Selim looked across and noticed that Sebastian seemed a little uncertain.

"Hold still," she said.

She reached her hand across and pushed a small patch onto the side of his head, on his temple.

"This will help," she said. "It will allow your brain to process information in a way that you can deal with more easily. We use it for creatures undergoing first contact. It will let you see things in a way that your brain is much more comfortable with."

She tapped the circuit on the side of his head and to Sebastian's surprise, Selim, Artun and the guards transformed into people.

Artun transformed into a large meticulously groomed black man still wearing his uniform and Selim changed into a medium–sized Chinese woman in her fitted white suit. They had both kept their approximate size and proportions. Sebastian felt decidedly more comfortable.

The two guards that had followed them stood looking like soldiers. Both were about six feet tall, one with well-trimmed, short red hair and the other with short brown hair and a goatee. Both looked rigid and alert.

"How do we look?" she asked.

"Much more normal," he replied. "Maybe the drugs are wearing off."

She smiled at him. "I wouldn't count on it just yet," she said.

Artun looked at the two men. "Return to your normal duties. I'll take it from here."

With that, the two men turned and walked back towards the hangar door.

"Well then, come with me," Artun said with authority.

Chapter 13

Artun and Sebastian made their way towards the entrance of the hangar. The sun, now rising in the sky, lit the hangar up with its morning rays. It was a vast building, rounded about the edges, that cast a long shadow. It sat looking like a four-hundred-meter-long reinforced jelly, with the identification VS3 written in large letters on its side.

A set of large ornate looking metal and glass doors stood in front of them as they approached the back corner of the building.

They entered through the doors. A beautiful staircase covered in a carpet that must have been an inch thick, rose majestically into the air on their left.

Directly in front of them was a far less ornate door with a keypad.

They moved towards the smaller door.

"What's up that way?" asked Sebastian, motioning up the stairs.

"Shortcut," came the gruff response.

"Shouldn't we just take the shortcut?"

Artun paused what he was doing in front of the panel and walked over to the steps. He reached down and ran his hand across a foot of carpet. From Sebastian's perspective, it looked as though the edges about Artun became blurry. He walked back towards the large metallic walls and stretched out his hand.

There was a deafening crack as a huge spark jumped from Artun's hand the two feet to the wall.

The crack echoed about the room for a few seconds.

"What just happened?" Sebastian asked, taken aback by the

spectacle.

"The carpet interacts with my fur. After about two feet the shock would likely kill you. After about twelve feet it might even kill me," he paused. "Although to be fair, I haven't tested it."

Sebastian just stared at him, still shocked.

"Do you still want to take the shortcut?" Artun asked calmly.

Sebastian shook his head, "I'm good".

'On Earth people are so backward that they teach their children that static electricity comes from friction.

This is wrong.

Throughout the Universe people know that static electricity comes about because temporary electric bonds are formed as different molecules come into contact. Electrons spend more time around one type of molecule than another and, as they are separated, the electrons have a bigger chance of ending up on the side they spend more time on. When two different types of material come into contact and are then separated, there is a good chance that one surface will become positively charged and the other negatively charged.

Thus, the charge is separated.

This is different to the creation of lightning. This occurs in clouds laden with miniature trans-dimensional sky penguins. They leave their dimensional pockets and throw charge at each other in a giant electron-snowball fight. Some penguins become positively charged and some become negatively charged.

Thus, the charge is separated.

With one exception among enlightened planets, this is what is known in the Universe.

The planet Stroomnalgen 3 is entirely inhabited by a sect of monks who eschew technology. They believe that static electricity is itself a vindictive attempt to destroy the

Universe by evil electric charges.

They take a vow to avoid all things electric and utilize natural materials for everything. Underwear made from mushrooms, clothing made from wood and shoes made from old underwear and clothing. They even developed a primitive electricity avoiding communication system by throwing notes at each other that they had wrapped around a rock.

As their communication needs increased in complexity, they eventually developed a primitive communications web. Since that time the number of concussions and other informational injuries has been growing exponentially.

It is the only planet in the Universe where getting the accurate answers to a question you've asked can actually make you dumber.

Stroomnalgen 3 is also the only planet in existence where plastic has been successfully banned. A side effect of this, of course, is that it is also one of the few places in existence that is not at risk of population extinction due to the plummeting sperm counts. It is believed that, in this unique case, the plummeting population levels are instead linked to the aforementioned mushroom underwear.'

Excerpt from: *Earth; just don't go–The engineers guide.*

Artun typed a code into the keypad and opened the smaller, more functional door. As they passed through it, Sebastian noticed the thick metal of the door attached to what seemed to be a thick metal wall. There were what looked like seams that stretched from the ground upwards located about the structure. Every part of the structure seemed to be honeycombed and reinforced.

Artun noticed Sebastian looking at it. "It's modular," he said, "each section of the building can be moved as an independent craft. If we want to build a base on another planet, we just pilot the appropriate building sections to where we want it built. We can set up a hangar like this in no time at all, it just needs to assemble itself as it lands. This entire base was set up in half an …" Artun's speech seemed to glitch for a moment, "hour," he finished.

Sebastian looked stunned "Half an hour?"

Artun grinned at Sebastian's reaction.

"They added extra time for the finishing," he said.

Sebastian and Artun started along the corridor as the door closed quietly behind them. The corridor seemed to follow the exterior wall of the building, with occasional hallways branching off to the left giving access to more rooms and more hallways. It seemed to lead to a labyrinthine rat's nest of more off-shoots and mysterious rooms all decorated in the same functional soul-crushing government grey. It gave the sinking impression that one wrong turn, and there was a risk you would find a secret entrance to a driving license politburo, from which you might never find an escape.

"Tell me a bit about your planet, then. What is it you call yourselves?" Artun asked.

"Humans," replied Sebastian, who was wondering why the drugs hadn't worn off yet.

"Humans." Artun mulled the term. "You travel through space?"

"Not yet, but somebody went to the moon," Sebastian replied helpfully.

Artun looked closely at Sebastian noticing the lines on his shoes and clothes. "How are your clothes made?" He asked, curious.

"They get sewn together by poor people working in sweatshops in other countries and shipped around the planet." Sebastian said.

Artun just shook his head. Sebastian noticed that Artun's uniform seemed to have no seams at all. Even his shoes seemed devoid of them. He looked as though he could have been preparing for the slip and slide world Olympics.

"How were your clothes made?"

"Everything gets printed directly, it's much more efficient,"

Artun replied.

Something occurred to Sebastian. "What about food? Do you grow it? Keep animals to eat?"

Artun turned to face him and looked a little surprised.

"Eat animals? No, not at all. We print the food with the printers. We construct and supply everything directly. There are groups out there who keep animals to eat but they're considered backward, and of course troops out in the field do it sometimes."

This took Sebastian a little aback as he considered himself somewhat of a meat frying ninja. "You still go to war, though," he said defensively.

Artun thought for a while. "We're advanced, not enlightened," he replied as they continued walking along the hallway.

Sebastian glanced at his watch; it was now 7:20 in the morning. and he was starting to feel uncomfortable.

"Is there a bathroom here?" he asked, his body now waking to the idea that he had been unconscious for several hours and, while he had been asleep, his bodily functions had been going about their business with great efficiency.

"A bathroom?" Artun inquired as he stopped walking. "We really don't have time, human."

"It's quite urgent," Sebastian replied.

"Ok," Artun muttered, still watching Sebastian closely.

Artun took the next corridor leading to the left. There was a sign above the corridor that read "crew quarters". He took Sebastian to an orange–colored door near the start of the corridor. Written on it was a single word "Bathroom".

Sebastian looked at Artun. "Do these chips in the brain also translate writing?"

"Of course," Artun replied.

"Well, why wouldn't they?" Sebastian said as he wandered through the door, well aware that this was more evidence that he was likely floating in some form of mushroom kingdom.

Artun remained outside.

"Hurry and bathe human, if you take longer than three..." he made a sound here, and his lips slowly went out of synch before correcting, as though the translator chips were struggling with at least one of their languages, "minutes." He said the lips syncing once more, "I'll have to take you out myself, we don't have a lot of time," he said as the door closed.

"Bathe?" Sebastian said as he turned to look about the room. It contained a large, recessed pool in the center about twenty feet wide and seemed to smell slightly of cranberries, elderberries and crabsticks.

There were two beautiful women bathing in the pool. They smiled at him and raised a hand in greeting.

Sebastian half waved back, but he was becoming really focused on finding a toilet. He tried to exit using the door and walked straight into it. He pushed it, pulled it, nothing happened.

Dammit, he thought, this was an embarrassing time to be trapped by a door. He tried to move it a couple more times.

Eventually, he shouted out and banged on the door.

The door opened immediately and Artun stood behind it, instantly ready to react.

"What is it human," he said urgently.

"Sorry, I couldn't open the door," Sebastian replied. He lowered his voice, "and I didn't really feel comfortable asking the ladies for help. It's embarrassing if I can't use a door."

"There's a little domed shape at the edge of the door. Just wave your hand in front of it," he said, and closed the door again with Sebastian still stuck inside.

"Wait," Sebastian said, but was only faced with the door. The door remained closed in front of him as if unwilling to accommodate his needs.

Sebastian looked around, examining the edges of the door. On the one side, about four feet up and glowing with a light that was actually quite relaxing, was a small domed object.

Sebastian moved quickly and waved his hand just above the dome. As his hand waved down the door started to open, but then closed as his hand waved back upwards.

He tried just waving his hand downward this time, and the door opened, revealing a slightly impatient looking Artun.

Something about what Sebastian had said was bothering him.

"The ladies?" Artun said, sounding confused.

An idea occurred to Artun. As Sebastian stepped through the door and it closed behind him, Artun put his hands on Sebastian's shoulders and turned him to face the direction of the pool. He reached across and opened the door again. As the beautiful ladies came into view, Artun touched the chip at the side of Sebastian's head, turning it off.

Sebastian flinched back as the two women rapidly changed into a pair of giant cuttlefish. One of them waved again, with the seductive allure that only eight-foot-tall bathing cuttlefish possess. Artun reached over and closed the door once more.

Sebastian turned to thank him and again saw the large alien covered in fur.

Seeing his response, Artun reached over and turned the chip back on again.

"You bathe quickly," he said.

Sebastian's urgency was increasing to the point of discomfort.

"Artun," he said as they began walking, "Perhaps I could have said it better. When I said bathroom, I really meant toilet."

"You wanted a toilet?" Artun asked.

"Yes." Sebastian said.

"To bathe?" he asked, deeply concerned that this human might be broken, and wondering if he could exchange him for a fresh one.

"No," replied Sebastian, a little confused.

"To keep?"

"Just to use." Sebastian replied.

"So, you want to know where a toilet is?"

"Yes."

"So that you can use it."

"Yes."

"Why didn't you just ask for the use of a toilet? Or is there a place I can go to the toilet, heck even a ..." There was a clicking and glitching sort of sound that Sebastian heard in his head. Suddenly he heard "... go potty," as the words seemed to catch up to Artun like a bad lip sync.

"It's a figure of speech where I come from," Sebastian said.

"You need to be careful with your communication," Artun responded. "The translation chips are struggling with your 'figures of speech,' possibly with your language structure itself. Ertic's waiting by the strike ships. The sooner we leave, the sooner we arrive. They have a toilet on board and they're probably the closest ones to our current location."

"Are there none in the crew quarters?" Sebastian asked.

"No, they tend to be near the food printers."

Sebastian wondered for a moment just how bad the food here actually was.

They increased their pace as they walked rapidly along the corridor.

"You are the first human we've ever had in this place," Artun said thoughtfully after a few moments.

"Are there any more of your species here?" Sebastian asked.

Artun didn't answer. Sebastian assumed it was a sore point.

A large round door sat at the end of the corridor. It was heavily reinforced and rotated up and out of their way as they approached, revealing the inside of a large aircraft hangar.

As they walked through, Sebastian could see that there were four main staging areas, each of which had an exit door for the ships which was twenty feet above the ground, and nearly on level with the mezzanine above them. The mezzanine stretched the entire width of the hangar. Each launching section had five ships lined up, pointed inward and spread out along the length of the outside wall.

The crafts were jet black and looked not unlike a sort of fat scarab beetle, pointed at the front, about ten feet high and forty feet long. The rear of these bug–crafts lifted like the rear of a small family car, if the small family car was a forty-foot-long spacecraft. People seemed to be moving quickly in and out of all of them.

They saw Ertic talking with a soldier near the rear of one of the craft nearby. As they walked towards him Ertic and the soldier finished talking, and the soldier went about his business. Ertic's tail wagged gently, enjoying the certainty of life once more. He stood watching the proceedings around the hangar as soldiers moved purposefully about.

There were four purple circles sitting horizontally on his sash showing that Ertic was in intelligence. He noticed Sebastian looking at them as they approached and reached out his hand to greet him. "It means Sub-Commander..." he began.

Sebastian took his hand, shook it and said, "toilet".

For a moment Ertic looked confused and then relaxed. "Come with me."

He walked up a wide silvery ramp at the rear of the ship and entered its interior. It opened out to a surprisingly spacious and clean room, not dissimilar to an office. The front section was composed of a semicircular control panel that stretched the entire width of the ship, following the viewport window above. There were five functional looking chairs with seatbelts by the long cluster of brightly colored instruments and readout screens. Separating the front from the rear of the craft was a four-foot-high bulkhead that stretched across the middle of the craft, just behind the captain's chair. Behind the bulkhead were two rows of five, spartan looking chairs. Each chair fitted with a five-point safety harness.

The captain's chair held pride of place just forward of the center of the craft. It was large, comfortable, and designed to inspire people to strive for promotion. It was a decadent indulgence surrounded by a sea of functionality. It contrasted in a manner not unlike a Belgian waffle in the middle of a weight loss meeting or a weight loss meeting in the middle of a giant Belgian waffle.

The floor was a sand colored, rubber like coating, with flecks of green and blue. It gave a firm grip to Sebastian's feet without being sticky. The walls were a mixture of silver colored metal and off-white colored paint. The entire room seemed light and airy. On the right-hand side of the craft a small selection of food sat on a long shelf with a lip about its edge, waiting to be eaten.

Ertic gestured to a small doorway located on the left wall of the craft, in the rear section with the two rows of seating. "In here," he said.

Sebastian's head swiveled from looking about the ship in awe as his eyes focused rapidly on the small open doorway and his brain switched back to the moment. He dove through the small door to the toilet.

"We would have been earlier, but the human asked to use the bathroom," Artun said. "I took him off to bathe."

Ertic chuckled. "It's a messy language."

"It was almost a messy bath," Artun responded. "There were a couple of Grethans in there."

Ertic raised his eyebrows.

Once he entered the toilet Sebastian took off his jacket and placed it on the shelf that extended along the edge of half of the room. He was very relieved to see something that extended from the wall as a unit and looked not dissimilar to a normal toilet. After a not inconsiderable amount of time, he was just very relieved.

Sebastian relaxed slightly. Wherever he was, at least he seemed to have found a toilet.

He examined the slightly odd, polished, seamless look of the room. There seemed to be no joins and all the edges were smooth yet slightly bulbous. It was as if an artisan had spent a century shaping and polishing a single perfect piece of flawless pink–ish marble and then decided that there, in this pristine, cistine, monument to stonework, was where they should put the latest, cutting-edge invention by Thomas Crapper.

He glanced around, looking for some toilet paper.

There was none.

But the room looked nice.

He glanced around again, looking for some toilet paper.

None appeared.

The room continued to look nice.

He started to twist and turn his body around, sure that there must be some toilet paper hidden nearby, but the smooth walls of the bathroom concealed nothing.

"Oh hell," he muttered.

He reached over and pulled down his jacket. He felt around inside his pockets and quickly found the stack of two–for–one pizza deal leaflets stuffed into his small book.

"Thank God," he said, genuinely relieved once more.

He cleaned himself up, found no washing facilities for his hands, and searched for the flush mechanism.

After a while, he looked up and noted another semicircular button on the wall by the door. He waved his hand in front of it and the toilet made some horrible noises, eventually sucking down all the contents under great protest.

He put the remaining leaflets and the book back into his jacket, draped the jacket over his left arm and exited the bathroom. The inside of the craft was empty. He walked back down the ramp and into the hangar.

Ertic stood near the ship, talking with Artun. They looked up as he exited the ship and approached them.

Sebastian decided he should just ask.

"I couldn't find any toilet paper."

"What's toilet paper?" Artun replied.

"It's how you clean yourself after using the toilet," Sebastian said cautiously.

Artun seemed quite surprised. "We're not on the battlefield. Just wave your hand over the button. It'll sense you're there and clean you up."

"Right," Sebastian said.

Ertic looked at the ship and paused as something occurred to him. "It isn't calibrated to deal with human waste." He said, "It won't recognize the enzymes and bacteria. We should close down the food printer."

"The food printer?" Sebastian asked.

"The food printer breaks down the waste and uses it as the ingredients to print the food. It's calibrated to kill off any dangerous bacteria while not destroying molecules that can be reused in the printing process. But it won't recognize your bacteria, so it'll need to be re–calibrated to rectify that. Otherwise, there's a risk it might just print your gut bacteria directly into food," Ertic responded. "I'll schedule it in, it's a low priority though. We'll disable the food printers for now,"

Ertic extended his hand toward Sebastian. "Now human," he said, "we have not officially met."

Sebastian took his hand and shook it.

"My name is Ertic, and you are not on Earth anymore," he said and waited for a response.

"My name is Sebastian," Sebastian responded, "and I'm pretty sure I'm on Earth, on drugs, and I'm just hoping I'm not on the bathroom floor."

"Why do you think that?" Ertic asked.

"Well," Sebastian began, a little concerned that he had to justify himself to his own hallucination. "You were a dog."

"Yes," replied Ertic.

"And now you're a human again," Sebastian continued.

"Not quite," Ertic responded, touching the side of his own head to remind Sebastian of the perception distorter.

Sebastian reached up and touched it, turning it off. Before him stood someone who looked very human, but also very green.

He turned it back on again, and everything returned to normal.

"So, you were a dog, and now you're not a dog, and I see you as a person. I just went to the toilet in a spaceship with a printer that recycles my waste to print food, but first it has to be calibrated to my behind," Sebastian replied. "I just saw two beautiful women bathing and waving at me and yet, if I touch the side of my head, they change from beautiful women into cuttlefish big enough to strike terror into the heart of even the most ardent sushi chef. Artun is covered in fur and can shoot lightning, and you," he motioned at Ertic once more, "are green. Really green. About the same color as an advert for lawn care," he said. "At this point, I haven't seen anything to convince me I'm not on drugs."

Ertic turned to Artun. "You can shoot lightning?" he asked incredulously.

"They put some expensive-looking carpets on the mezzanine. They interact with my fur," he replied. "It's a sore point."

Ertic shook his head and focused back on Sebastian.

"Our nurse tested you."

"The large female lizard, yes," Sebastian replied.

"She says you're clean."

"Yet talking female lizards are not my usual port of call to prove I'm not on drugs," Sebastian said. "Also, you have a tail."

Ertic looked back at it and appeared to shrug. "A fair point," he conceded.

"I think it may take you some time to adjust," Artun said.

Just then, some troops in their regulation uniforms bounded around the edge of the ship and began boarding. They had a mixture of red and green vertical lines on their sashes.

The team leader approached Sub-Commander Ertic and saluted him. On his sash were three green vertical stripes.

"We're taking them all out, Sir," he said through his visor, "we're almost finished updating the meteoroid orbital map."

"Mapping the meteoroids?" Ertic exclaimed. "Why wasn't that finished months ago?"

"The orbits are unusual. The creature seems to keep them in an unpredictable orbit about itself. Sometimes they speed up, slow down, even change direction. We can get an approximate map of the meteoroids, but it quickly changes," he replied.

Ertic nodded his head and thought for a moment. "The printer needs re–calibrated Flight Sergeant, and the tank will need physically drained, so don't use it, but the toilet should work fine for the moment," Ertic said and then stopped as something troubling seemed to cross his mind.

"How did you clean yourself, human?" He asked cautiously.

Sebastian reached into his pocket and pulled out the remaining thin cardboard leaflets. "Needs must and all that," he said hopefully.

Ertic shook his head gruffly, "Don't use the toilet. Watch the back pressure. We don't know how the new bacteria will interact with the material in the holding tank. I don't know if there's an internal blockage. The system might need to be stripped down and rebuilt. Once you've returned, put the ship out of service," Ertic growled.

"Not much time for food, or the toilet at the moment, Sir," the Flight Sergeant said. Ertic nodded in response, still looking a little frustrated, as the troops boarded.

They exited the ship and stood next to it as the ramp retracted and the door lowered and closed, sealing the rear of the ship.

Sebastian reached out to the edge of the ship and began running his right hand across it. Its surface felt like a frictionless golf ball.

Artun and Ertic backed away a little from the ship.

"Should we tell him to move his hand?" Artun asked quietly.

"Right now, he's in denial," Ertic said. "He needs to understand that things are different if he's going to adjust. He can't ignore this. If he does something stupid because he thinks he's hallucinating, he could get seriously hurt, or worse. He needs to accept his new situation."

Ertic continued watching him for a moment, "Put in a request for a couple of guards to keep him safe. He doesn't know how anything works yet."

Inside, the captain had moved to the viewport and was

watching how close Sebastian was to the ship. Ertic caught his eye and nodded at him.

The captain understood and nodded back. He walked over to his chair, sat back down and gave the command to turn on the shields. Sebastian's hand and arm were thrown forcefully from the edge of the ship as he found himself being spun around.

He looked down at his arm, surprised that his sleeve was missing. His arm was uninjured, but his shirt had been completely removed just below his elbow. The skin on his forearm was smooth and hairless. He glanced at the edge of the ship, and he could clearly see his shirt sleeve and his arm hair was held there, as if frozen in time, but flatter.

He turned to Artun and Ertic. "What just happened?" he asked, looking at his arm.

"Welcome to the future," Ertic said with a flourish.

Artun saw his confusion. "The shield creates a section where time runs more slowly about the ship. It's a chrono-bubble. Along the center line time slows to a tiny fraction of its normal value. It creates two separate sections, inside the bubble and outside the bubble. Things inside the bubble are kept safe, like the passengers, and things outside, are kept outside, like us. Living material is ejected from the shield while inorganic or dead material like dust, small rocks, hair or sleeves, accumulate on the center line in flight. They become a part of the shield adding to its strength. It ejected your arm, but your sleeve and a few hairs remained."

Sebastian looked over at the ship as it took off, rising slowly. The dark blue shirt sleeve seemed frozen in position completely flat and held about a foot from the edge of the craft, taunting him with its absence.

Artun looked at Sebastian as he watched the sleeve. "It'll remain there until the shield gets switched off. It experiences a sort of temporal redirection. As time moves faster outside the line, anything along it experiences a force that pushes it back into the center if it starts to drift away. As time slows down a lot, the forces holding it in place are extreme."

Sebastian looked at the ground where the ship had stood, pondering the slight chill he felt on his arm. The ship continued majestically toward the exit portal some twenty feet up, almost on the level of the mezzanine above, still pointing inwards. It rotated itself to face the outside opening and then glided silently out of the launch window, high on the building's side.

Once it passed through, the next ship began its ascent to the launch window. This was happening across all four of the launch bays and continued until all the ships had left.

Sebastian put his jacket back on to placate his now cold arm.

Chapter 14

A couple of guards arrived, ready to escort Sebastian, as
Ertic, Artun and Sebastian left the hangar.

Ertic turned to Sebastian. "The ship carrying the Decimator
is due to arrive," he began, "You will need to stay in a safe
location during its arrival. I think it's best if you wait in the
Ambassador's lounge. There is further work required before I
join you."

"Stand guard by the door until I arrive," Ertic said to the
guards.

"Is there anything to eat?" Sebastian asked, feeling a little
hungry. He looked at his watch. It was now fully morning,
and despite having briefly passed out, he hadn't properly
slept.

Ertic nodded. "The lounge is always fully stocked. Just try
not to use the toilet until we can calibrate it to you," he added
cautiously.

The two soldiers started on their way to escort Sebastian to
the Ambassador's lounge.

"Do you want me to stay with him?" Artun asked.

Ertic thought for a moment. "No, the diplomatic station is
fully surveilled it keeps the diplomats contained. He can't do
any damage and he can't get hurt. I wanted the chance to talk
with you."

Artun and Ertic began walking quickly toward the main
control center.

"Did anyone else return from any of the missions?" Ertic
asked.

"No."

"All the six trackers sent out ceased working when they

were off planet?"

"It was an untested tech, developed too quickly and without due care. After a couple of weeks, they all just switched off. We're just lucky nobody exploded, is my guess. That's assuming that nobody did explode. First time anything like it has ever been created," Artun replied.

He looked at the tracker on Ertic's wrist.

"I had the computer scan the one you're carrying," Artun said. "Most of its circuits are dead."

"Could be the power supply," said Ertic.

"Maybe," said Artun, his voice a little distant.

"Only problem is, we can't rule out sabotage," Ertic said.

"I know," replied Artun, "but there's no way we can have it examined. We're on a war footing with an imminent attack. This is low priority." Artun finished.

"If someone sabotaged them, how could it have been done?" Ertic wondered aloud.

"As long as somebody was close enough, they could make anything happen," Artun said, "bit of a distraction here, bit of destruction there."

"But who would have the opportunity?" Ertic asked.

"Anybody with access would be a suspect. Anybody who knew somebody who had access. Anybody who knew where they stored them..." Artun began.

"I get the idea," Ertic said.

"Anybody who knew someone who knew someone who was important to someone who had access," Artun continued.

"I see," said Ertic dryly.

"How about people who know of someone's pet when that pet was important to another person's pet..."

"I take your point," Ertic said a little more forcefully.

"Point is," said Artun, "it doesn't matter. We're in imminent danger of attack. The fact your fancy locator stopped working is less of an issue. Fix the major problems first, then deal with the less time dependent ones. After all, you don't even think someone sabotaged it, just that it might have been. No point heading into that tunnel.”

Artun paused and looked at him closely. “Keep your eyes open and see what’s around you. Do you want me to keep watch on your human?” he asked.

“We can rule him out,” Ertic responded, “humans don’t have the technology, or anything even close. They wouldn’t know what it was, how it worked, how to sabotage it or why it doesn’t take pictures.”

“Watch for anything out of place,” Ertic finished, as they began making their way to the command room.

Chapter 15

On the viewscreen at the front of the control room a small dot slowly grew larger as everybody stopped to watch it. The artificial sun now sat high in the sky. Groups of engineers busied themselves with the information coming on their terminals, pushing buttons in response to the changing readouts.

Triven adjusted himself to a position that he thought looked more authoritative. Sardok gripped his armrests a little more tightly, trying to look relaxed. The little pyramid basked in the light from the screen as it waited, happily enjoying the moment.

Ertic stood with Artun, carefully watching everyone as the screen held the attention of the room. He watched the people working, looking for anything out of the ordinary.

One of the junior officers knocked some items from the top of his desk and then nervously bent to pick them up. Ertic felt his frustration rise. It was almost useless trying to identify a saboteur. Any traces of nervousness meant nothing. Everyone was on edge. These moments may be among the most important and dangerous in the Empire's history.

The ship on the screen had grown to about the size of a baseball. On board that ship sat the Decimator, straight from the Emperor's own vault. It was a device that, if it activated early, could obliterate the moon entirely and any nearby planets that just happened to be in the wrong place at the wrong time.

The glow of the engines was visible on the screen. The drive was working hard to slow the ship as it approached the base.

"Open hangar doors," Sardok said.

"Hangar doors open, Sir," came the response from a Navigation Officer who looked like he would not be out–of–place wearing a scarecrow outfit and standing in the middle of a field.

"Clear the area and get ready to receive," Sardok ordered.

"Ready to receive," the scarecrow responded, nervousness sounding in his voice.

Sardok looked to Triven for further instruction.

Triven paused for what he believed to be a length of time that communicated gravitas and authoritative intensity. "Bring the ship in," he intoned trying to use his most serious voice, the one with a mild gravelly undertone. For posterity this moment was being recorded, and he wanted to ensure that future generations could fully appreciate his presence. This was unfortunate because it sounded like his tongue was trying to secure a marble desperate to escape the sand in his throat. He felt it didn't quite sound important or gravelly enough.

"Bring it in," he boomed in the voice that he used on recruits when he was ordering them to march in circles. Which he thought sounded much better.

Sh'ockley passed the landing data over to the incoming ship.

The ship on the viewscreen got closer, becoming larger until it took up about a half of the monitor, slowing to a halt and hanging in the sky like a fat silver falcon.

Slowly, the ship turned and began its final descent towards the hangar.

There was silence as the ship slowly approached the ground. Even the atmospheric recyclers seemed almost to quiet down for an instant, as carefully, the most dangerous ship in the galaxy, slowly and awkwardly, continued on its approach.

Nobody let out a sound.

The silence hung over the room like a giant death squid, palpable and moist. The giant death squids were themselves elsewhere however, waiting on their watery planet for an unwary passerby to travel beneath them. At this point the death squid descends upon their prey, devouring them whole. This had been their tactic for millions of years - wait and drop, wait and drop and it seemed likely to continue. Interestingly their natural prey was slowly evolving a type of primitive biological shotgun, while they themselves appeared to be developing rudimentary gun control legislation.

The ship slowly paused outside of the largest of the hangars on the base, the only one capable of holding it, and turned itself around. The rear entrance of the ship jutted out beneath the massive engine exhaust which, along with the engine, took up most of the rear of the ship. The exhaust stuck out like a giant industrial satellite dish, a massive speaker cone or a very confused barnacle. The ship hummed as it slowly entered the hangar backwards.

Only the gentle sound of a whisper drive, and the horrifying deafening screech of the metal edge of the ship grating extensively against the side of the hangar, along with the occasional pop as a supporting strut was ripped apart could be heard.

"Can the AI pilot it in Number Two?" hissed Triven over the hellish noise.

"It can't," he called back, "if we try to interface the systems their AI would detect an intrusion from another AI and either destroy itself, and us, or destroy us, then itself. They've supplied us with their flagship. It only has about three feet on either side. It has to perform the task itself just using the supplied coordinates."

For a brief moment the screeching and popping stopped, before starting up again as the ship started to scrape against the other side of the hangar instead.

After what seemed like altogether too long, the ship finished entering the hangar, and sat down gently, in silence, onto the cold, hard floor. The front end of the ship protruded slightly from the hangar, which allowed it to fit.

"The ship carrying the Decimator has docked," announced the scarecrow.

The relief broke the tension in the room like an overweight man undoing the top button on his trousers after a large meal. The atmosphere relaxed immediately in a manner which was deeply tangible.

"It has been delivered?" Sardok asked.

"The Decimator detonation delivery device has been delivered," came the reply from Sh'ockley this time.

Artun sighed. He hated being in the command room. Too many people who like the sound of their own voices creating little jokes to pass the time.

He paused, reflecting on the idea that at least there seemed to be some hope creeping into the room.

"The Decimator detonation delivery device has been docked and delivered," came another reply with a giggle from the long-range monitoring station.

Ertic tilted his head. "Do you mean that the ship carrying it has been successfully docked?" He asked carefully.

"The Decimator is on the ship, so clearly, yes," replied Sh'ockley, annoyed that she had been interrupted from thinking about a longer reply with more d's in it.

Triven decided that he was not to be outdone.

"Prepare for ship inspection, prior to deploying the docked, delivered, Decimator detonation delivery device," he said, sitting back smugly.

A general air of unease set about the bridge. Nobody really liked Triven, so nobody wanted him to win the competition, however trivial. A look of deep concentration crossed the faces of at least half the people in the command room, as each wanted to be the one to beat him.

"Ready to inspect the docked, delivered, Decimator delivery detonation device, to prepare for delivered Decimator detonation," Sardok blurted out with an enormous smile.

Triven glared at him and made a mental note to write him up for insubordination if this didn't go as planned.

"Is the ship secured?" Triven growled.

"Secured, Sir," came the response.

"Begin the inspection," he commanded.

A handful of the people in the control room, all of whom had the orange engineering colors on their sashes raised themselves up and left the room, heading down towards the docked ship.

"Can we set the ship course from here?" Triven asked.

"It has to be done from inside the ship," Sardok replied.

"I'll go down and oversee the process," came the response from Triven. "You have control of the room," he said to Sardok as he stood to leave.

"If I may interject Number One," Ertic said carefully.

Triven paused, looking a little irate.

"What is it, Sub-Commander?" he asked sharply.

"The human who traveled through the transport tunnel …" he began.

"That's right," interrupted Triven. "He's in the Ambassador's lounge, isn't he?"

"Yes, Sir," Ertic replied. "However, as the first Ambassador from Earth, we may wish to bring him out and show him what we're currently engaged in. That way we will avoid any future diplomatic concerns, as their species becomes more aware of the weapon we're about to deploy."

Ertic's tail gained a little momentum with a cautious 'wag'.

Triven stopped dead in his tracks. The entire diplomatic process was one of the top priorities for the entire civilization and had been ever since the Emperor almost started a war when he was offered the glass of sacred wine by the leader of the Sallasins.

The offering had been symbolic. He was supposed to hold it, lift it towards the gathered delegation as a sign of respect, before returning it, once more, to the high priest. Sadly, this small detail had been left out of his briefing after some of their delegation had gotten drunk the night before and sent pictures of themselves in their underwear re-enacting historical battles, to the chief liaison officer's mother.

It wasn't that the Emperor had drunk the sacred wine,

although that was definitely not appreciated. It was more that he spent the next three hours throwing it all back up again. And why wouldn't he? It was made from the fermented mucus of the last twenty high priests.

He had tried to only sip the wine, however it slid into his mouth and slurped down his throat like a proactive oyster on a mission of revenge.

The Sallasin home planet nearly threw itself into civil war, one half believing it was a stupid mistake and the other half believing the Emperor was a creature of evil who should be attacked on sight. There was a third, much smaller group, involved in the marketing of tissues, who tried to put a positive spin on it, but nobody cared what they thought. In the end the only glue that held their entire society together was the idea that nobody wanted anything else to do with the Empire.

As the Emperor's first project, it was still brought up whenever he visited with other civilizations, which really got under his skin. It was among the highest priorities of the Empire's alliance structure. At all times their galactic civilization relationships were key.

"Get your Earthman," he muttered.

Chapter 16

Sebastian sat on a long padded white bench so soft that his hand just sank into it, as though it was a four-inch-thick marshmallow that covered the seat and the backrest. A huge viewscreen was suspended on the wall opposite him, in front of the bench. It gave the impression of being a giant window. It showed the view over the top of the base as the buildings sat like large puddings with no sharp edges.

To his right, along the wall, was a selection of what looked to be food. An entire set of tables covered in all manner of delicacies, of all different colors and shapes. Occasionally a large nozzle would remove some intricate looking design by sucking it up while a little brush cleaned the table and then another nozzle seemed to print it out once more, likely to keep it fresh.

Sebastian had sat and watched this dance across the food table trying to decide whether or not he should risk it and actually try the mysterious food.

He had been playing a little game with the printer nozzle. First the food would get sucked up, then it would start to print it once more. Sebastian had taken it upon himself to see how many times he could interrupt it and have it pull away from his hand before it gave up on the piece of food it was printing.

After twenty minutes a reasonable portion of the table was starting to fill with unfinished delicacies. The nozzle head began printing a curiously complicated item of food made of geometric designs. Sebastian put his hand near the nozzle again, it pulled away. He waited until it was about to print again and then put his hand near it. Again, it pulled away.

Sebastian continued this for another five minutes, and then he misjudged where his hand should be. The nozzle, by this time, had now finished printing the main body of the food and was squirting some type of blue sauce that looked like icing over it. As his hand approached, the nozzle had pulled away once more but this time some of the sauce ended up on his finger.

He paused and looked at it. He was getting hungry, and he knew sooner or later he would have to try it. He brought his hand near to his face and licked the sauce. To his surprise it didn't taste like icing but instead tasted like the meatiest barbeque sauce he had ever enjoyed.

He reached over to the now finished piece on the counter and picked it up. Carefully he started to eat it. The flavors were amazing. He ate another piece, then he tried a small blue piece from another pile, this time it tasted like butternut squash, another pink and yellow one tasted like sunflower seeds.

After trying the first few pieces of food he realized just how hungry he was and proceeded to treat the counter as an all you could eat buffet.

By the time he had finished he was just about able to sit on the bench and regret the quantity of food he had enjoyed. To help take his mind off how much he had eaten, he had decided to focus on the viewscreen. He watched as a distant speck in the sky had quickly grown to become a large, white, gleaming starship. At least he assumed it was a starship and not just some sort of giant airship or mirage brought on by eating too much.

Sebastian watched as the large white ship descended slowly from the sky in a majestic sort of way. It looked a little like someone had sanded a giant white space armadillo, to make the armored segments smoother and less pronounced and now it was shimmying its way to the ground.

The impression was like gentle stripes on a sleek cat stalking through long grass. He had watched on the viewscreen as it turned gracefully, pivoting in the sky like a hunting cat and changing direction, its prey in sight. He had covered his ears and cringed when it let out an unholy screeching and popping sound as the side of the ship rubbed up against the side of the hangar. The screeching sounded like a cat's chorus being broadcast through a low quality megaphone.

He had released his ears briefly as the noise stopped for a few seconds, as though the cats had stumbled upon a stash of catnip, and then covered his ears once more when the catnip was taken from them, and the screeching and popping resumed as the ship now grated against the other side of the hangar.

The giant screen switched to show the inside of the largest hangar on the base, as the arriving ship gently touched down.

He stood by the viewscreen watching the ship settle into its final position, as several people in uniforms with thin vertical orange stripes, indicating technicians, formed groups and stood about waiting. The front part of the rectangular section beneath the rear engine, silently lifted inward a few feet and then angled itself downward and extended to the ground to become a ramp to the entrance.

Immediately inside the rear entrance was a large rotating sphere and behind that was a row of consoles.

A small technician boarded the ship as the other waited until some engineers from the control room arrived. Then they began running checks and tests on the exterior.

He watched for a while as the technicians moved about the ship inspecting the outer panels. The members of the crew seemed to be waiting for an all clear to enter.

The technician emerged from the ship and approached the group. With a nod, the other groups entered the ship.

Sebastian continued to watch the viewscreen, staring at the almost hypnotic dance between the workers as they moved fluidly about the exterior of the ship, checking and recording as they did so.

The door behind him in the Ambassador lounge opened with a calming 'bong' sound as Artun entered.

"Earthman," he said in a grandiose greeting.

Sebastian turned to him.

"You know you could just call me Sebastian," Sebastian replied.

"Noted," Ertic said with a nod.

"Tell me, human," he began.

"Sebastian," Sebastian corrected.

"Tell me Sebastian," he began again.

"Don't get me wrong, I know that this is likely just the result of some crazed hallucinogen, but still, as a hallucination in my head, I rather hoped you'd call me Sebastian," Sebastian concluded.

"Very well," Ertic continued, a little irritated that the moment when the human saw his first alien spaceship was being relegated to a place of less importance than someone using his name to identify him and not his species. Ertic cleared his throat.

"Tell me, Sebastian," he began using his important voice. "Have you ever seen an alien spaceship?"

"Yes."

"Yes?" Ertic said incredulously. He had been pretty sure that there were no aliens on Earth. Had he missed something? He'd spent almost five months disguised as a dog watching TV and studying Earth. He would know if they'd made contact with aliens. They would have aired a special.

"There's one over there," Sebastian said, pointing at the large ship on the viewscreen that Ertic had been hoping to impress him with.

Ertic sighed. He always enjoyed the big reveals from the shows on Earth, but he had been busy, and now the moment was gone.

Still, he thought, the human hasn't been inside one yet, and Ertic really needed to go inside.

This thought cheered him up immensely as it gave him

another way to impress the Earthman.

"Have you ever seen inside of an alien spaceship in person?" Ertic asked, using his important voice again.

Sebastian thought about it briefly and quickly excluded the various shows he'd seen and games he'd played.

"I went to the toilet in one." Sebastian responded.

Ertic muttered under his breath and tried again. "The last spaceship you saw was like a work van. This one is like a cruise liner, have you ever seen inside of a ship like that?" He said pointing at the ship on the viewscreen, exasperation clear in his voice.

"No," Sebastian said with certainty.

"Well, human, come with me. We can't very well have a diplomatic incident now, can we?" Ertic said happily.

"A diplomatic incident?" Sebastian said, a little confused.

"As the first representative of Earth, you are now an Ambassador for Earth," Ertic said. "Congratulations."

Sebastian thought about this for a moment. It didn't seem at all realistic.

"Do I get paid?" he asked.

"Nope," Ertic said happily, "think of it as an internship or a bad trip. Those two seem to have a lot in common." He grinned, showing what appeared to be more than a normal number of teeth.

"Do I get diplomatic immunity?" he asked.

"You can get it, but if you commit any serious crimes, you get shot." Ertic thought for a moment, "although I believe we could put it on an inscription on your tombstone."

"After I'm shot," said Sebastian.

"And we'd probably invoice your planet for it." Ertic continued.

"You'd invoice the Earth?"

"It's a nice tombstone."

"So, you'd shoot me, then invoice my planet, but I get my name on the tombstone."

"That's right," Ertic responded, "and we'd probably have to

go to war with Earth as well, if they didn't reimburse us for the costs."

"So, what are the benefits of it, then?" Sebastian asked suspicious.

"You get to see the inside of an alien spaceship," he turned and pointed at the screen, "that one. Just before it goes off to be destroyed in the largest controlled explosion any of us will ever see up close. As you still think you might be on some sort of drug induced vision quest, this could really be good for you. Explore the Id and all that."

Sebastian paused for a moment wondering what in his Id was going on.

Ertic was enjoying this. He was going to show this human more than any human had ever seen before. What Ertic didn't know was that spending so much time as a dog had left him with somewhat of a desire to please. But that wasn't his main motivation.

As he stood there, his tail started wagging. "Let's go human," he said, pushing Sebastian out through the door in a firm, yet friendly manner.

Chapter 17

They entered the hangar and approached the large ship, its sleek lines seemed to almost dare the onlooker to test it in uncharted waters, yet it sat there giving an impression not unlike a swordfish sitting in a puddle. It just looked out of place. Its sleek yet oddly bulbous carcass wallowing atop three stanchions that had emerged from the enormous body. At the rear, a ramp had descended to the ground and people were walking up and down it with purpose.

As they walked closer to it, Sebastian watched as it appeared to almost pulsate, slight undulations that passed down the length of the ship from the nose to the rear.

The hangar was four hundred meters long, closed on three sides and lit from above. There were no rooms, no mezzanine and no corridors. This building was as large a hangar as you could get and even then, the ship barely fit inside it.

They paused for a moment to take it in. It was nearly three hundred meters long and glimmered under the hangar lights as though it had gone through a car wash. It's scale so large that it looked as though someone was hiding a glacier.

"What is that?" Sebastian said, his breath taken away by its size.

"Looks bigger up close, doesn't it?" Ertic said.

"We weren't that far away," Sebastian said in a hushed voice.

"The room is for diplomats. It's important to have them able to view everything and even more important to give them exactly the wrong impression until you need them to think otherwise," Ertic answered. "The default setting is to make the ships smaller and less impressive, but there are a couple of other settings too, larger and more like transports, covered in skulls and, my personal favorite, oddly purple."

"Oddly purple?" Sebastian said, almost wishing he hadn't.

"Yes, everything of interest shows up as purple, but really oddly," Ertic replied.

"Why's that useful?" Sebastian asked.

"A surprising number of species can't see purple," Ertic responded.

"How many's a surprising number?"

"One."

Sebastian paused for a second and thought about it a little more.

"So why make it oddly purple and not just purple, then?" He asked.

"Because one species that we deal with, the Beekans, can't see purple and all they can sense is that it's really, really odd. It's very disorienting for them." Ertic responded proudly.

"Why would you do that to diplomats? I thought it was all about maintaining peaceful relationships," Sebastian asked curiously.

"They're pacifists," Ertic said.

The Beekans are unique in the history of the Universe. Due to their pacifism, they have been conquered by over one hundred different empires. Nobody knows the true extent of the wealth on planet Beekan except for every single Beekan and about a hundred, very quiet, civilization level governments and rulers.

It is precisely zero.

They have no natural resources of any use, little agriculture to speak of, and their music is derivative. They sit on their planet all day long doing nothing, because there is nothing for them to do. The only way they survive on the planet at all is through the beneficence of their invaders. This is because the Universal Treaty states that: 'the welfare of all conquered worlds is the absolute responsibility of the conquerors.'

The Beekans had discovered, a long time ago, that once conquered, whomever conquered them has to provide them with food, education and water. They took this opportunity to become well fed, well–watered and very well educated.

They have the highest number of economists per capita of any race in the Universe. Thus, they are an enormous drain on whoever conquers them. In fact, before coming under the purview of the Empire, the last time they changed hands was during a drunken game of cards when the title deeds were snuck into the pot.

The empire that lost the game had once been the richest in the sector and was now the poorest. Their entire government moved home planets during the night and went into hiding for two years until the change of ownership was crystallized in the Interplanetary Treaties. It is believed that everyone who is aware, keeps the Beekans' finances secret, in case one day, they need to pass them on to someone else.

It may be the best kept secret in the galaxy. The other, deeper problem with the Beekans is that being economists, they are very bad with money.'

Excerpt from: *The Beekans, A top secret report.*

They walked closer to the ship and Sebastian reached out and touched it as they walked past. It felt frictionless but dimpled, just like the smaller space craft.

"I thought it would be smoother," he said, his voice trailing off.

"The surface encourages extra–dimensional bubbles to stick to it," Ertic responded.

Sebastian looked at him questioningly.

"Look, we can only travel faster than light when we put things outside of this dimension, so we put them into extra–dimensional bubbles. Things can sit slightly outside of this Universe with a small connection, the cross–sectional area of one of the bubbles."

"Okay," Sebastian said.

"It takes an exponentially increasing amount of energy to maintain an increasing bubble size. If we wanted to make a bubble large enough to hold a ship, we'd need to burn up a sun just to get the energy. What we can create much more easily is billions of tiny bubbles, borrowing the energy from the Universe itself. As we go faster, more energy builds up on the edge of the bubble that bridges into this Universe. That energy is passed through to the rest of the extradimensional bubbles. These surround the surface of the ship and get maintained as energy seeps in from our Universe. That way, the ship is inside of an enormous bubble that is actually a huge number of smaller bubbles, sort of side steps the energy requirements and we get to keep our suns," he paused and looked closely at the ship. "It's a nice ship, though," he said appreciatively.

Ertic looked at Sebastian levelly. "You don't need to use the toilet, do you?" Ertic asked.

"I'm good, thanks," Sebastian responded.

"Or bathroom?" he asked suspiciously.

"Nope," Sebastian said.

"And you realize that peeing on something doesn't make it yours?" Ertic said, watching Sebastian carefully. His hackles raised slightly as his tail stopped its gentle wagging. That was his plan. He wasn't showing the human the ship to solve a diplomatic issue. He had every intention of somehow peeing on the largest explosive device in history. He just wasn't sure how yet.

"I'm okay with that," Sebastian replied cautiously, wondering if he'd accidentally stumbled into the wrong conversation.

"Alright human, follow me," Ertic responded, continuing to watch him with suspicion.

Ertic found himself fighting a powerful urge to pee on the support stanchions that had descended from the ship. He had spent much of his time as a dog peeing on things and thereby

owning them, and he had to admit he rather liked the look of
the ship.

On Earth, he had taken great pride in the sheer quantity of
things that he 'owned'. They included road signs, coats in the
park, the park itself, skyscrapers, houses, garbage, a sleeping
cat (although it had not taken kindly to its new owner) and
once he even found himself by the railings on the edge of a
roof garden and took ownership of the top two tiers of a
wedding cake and some of the guests.

Now, finding himself once again as an unabashed bipedal
capitalist, he was trying to merge his two distinct drives and
had to hold back on the need to assume ownership by making
it rain.

They walked to the opening at the rear of the ship where the
ramp stretched down to the ground, its end smoothly sealed
against the floor. As they rounded the base of the ramp, they
could see into the entranceway. It seemed to be a room about
thirty feet by thirty feet and about twelve feet high. From
their vantage point they could see the tops of some the
consoles at the other end of the room. Beyond the room it
seemed to open into a cavernous space.

A large spherical metal object sat just inside the entrance,
about ten feet across and covered in lights, flashing as it
slowly rotated. A dull hum radiated from it as if it were
almost alive.

They stood entranced at the sight. It's almost hypnotic
sounds removed the noise of everything else happening
around it. The maintenance crew watched it nervously while
some of the crew from the control room watched it with an
innate sense of horror.

"That must be the Decimator," Ertic said.

"Is it the first time you've seen it?" Sebastian asked.

"This is the first time one has been deployed. Nobody knows
how many of these even exist. They stored this one in secret
beneath the Royal Palace. It may be the only one in
existence," Ertic responded, transfixed by the machine. "I

think I'd be fine with that; nobody should be able to destroy a planet."

They stood for a little longer, watching it.

Ertic noticed the look on Sebastian's face as he stared at it, with a sort of curious awe. He looked at the Decimator again and then once more at Sebastian, this time with a sly smile. Sebastian wasn't the only one who could 'use the bathroom.' An idea was beginning to take shape in Ertic's head. A way that he could lay claim to the Decimator. It was a simple plan but there was a very good chance it would work.

"This way Sebastian," he said leading him onward to the ship.

They walked up the ramp and started to round the large, spherical object which took up a sizeable amount of the entrance. Close behind it was a row of instrument panels that sealed the Decimator in the entrance structure below the engines. The twelve-foot-tall ceiling trapped the Decimator in a colossal cubby hole. As they skirted the Decimator, they noticed there was not just an audible hum emitting from it, they could also feel a sort of deep vibration as they passed by.

It was beautiful but gave a sense of deep–seated dread that appeared to increase with proximity. It seemed to stop rotating at random intervals before starting up again.

None of the maintenance workers or engineers from the control room watched them as they passed. Too fixated were they on their own tasks and checks, each attempting to ensure that everything was completed to perfection, and they didn't accidentally blow up the base, the moon, the planet and this sector of their solar system.

Beyond the instrument panels, a group of maintenance workers were fixing large metal bars and plating, between the row of instruments and the rest of the ship to ensure that the trapped decimator remained trapped in position, in its space.

Ertic and Sebastian reached the main part of the ship's interior. It seemed to go for a hundred and fifty feet, the roof extended majestically upwards revealing six different levels to

the ship, each looking down into the entrance from panoramic
balconies in the giant atrium.

It looked a little like a cross between a cruise ship and a
five–star hotel.

"Checking auxiliary power to the control units," said a voice
under one of the units.

"Auxiliary power provision successfully tested," said the
same voice again.

"That's all we can actively test," said what appeared to be a
foreman with a slightly bigger note–taking board. The crew
continued recording the data from their instruments as they
breathed a collective sigh of relief.

For a brief second, after they passed by it, the sphere
stopped slowly rotating once more and the crew froze in
position. Then the moment passed, and the sphere began its
journey once more.

Sebastian turned and watched as they continued their well–
choreographed dance.

Point at instruments.

Read instruments.

Record results.

Point at instruments.

Read instruments.

Record results.

"Why do they need clipboards?" Sebastian mused.

"They developed the plan for using the Decimator with great
care over the last few years," Ertic began. "In order to deploy
it, it had to be loaded aboard a vessel and moved from the
Royal Palace. The Emperor himself loaded it before it began
the journey here. He was the only person who had access to it.
Another race provided the only ship allowed to carry it. Then
it can only be deployed with cross species agreement."

"So why the clipboards?"

Ertic thought for a moment about how to explain the
complexities involved to a human. "Think of it like two
political parties. They can pretend they are working towards

helping the same people, but if that's true, then why do you need two of them?"

"Because they might disagree on the best way to implement the policies that can best effect positive change for people." Sebastian answered, he was feeling quite proud of himself after having taken an online course in social engagement and donating a bit of his cash to a small political drive.

"Then why don't they give the money back if they're unelected? And why do then end up so wealthy when they leave office?" Ertic asked. "Basically politicians, like many of the species that can traverse space, don't like each other, but they do like themselves. This ship is here to move a Decimator from one location to another. It comes from a fleet of ships that are of an equally high caliber. They pulled it from active service, showing it's tested and ready."

"This action is designed to save this species here, in this star system, or at least to look like it, which will make politicians here, and there, look good. They supply it with an advanced AI from the other star system. This will help to protect their technology from us. The politicians there do not trust the politicians here anymore than they like, or trust, each other. This maneuver helps to ensure, then, that they use the Decimator only where it is supposed to be, and not against the species supplying the ship."

"That seems sensible," Sebastian responded.

"The problem with this is that our AI can't interface with it without this AI assuming it's been captured and self–destructing which will kill everyone. The group supplying the ship appears to have done everything possible to help whether their ship kills everybody or not. The politicians both supplying the ship, and agreeing to receive the ship, look good regardless of whether we all live or die. Just like politics."

"So, everything has to be checked manually," Sebastian said aloud. He was also thinking that it also helped to explain why the course in social engagement was being run by the small political group he donated to.

They remained silent for a moment.

"So, what do they do with the money?" he asked, unable to let go of the idea that his money might have vanished.

"On Earth? Either the black hole of an untraceable retirement fund, probably via a charity that the politician is affiliated with, or they do love their hidden trusts in other countries. Sometimes they donate it to a similar party as they can't compete. Then they get a kickback to a bank account registered under a company name in some place with strict privacy laws. Sometimes they just keep the money, but, if they're really lucky they can get their entire country to send money to another country so that either there are no books to check or too many to choose from. Why do you think politicians are so keen on sending money to other countries?"

"They use their supporters to continue political attack maneuvers whenever anyone asks questions, and they get to keep all the money they received. They just have to hide it. Despite the attacks, politicians, unlike the soldiers they direct, never really die," Ertic said with more than a hint of distaste.

"They can't be that bad," Sebastian said.

"Show me a war that wasn't started by a politician." Ertic muttered. "Hell, even once the war's ended, it suddenly becomes very important to show how the prevailing justice works. This means that they are at most given a show trial and then put under house arrest, while the soldiers they sent to war get shot for going to war, even though they would have been shot for not going to war. So, although politicians dislike each other, they protect their own. They know too many of each other's secrets," he said coldly. "Whether it's here or on Earth, never underestimate them."

"So how do you deal with them?" Sebastian asked, a little nervous as to the answer.

"The Emperor deals with them but the balance of power is," he paused, "fragile. "Come with me human, we only have a few minutes before this ship takes off. It's on a bit of a deadline," Ertic said.

They continued along a wide corridor illuminated by gently pulsating light from the ceiling that seemed to emanate in all directions. Ertic was reading the signs on the rooms as they passed. Eventually they came to one that said, 'mess room' and they entered through a wide door.

There were rows and rows of benches ready to seat hundreds of soldiers. Ertic rushed to the back of the benches, where there was a large serving platform that appeared to be full of food that sat above rows of drawers and cupboards.

"If they're destroying the ship, why is it full of food?" Sebastian asked.

"The food printers are all on automatic," Ertic responded as he rifled through the drawers beneath the food, eventually finding what he was after and holding up a metallic jug in triumph.

"What's that for?" asked Sebastian.

"Important business," Ertic said almost to himself. "Right, let's find a bathroom, Earthman,"

They exited the room and followed the corridor to a sign that clearly read 'bathroom'. Opposite was another that read 'toilet'.

"It's been a couple of hours," Sebastian said looking at the toilet sign, "I might quickly use it."

"You're fine. The ship's not calibrated to you," Growled Ertic. "Wait here," He said as he entered a door labelled bathroom, trying not to smile at the irony.

"Wait, I thought you were about to blow it up," Sebastian said. "Can't I just use the bathroom and avoid snacking before we leave?"

"Nope," Ertic said as he continued through the door.

Sebastian waited for a few moments and then it occurred to him that this ship belonged to an entirely different race of aliens. If this was real, he wanted to see what their toilets looked like and if this was a hallucination, he wanted to see what their toilets looked like.

"If I can't use it, I still want to see what it looks like," he shouted out. After all this was a toilet for a whole new species. It could have handles, or nodules or fake plastic trees.

Sebastian entered the door labelled 'toilet' and was disappointed to see that it bore a striking resemblance to the other toilet that he had already used. There was a very slight lemon smell in the air. He looked about the surfaces, which were rounded, smooth and calming, then he started pushing in on the edges, about the sink. One way or another he was going to figure out how these things worked. He moved his hands about dramatically and the toilet flushed. He thought that was a good start. He kept pushing on different surfaces, poking, slapping and waving his hands about. Gently a small drawer opened. In it was a little round metallic ball. It smelled like lemon and pine.

He picked it up and looked at it as it gleamed in the light from the ceiling, before exiting the room and waiting for Ertic.

Ertic emerged a few moments later, appearing triumphant. Having now used a bathroom to get the privacy to pee into a jug, he felt freer than he had all day.

"Well, human, are you ready to escape before the ship blows up?" he asked carefully, holding the jug, that now appeared to be full of liquid.

Sebastian watched it cautiously.

"If the ship's about to blow up," Sebastian began.

"Yes," said Ertic impatiently.

"Does it matter if I take anything?"

"Not really," Ertic replied.

"I found an air freshener," Sebastian continued and pulled the small lemon scented ball out of his pocket. "Can I keep it?"

"You didn't use the toilet, did you?" Ertic demanded.

"No, I just wanted to see it," Sebastian said as Ertic visibly appeared to relax.

He looked at the little round ball. "I think we'll be fine in the long run; we should be able to crash the ship without the air freshener," Ertic said, he was starting to look a little distracted. Very soon they would send the ship off to explode, and, with a bit of luck, he would own the biggest bomb in this corner of the Universe.

Ertic looked at the ball again and shrugged, "smells nice."

Ertic's wristband vibrated gently.

"It'll probably smell less nice if we explode. We really need to leave here now," he said.

His wristband let out a few beeps.

It was time.

His plan had been simple. Pee in the jug then wait until everybody left. The beeps were the final evacuation warning. All the other staff would be out of the ship or running for the exit. It was a simple game of intergalactic chicken with a massive bomb and a ship that would be impossible to escape if he lost.

Now all he had to do was get his jug to the Decimator.

"Quickly," he said with urgency and started running down the hall, carefully trying to balance the jug in his hands. Sebastian ran after him.

They ran back through the corridors towards the exit and the Decimator. Ertic was doing his best to keep the contents of the jug from spilling, as urine splashed over his shirt and hands. As they approached the Decimator, Sebastian noticed that everybody was gone.

Ertic ran to the desk nearest the Decimator and placed the gently steaming jug of warm liquid on top of it.

"Why are you putting that there?" Sebastian asked.

Ertic looked at him with an almost rabid wide–eyed expression, "It doesn't matter, we need to go, now," he said curtly, a crazed grin on his face. Inside his heart was soaring.

He ran towards the ramp, and Sebastian followed. By the time they reached the ramp and began to descend, it had already started to pull back into the ship, and they had to jump the remaining five feet to the ground.

They landed and lay on the ground. Ertic lay there with a very large grin on his face, wet shirt and damp hands. Two technicians that had remained to report on the launch helped them to their feet.

The one who helped Ertic up was left wondering why his hands were damp and smelly.

"Let's go watch the action happen," Ertic said, still grinning.

Chapter 18

A general silence fell on the bridge. This would be the first time in recorded history an activated Decimator had launched.

"Send the ship on its course," said Triven.

The general silence in the room was soon joined by major discomfort and general acceptance. The room was silent, but for the occasional voice issuing commands or updates.

The Navigation Officer watched the readouts closely, carefully confirming the information on her screen. "The ship has begun to exit the hangar."

Silence pervaded the room and thankfully, this time, the ship avoided the edges of the hanger. Slowly it moved outside and turned, ready for launch.

The Navigation Officer carefully studied the readouts. "Launching in three, two, one." There was a pause. "Ship launched."

The crew watched the large screen at the front of the room as the image switched between different views of the ship as it launched, before finally settling on a rather nice one from an elevated height in the distance.

Ertic and Sebastian had moved back to the diplomatic lounge. They stood and watched as the large vessel, which appeared significantly smaller from inside the lounge, began to exit the hangar, ready to take off.

"It looks so much smaller," Sebastian said.

"Accept command override, show external view, no filter," Ertic said loudly.

Suddenly the image of the ship on the screen, was replaced by the image of a ship that was easily four times the size. It barely passed through the sides of the hangar in which it had sat.

"Now that's impressive," Sebastian said.

Ertic nodded approvingly at Sebastian's surprise.

"Watch this," Ertic said. "Strangely purple filter."

Suddenly, the ship turned various shades of purple and there was something about it that just made it feel deeply strange.

"Why does it feel so strange?" Sebastian asked.

"A lot of work went into that effect," Ertic said proudly. "It targets both the fear center in most brains and also, rather oddly, the part of the brain that recognizes humor." He tried to think of a way for Sebastian to relate to it. "Like if you went to a comedy show and someone was nice to you."

"No filter," Ertic said again, and the screen immediately reverted to normal.

The enormous ship finished leaving the hangar and slowly turned with the stoic grace of an iceberg chasing a herring.

It continued to turn and began to rise into the air, like a very determined iceberg following a seagull that had stolen the herring it was chasing. The ship moved farther and farther into the distance, seeming to disappear faster as it did so.

"Replace view with command readout" Ertic said and immediately the view changed once again, showing the readouts that were being viewed in the command center.

"One of the perks of being in the diplomatic lounge," Ertic said, "is access to all the information."

He walked to the readout and entered a command code into the screen. Immediately what seemed to be a random set of numbers switched locations on the screen.

"And now the information is accurate," he grinned, "Before, it was just complete."

"Are there any other perks?" Sebastian asked.

"Open buffet," Ertic responded, gesturing to the table filled with food.

"Private toilet facilities," Ertic nodded over to another door.

Sebastian found his gaze travelling between the two parts of the room, caught somewhere between wonder and curious disgust, with a strong memory of how much he'd enjoyed the food.

"How long before I can have the toilets programmed for me to use them?" he asked.

"Soon enough," Ertic said. "Although I suspect there'll be a meeting first."

There was a determined silence in the command room, interrupted only briefly and poignantly as information flowed across the group.

"The course was manually updated and accepted by the AI," said the Navigation Officer.

The camera view on the screen switched to show the ship's exterior as it began moving higher into the atmosphere, heading towards the approaching creature.

Triven leaned forward in his chair, watching the large screen at the front of the command center intently.

"I need a status report on the Decimator," he said.

"All working within safe parameters," came the reply from the Science Officer, a gentleman who shared more than a few attributes with an old–timey homesteader. He had slightly crazed hair, a nervous look in his eyes and his uniform appeared about two sizes too large.

"Do we actually know these parameters?" Sardok asked.

"Not exactly Sir, no," he replied.

"Then how do we know it's all working within 'safe parameters'," Triven said with an edge to his voice.

"Alright," began the Science Officer, "The Decimator is behaving exactly as it did when the ship was docked."

"So, no change then," said Sardok.

"And we're still alive," said the Science Officer.

"Aha, so within 'safe parameters'," Sardok appeared to be quite pleased with this. "Good update."

"Thank you, Sir," the Science Officer responded.

"Give me a countdown to the collision," Triven commanded.

The Navigation Officer manipulated her console a little and a small timer of blinking lights appeared at the bottom right of the screen.

A silence slowly descended on the group as they continued to watch the ship as it rose through the thin atmosphere before heading out to space on its last flight.

Triven watched intently on the viewscreen and then examined some readouts that were being fed directly to a smaller screen on the arm of his rather luxurious chair.

"The ship has cleared the atmosphere and is accelerating toward the intercept coordinates," the Science Officer stated.

Triven watched the numbers as they appeared and then seemed to relax a little as they continued to feed onto his personal screen, making minor adjustments on his controls. "Chart the course and prepare to engage FTL engines."

There was an awkward silence in the room. Normally this would have made Triven quite happy, but, as it was one he hadn't expected, he felt it lessened his 'gravitas'.

He repeated himself, "chart the course and prepare to engage FTL engines."

There was a sound of someone clearing their throat.

Triven was a team player in the way an alligator worked well with gazelles. It was for this reason, which was now starting to dawn on everyone in the room, that nobody had actually told him that there was going to be an issue.

The silence remained in the air, generally making everyone uncomfortable, until it too decided it would rather be elsewhere.

"There aren't any," said the Navigation Officer, watching him carefully.

"Excuse me?" Triven replied, glaring at the Navigation

Officer.

"We don't have any, Sir," said the Science Officer.

"What do you mean?" Triven said icily.

Triven turned to face the Science Officer, and, for a moment, it almost appeared as if the wind was whistling gently over the fields and lightly rustling the homesteader as he stood by the science console. The sight of tumbleweed slowly traversing the control room would not have been amiss.

"The Vertids didn't want to share their technology when they provided the ship, so they removed it," he replied.

Triven felt irritated. This single act was making his very important task take longer than required, and he was not pleased about it.

"Well, it obviously arrived here, so what does it have?" he asked impatiently.

"Sub light drives Sir, they're fully operational, but there is a possibility they could set off the device," the Science Officer responded.

"I thought you didn't know how it worked." Triven fired back.

"They have a level of vibrational instability…" the Science Officer began, his voice becoming quieter.

The room suddenly became more tense, as if someone had just stolen Triven's socks.

"How long until it is at a safe distance?" Triven demanded.

"A few more moments until we could survive the blast," the Science Officer replied.

A silence descended on the command deck while Triven's mood deteriorated. He glared at the viewscreen and anybody who dared to catch his gaze.

"Reaching a safe distance now, Sir," the Science Officer said.

"Engage the sub light engines," Triven growled with the tone of a being who knew where his socks had gone and that they were no longer either on his feet, or coming back.

Sardok looked at him a little uneasily.

"Shouldn't we wait until it's a little farther out?" he asked nervously.

"Engage the sub light engines," Triven repeated with an intensity that might frighten a small rhino and make a larger one question its life choices.

"Engaging sub light engines," the Science Officer responded, just glad to no longer be a part of the conversation.

Everyone stared intently at the main screen, breaking their view, only to read outputs on their individual screens or to input data.

After a few minutes, when everyone realized they were still alive, they began to relax. Even Triven seemed to lose some of his intensity.

Ertic's eyes kept focusing back on the image of the ship on the screen.

"It's travelling sub light," he said, surprised.

"Is that a problem?" Sebastian asked, not really sure what he was supposed to be looking at.

"When ships travel faster than light, they are covered in a structure that separates them from this Universe. That means that they can't hit any meteoroids that could destroy the ship. At that speed, even dust would destroy a vessel. Inside that structure you could travel through a planet," Ertic responded. "If the ship's travelling slower than the speed of light, then it's vulnerable. It isn't protected inside the structure."

"The bubbles?" Sebastian said.

Ertic nodded. "You can use the shields, certainly for smaller obstacles at slower speeds, but to do this? It's more likely to go wrong."

Sebastian pulled out his phone and loaded up his game. "I just need to check something," he muttered.

Sebastian looked at the screen as his game loaded. He started to play it again. Everything in the game looked just as it always had, and it troubled him deeply. He threw the ship in his game from side to side, passing over and around objects as they came at him. He was desperate to see something missing or glitching that would tell him it was all in his head. There were no glitches or any parts of it that seemed affected.

Ertic watched the game briefly and then looked back at the readouts.

"Wait here," he said as he left the room and made his way towards the command center.

"This had better be a drug induced trip," Sebastian said quietly to himself. He continued to play the game, hoping that something would just start looking wrong.

Chapter 19

Ertic entered the command center and nodded to Artun, who stood by the wall. Artun nodded back and then shook his head ever so slightly. He hadn't seen anything suspicious.

Ertic looked about the room and then walked over to the engineering section.

"Why are we travelling sub light speed?" he asked.

"There are no FTL engines. The Vertids took them out when they gave us the ship," the Science Officer replied.

"Dammit," Ertic responded.

He looked at the readouts. Everything else seemed in place. Ertic breathed a sigh of relief. On the viewscreen, the timer continued its countdown.

"How is our guest doing, Sub-Commander?" Sardok asked, a joviality in his voice that never quite seemed to fade.

The pyramid next to him just sat there and watched everything.

It waited.

The fun was due to start soon.

"He's adjusting. It might take him a little longer to acclimatize," Ertic replied.

"He should be locked up until we're finished." Triven said, clearly unhappy.

"That would violate the protocol for dealing with Ambassadors," Sardok responded with an air of cheerfulness.

Triven glared at him.

On the screen, a flash engulfed a part of the ship.

"Report. What was that?" Triven demanded as he jumped up from his chair.

"A small meteoroid collided with one of the fuel structures,"

The Engineering Officer responded. "One of the starboard engines is non–functioning, the other engines are adjusting to compensate."

"Why didn't the shields stop it?" Triven demanded.

"Unknown, they should be fully functional," the Science Officer replied. "It was not a large rock; the shields should have had no difficulty stopping it."

"Engineering," Triven shouted, "run a diagnostic on the shields of the ship."

"On it," came the response from the engineer. a small blue person with pristine hair like a 1970s rocker.

"The readouts are positive but there are no fuel drains for the shields. It's as if the readout is jammed on, but it's just for show," the engineer responded.

"Can we interface with the AI and activate them?" Sardok demanded.

"Not without the ship destroying itself," the engineer said, his hair moving dramatically.

"What are our options?" Triven said, still standing.

"We can't interface with the AI to turn the shields on, and the AI on the ship is course locked now. We can't change it without an interface. The Decimator was primed when it left the home planet so one wrong collision and there's a good chance it will explode. If it explodes in the wrong place, we'll miss our opportunity." The engineer responded.

"What are the chances the ship can survive the meteoroids?" Sardok asked.

"The meteoroids will get thicker as the ship gets closer to the creature. They surround the creature. There's no way that the ship will reach the creature without being destroyed. The AI will continue along the course that was manually set."

Triven sat down, his frustration evident.

"Are there no other options?" he asked.

"Do we have anything else that can communicate with the ship without tripping the AI," Sardok asked.

"Everything here ties directly to our AI," the engineer

responded. "We'd need something that doesn't come from the ship."

"Come with me" Ertic shouted to the engineer. "The human has a primitive controller. Connect through to the diplomatic lounge," Ertic said to Triven, as he ran from the room quickly followed by the engineer.

Chapter 20

Sebastian put down his game and watched as the explosion on the side of the ship seemed to break off a small section. Half of the screen was showing the readouts, and the other half was showing the video feed from the ship.

"That can't be good," he said, watching as the explosion seemed to die down, almost hypnotically, in the vacuum of space.

He moved to stand next to the viewscreen and, reaching out, ran his fingers over the image of the ship spewing out glowing white–hot embers from the reaction of whatever chemicals had been stored inside. He brought his face close to the viewscreen, trying to see the damage.

He stared with absolute fascination at the image of the ship.

The viewscreen suddenly flickered and an eight–foot–tall image of Triven's head appeared across the screen, looking at him disapprovingly. Sebastian's hand was resting on his fine line moustache. He instinctively jerked away from the screen and stepped back, dwarfed by Triven's huge head, mere feet from his face. He found himself staring at Triven's nostrils, which were the same height as his eye level. "Human, we are about to make some demands of you. We expect your complete cooperation," the voice from just below the giant nostrils said.

"Sure?" Sebastian said, uncertain.

The door opened and Ertic and another, smaller man with fabulous hair ran into the room.

"Sebastian," Ertic said quickly, "have you got your phone?"

"Sure," Sebastian said with more certainty this time, pulling it from his pocket and offering it to him.

Ertic grabbed it and passed it rapidly to the engineer.

The engineer looked at it, turning it over in his hands.

He looked at Sebastian. "Does this have an AI?"

"Yes," Sebastian said.

"No," said Ertic. "An AI that could interface with, and run, a planet, not one that tells you if there are discounts at the ice rink."

"Probably no, then," said Sebastian, curious about what was happening.

"You said you were good at that game you're always playing," Ertic stated. "How good?"

"I won some money in a competition,"

"Perfect," Ertic said. "Can you patch in the controls and interface to mimic the game?"

"The AI is analyzing it now," the engineer said.

"You may be about to play for higher stakes," Ertic said to Sebastian.

"The adaptations are being made." The engineer paused for a few seconds as he worked to interface the system with the phone. "It's done," he said as the interface finalized.

Ertic took it back from the engineer. "Can it communicate safely?"

"I've adapted the device so that it uses the same carrier wave as the ship carrying the decimator, but as it contains no real AI to speak of, the ship should not view the interface as an attack or intrusion. The AI of the ship should just see it as a passive controller. The power has been updated to run off the power transmitted about the ship," the engineer responded.

The screen in the room behind Ertic still held the giant, disapproving head.

"What's happening, Sub-Commander?" Triven's suspicious, bulbous, giant head said testily, looking a lot like it belonged somewhere on a scale between evil villain and electronic engineer.

"We have a means to control the ship," Ertic responded.

"Then bring it to command and we can use it."

"We have to use it now Sir, before the ship's destroyed," Ertic responded.

"Then pilot the ship back to the base so we can regroup."

"We'd still have to pass the ship through the meteoroids drifting out there, it's already starting to pass through them and the moment we disengage the controller the AI will target the creature again and take off. It's been hard-coded now."

"That was an order," Triven shouted, furious that someone else was trying to steal his glory.

"There's no time, we need to start it," Ertic shot back.

He handed the phone back to Sebastian.

"It should work exactly as before. The AI reprogrammed the interface to respect the game rules and update it with the real–time meteoroid positions," Ertic said.

Sebastian took the phone carefully and began the game.

On the big screen, Triven ordered Artun to drag Ertic to the brig and bring the controller to the control room.

Ertic looked up at the screen and changed it to show the view from the ship as it flew towards the creature. He turned to the engineer.

"Do you have a fuser with you?" he asked.

"Yes," the engineer responded, "but I can't give it to you. You're under orders."

"I understand," Ertic said. Then he reached down to the engineer's bag and pulled out a small square device with a handle that came off to the side.

"I'd like you to leave now," Ertic said to the engineer.

The engineer left and Ertic sealed the door with the fuser behind him. Then he flipped a small switch at the side of the door and a message flashed up 'Door Secured.'

A few moments later, he heard Artun as he attempted to open the door.

"Open the door Sub-Commander," he said loudly from the other side.

"Can't do that Artun, we need to do this now. The meteoroids are about to come thick and fast. Any pause we take means failure," Ertic replied, loud enough to be heard through the door.

He looked at Sebastian, who was moving his fingers rapidly about his phone, redirecting the ship on the viewscreen.

He was staring wild-eyed at the small screen in front of him.

'Dammit,' thought Ertic. He walked to Sebastian and crouched down beside him.

"You look tense," he said. "Does that help with your game play?"

"It doesn't," Sebastian replied.

"Alright human," Ertic began. "It seems you understand the gravity of the situation."

"It crossed my mind," Sebastian replied, narrowly avoiding a meteoroid flying towards him on the screen.

Ertic started to wonder if Sebastian could fly the ship safely.

Artun banged on the other side of the door. "My orders are to come through the door and pass the controller to Number One. You've got maybe three minutes," Artun said from the other side, before a loud screeching, grinding sound emanated from the corner of the room.

Ertic looked at Sebastian and thought carefully, "Well, human, that's not helpful. I need you to believe that you're definitely not here and go back to believing that this is all in your head. What's more likely - that you appeared in another part of the galaxy, or that you are still struggling to get through the effects of whatever you were given?"

"But the game hasn't changed," Sebastian said desperately "Everything's different, but the game's exactly the same. If I'm hallucinating why has everything changed but the game's the same? Why don't I have a giant controller shaped like a hedgehog moving a dump truck through spaghetti?"

"That would be a good solid hallucination, but what about this?" Ertic gestured about. "Apparently, you're a diplomat. You're using your phone, to play a game, to fly a spaceship into a giant space creature because some super advanced aliens really need to use a cellphone. Your cellphone. Are you sure it's not a crazy hallucination?"

"Not really," Sebastian replied.

"Then just assume that it is and play the game a while to relax," Ertic said calmly.

"What about the time delay?" Sebastian asked. "If it's that far away the signal should take at least twenty seconds just to reach us…" he began.

"Well, now you know you're having a hallucination. Either that or the communications would need to be shunted through a miniature artificial wormhole so that you could have immediate feedback," Ertic said, "And that just sounds unrealistic now, doesn't it?"

Sebastian's shoulders visibly relaxed and his movements became more fluid, gliding smoothly across his phone as the ship on the viewscreen in the Ambassador's lounge mimicked the movements of the biplane in the game.

"That's better. Enjoy yourself, just remember that you're most likely stoned off your tits," Ertic said, slapping him on the back with a grin.

The grinding grew louder from behind the door and then quieted for a moment.

"It'll be easier on you if you come out now," the voice from behind the door said.

"Sorry Artun, it's all going smoothly, and the human is on track," Ertic said through the door. "Don't worry human," he said focusing on Sebastian again. "You're still on the floor and you've probably soiled yourself. In fact, I'm certain of it, and I'm not even real."

"I can't disobey orders," Artun said from behind the door.

"You shouldn't. No need for us both to be at the wrong end of this," Ertic responded.

Ertic heard a sigh from behind the door as the grinding started up once more.

Sebastian's fingers were gliding across the screen at a rate that made them blur. Ertic watched him, genuinely impressed, as the ship on the viewscreen darted from side to side.

Ertic danced about the room making ghost noises and chanting nonsense only occasionally stopping to say, "this is a dream," in what he thought was a spooky voice.

The viewscreen changed from the view of the ship to show that the engineer had once again joined Triven in the command room.

"The ship is undergoing dangerous levels of acceleration. It'll tear itself apart," Triven growled, still fuming.

Ertic stopped his dancing, "What choices are there? Either it reaches the creature because we avoid the meteoroids, or it explodes, whether it's because of the acceleration or it hits one of those rocks seems like less of an issue," Ertic responded, "Watch him. Do you think anybody else could do a better job here? He's spent years training."

"We could just attach the controller up to the AI here and the control would be far more effective," Triven responded, his frustration evident.

"The risk is too high. Their navigational AI will be constantly monitoring for input that can only come from another AI. This is the only way," Ertic said.

Triven looked at the engineer, who nodded in agreement with Ertic.

The grinding on the door grew louder as some machinery created a crack in the door.

"Look, you've got two choices," Ertic said desperately. "Either let the human do this," he paused, "or accept that this collision won't happen and explain it to command later. Which one will you choose?"

Triven looked furiously to the engineer.

"Is he correct?" he demanded.

"It appears so," the engineer responded carefully.

"This is an unacceptable breach of protocol," Triven spat. "Tell security to stand down," he called out. "Send up the attack ships to help clear the path of those damned rocks, defend the delivery ship."

Ertic started dancing about the room again and making spooky noises once more. He interspersed these with the statements "This is a dream", "I have a dogs tail" and "I'm bright green" at random intervals. At one point he even broke into slam poetry with an off the cuff creation - 'my friend is a hairy creature.'

The grinding from outside had stopped as all eyes in the control room focused on the giant viewscreen. On one side was Sebastian as he moved his fingers about his screen, while the other side showed the ship as it mimicked his movements, darting between the meteoroids that had accompanied the creature across vast regions of space, drawn in by its immense mass.

Triven's giant head still sat on the viewscreen watching Ertic with deep suspicion. "What are you doing?"

Ertic flipped the view on the screen to show the outside of the ship once more, barreling towards the creature. He continued dancing about the room but was slowing down as he became ever more focused on the screen.

His tail began to wag.

Ertic felt himself relax as he watched the ship dance impossibly about the screen. And, for a moment, he allowed himself to dream.

He was about to pee on a huge bomb.

Ertic's tail was wagging hard as he felt the Universe give him hope that his dream might actually come true.

As they watched, a dozen ships dropped out of faster than light travel and joined the main delivery craft. They took up positions about it and started to shoot at meteoroids as they approached.

The setup was effective as the minutes passed and the small attack craft were able to destroy the rocks before they hit the larger ship.

"Watch out," the engineer's voice screeched out over the communications array as Ertic found himself dragged back into reality, reminded that the situation was being closely monitored.

Rapidly the smaller attack craft peeled off, away from the larger ship.

He looked straight at Sebastian, who was so focused on the phone in front of him it was as if nothing else existed. He quickly turned to the viewscreen to see a three-hundred-meter-long ship pull off a near impossible barrel roll to avoid a huge meteoroid, as it followed a corkscrew shaped path through space, then it spun seven hundred and twenty degrees as three more sizeable meteoroids brushed past it, the last one so close that it almost took out the communication tower at the head of the ship.

Several of the smaller ships had taken heavy damage from the pieces of rock thrown out by the meteoroids as they disintegrated. The most damaged of them began jumping back to base.

"Watch out for the ..." the engineer's now shrill and panicked voice began shouting over the communicator.

"Communication off," Ertic shouted, and silence descended on the room. He couldn't allow Sebastian to be distracted.

From his vantage point, he saw that Sebastian had gained a thousand extra points and, for some reason, three bananas, for the maneuver.

Sebastian continued to focus on the ship, dodging the meteoroids ever more frequently. The minutes seemed to grow longer as the ship approached the creature.

He was becoming aware of the monstrous presence of the giant slug as the nothingness that existed between the largest of the chunks of rock honed silently into view.

The creatures location in space came into focus only when you realized not to look for it, but for what was missing. The absence of the stars and galaxies obscured by its immense size.

It was vast, and they were closing in on it rapidly.

Sebastian's hands raced as he moved the ship, now more of an extension of himself than a separate object. It darted about in the space that separated it from its target as it raced ever closer to the creature.

His brow was furrowed and glistening with sweat as he focused all his concentration on the game in front of him, perhaps more than he ever had before. The game began awarding him pizzas and was threatening to upgrade this to anchovy toppings.

The seven smaller ships that remained continued to hold their position, raining out fire and destroying the meteoroids, but now the rocks were getting bigger and more dangerous.

One of the attack ships fired at a large rock heading straight for the delivery ship, shattering it. Some of the fragments flew towards the larger ship and embedded themselves in the hull, tearing holes into it. The crew in the control room watched as atmosphere leaked from the side of the ship through the multiple punctures in the skin.

The smaller attack craft also continued to take a heavy pounding from the rocks. They were starting to falter as the collisions with the debris continued to take their toll on the remaining vessels.

"Pull back the attack ships," Ertic said. "The meteoroids are too large. They're starting to do more harm than good."

Triven gave the order, and the craft peeled away and engaged their FTL drives to return, leaving the main ship alone to face the meteoroids and the creature.

There was silence throughout the command room as everyone watched, frozen, staring at the ship as it traversed the meteoroid storm that surrounded the creature, edging ever closer to it. Occasionally small chunks of rock made it through and took off a panel or smashed into a wing, but the ship was far outside any atmosphere. This made the small wings purely aesthetic and about as useful as plastic stickers on fruit. All it needed were the engines and enough of a body left to push to the finish line.

The high acceleration maneuvers were taking their toll on the ship's structure however, as cracks began to form through the mid-section of the ship,

The number and size of meteoroids grew with proximity to the creature, and it became impossible to avoid them all. This focused Sebastian on only avoiding the large ones. The ship was becoming more and more riddled with holes and missing sections.

The ship was almost upon the creature, which sat, surrounded by an impenetrable halo of massive chunks of rock the size of mountains. It was impossible to fly through them.

Sebastian decided to perform a large loop to get more time to look for any gaps in the final shield of huge meteoroids that formed the last obstacle between the ship and the giant slug. He pulled his fingers back, and the craft lifted upwards starting the giant looping maneuver.

This proved to be too much for the structural integrity of the ship. The cracks that had been growing through the superstructure and frame of the ship finally completed their journey, meeting with the cracks that traversed the skin.

The cracks shook hands, dislocated their joints and then their arms fell off at the shoulder.

The entire front four fifths of the massive ship broke off across the atrium, leaving Sebastian with control of the remaining fifth of the ship, the engine section and the entranceway at the rear. Thankfully the controls remained functional.

"What they hell?" Sebastian muttered as the game interpreted the event by showing him that he was now flying the tiny tailplane of his biplane as the main body of it, still being driven by the dog in goggles was moving away from him.

Sebastian continued to perform the loop as the huge front section, now fully separated, moved onward toward one of the massive meteoroids that shielded the creature. This monster meteoroid was the final defense that separated the rear section of the ship, holding the decimator, and the creature itself.

Sebastian completed the loop and lined the tailplane up with the rest of the biplane in the distance. His game showed the front of the plane rapidly heading towards a giant rotating silver star. At the same time as the plane hit the star the huge front section of the delivery ship introduced itself to the massive space rock.

It was as formal an introduction as one might expect as the near light speed of the massive fragment of ship created an explosion so powerful that it fully punched a hole through the huge meteoroid vaporizing a large amount of it and throwing the remaining enormous chunks of rock out of the way. This also vaporized many of the remaining parts of the atrium that hung on the rear of the ship, as it followed in the path of section that went before it. The external cameras on the rear showed a bright flash before becoming atomized, their last action before forming a small gas cloud.

Sebastian seized the opportunity and accelerated the ship forward with everything it had left. The only remaining working camera on the ship showed occasional glimpses of the Decimator being flung about inside the rear of the ship. He knew that, if the ship continued to function, then flying it forward created the most likely chance that it would fit into the gap in the meteoroids, passing through the creature's rocky shield. He continued onward, with nothing separating him from the creature.

Accelerating hard, he crossed his fingers and hoped that that he was still aiming the ship towards the gap he had created.

Ertic watched, his mouth open in wonder, as Sebastian performed maneuvers that would have killed any creatures on board. The Decimator had remained intact. If it had exploded, the cameras would have ceased, and the light would have filled the sky.

He watched, and he waited, half astonished at Sebastian's flying and half amazed that his plan might have already succeeded.

His mouth stayed open as Sebastion performed the loop.

It salivated as he cleared the meteoroids.

His tail wagged rapidly as the ship reached its final approach.

And the screen went black.

Sebastian dropped his hands, still holding the phone, clearly exhausted.

Ertic let out a series of excited barks as his tail wagged like a dog that had discovered where the treats were hidden. This was epic. He was now the only dog in history, across the whole Universe, that had ever laid claim to a Decimator, and he had done so just as the Decimator had saved his home world.

He flipped the view to watch the sky on the viewscreen and waited.

Sebastian raised his head back up and looked down at the phone. Apparently, he had gained enough points to upgrade to level two, and he now possessed a fruit cannon.

So now he could fire fruit.

"Did we do it?" Sebastian asked.

"It'll take a few minutes for us to see the flash of the explosion if everything was successful," Ertic said, still staring at the sky and desperately hoping that his urine would bring them the luck they so desperately needed.

In the control room everyone was on their feet watching and waiting for the readouts to change. The cameras pointed at the sky fed an image through to the screen.

As the minutes ticked by hope was returning to the room, the officers were alternating their focus between the readouts at their stations and the image on the screen.

The Science Officer turned to Sardok. "If the collision was successful, we should experience a massive burst of energy in ten seconds."

Triven's voice came over the base. "Brace for collision."

They watched in silence as slowly time ticked past.

The time kept ticking.

In the sky a little flash followed by another little flash showed the collision between the front of the ship and the meteoroid, and then the rear of the ship and the creature.

Then nothing changed, no massive explosion, no moon shaking earthquakes.

Nothing.

The viewscreen sputtered into life once more, showing an image of Triven that took up a half of the viewscreen.

"Why hasn't it exploded?" he yelled.

"Any time now," Ertic responded, the hope slowly fading from his voice.

They continued watching for a few more seconds as Ertic's tail gradually descended, no longer wagging as it started to look more and more limp. It looked like the tail of a dog who tried, unsuccessfully, to pee on a cataclysmic weapon. Or worse, and this was what was gnawing at him, a dog whose pee may have prevented a cataclysmic weapon from working.

The view of Triven on the screen switched off, replaced once more with the view of the exterior of the building.

They sat a while in silence.

Ertic and Sebastian continued to stare at the image on the screen, each of them slowly gaining the certainty that something had gone very wrong indeed.

"Get them onto the cruiser and straight into the brig," Triven's voice rang out over the communicators outside the diplomatic lounge.

A Fzzt sound came from the base wide communications followed by the message, "all hands abandon the post. The explosion has sent a number of meteoroids in this direction. The surface of the moon will not escape what's coming, I repeat it will not escape what's coming. All autonomous segments of the base will begin launching to Callaxia."

In the command room, Triven turned to address Sardok.

"They will be held accountable for this debacle," he muttered angrily. "Move everyone to the cruiser. Prepare for immediate take–off," Triven called out as the room rapidly emptied.

The pyramid was watching everyone as Sardok picked it up and placed it in his pocket. Then he picked up his papers and quickly carried them to the ship.

In the diplomatic room, Ertic looked sullenly at Sebastian.

"This did not go as it should have."

As they watched, sections of one of the large exterior hangars began to slide upwards, separating the building into independent parts. They continued to rise upwards into the air.

"What's happening?" Sebastian asked.

"They're reallocating the resources. That's the attack craft and the hangar launch sections they're contained in. They'll be sending them back to Callaxia so they can help with any attacks or evacuations. The hangar breaks into autonomous parts that will travel back at sub light speed. They should arrive shortly after us, if they make it through the smaller meteoroids."

"Are we going to your home planet?" Sebastian asked.

"Yes." He replied.

From behind Ertic, the cutting sound at the door started once more.

Ertic got up, went across to the door, and removed the entry restrictions.

Chapter 21

They sat in a stunned silence on the evacuation ship. The firmer benches in the brig were long and only lightly padded. They had been designed specifically to lower the resolve and the resilience of whoever used them. To slowly grind them down, to make them placid and desperate for relief, in preparation to accept whatever Faustian bargain was offered. They were about as comfortable as airport seating, but without the bars to prevent sleeping. The Callaxians were pragmatic, not cruel. The gentle hum of the engines was the only signal they were moving at all.

The brig itself was a rectangular containment room that was held inside of a larger room. It had a large glass fronting, some sixteen feet by ten feet, with three beds in it. In one corner was a door to access a toilet. The room itself felt cold and unwelcoming but provided the essentials for the prisoners. In the larger containment room outside of the large glass window they could see the food printer and a very unhappy-looking guard.

Not unhappy the way that someone might be had they recently lost their car keys, but the sort of general deep-seated anger that one might expect of a person who had bent down to pick up their car keys, and then for no reason, their trousers exploded, rendering their winning lottery ticket unreadable.

This was not a happy-looking guard.

"Did the Decimator explode?" Sebastian asked.

"No." Ertic responded, his usually upbeat demeanor gone as he sat morosely on the bench.

The silence pervaded for a while.

"Why not?" Sebastian asked.

The silence put on a light summer jacket and sat staring at Ertic.

Some time passed.

After a while, the silence brought awkwardness, and then they both invited brooding.

"Something went wrong," was all he could muster.

The mood in the brig felt so somber that even brooding was questioning whether it should stay.

Ertic's tail seemed to have lost any life of its own and now hung off him like a wet towel.

His mind was racing. All the pieces were in place. Sebastian had flown the ship to perfection, and it had collided in a way that should have brought an end to all of this. Was it possible that the jar of urine he had left there had smashed into the bomb, wrecking the circuits? Why had the shields not been up? Why was there no faster than light drive?

Ertic was suspecting that once again the mission may have been compromised, but he was deeply troubled that it could have been, in part, by himself. He gripped on tightly to the edge of the bench and waited.

Sebastian sat and played his game some more, trying to take his mind off the events. The batteries on his phone were still fully charged and Sebastian was starting to wonder how the engineer had actually altered the phone. He was feeling rather good about his score, though, the failure of the mission notwithstanding.

Triven entered the room. His face looked like thunder and his eyes flashed with rage.

"What have you done?" he screamed.

"The collision was perfect," Ertic said, staring at the floor still gripping the bench.

Triven stared at him, his face still radiating anger as he stood flanked by a couple of guards.

"We'll meet to discuss it then," he said carefully, picking the timing of his words to communicate his anger. "Come with me," he demanded as the door opened and the guards moved to the side making way for Ertic to pass.

Chapter 22

Ertic sat down at the middle of the long table in the small conference room. Triven and Sardok were there, sitting opposite him, while Artun remained in the room's corner, his fur a little raised. Two guards stood by the door.

"Why don't you tell us what you think happened?" Triven hissed.

"The ship went up, the shields weren't working, and the ship had to be flown manually," Ertic replied.

"And did it reach its destination?" Triven asked, his voice raising.

"It reached it perfectly," Ertic responded. "It should have exploded."

"Unless you damaged it by giving it to the human to fly," Triven stated poignantly.

"The human performed perfectly. I'm not even sure our best pilots could have pulled off some of those maneuvers." Ertic responded.

"Indeed, I doubt that they could have, or would have," he growled with suppressed rage. "Those maneuvers took the ship far beyond tolerance. There was barely enough of the ship left to hit the creature."

"But it did hit it," Ertic responded. He caught Triven's eye and held the stare. "He performed perfectly."

"What happened to the shields?" Triven asked. "Was it you? Did you sabotage them?" he demanded.

Ertic paused and looked forcefully at Triven. "I wouldn't make that charge again," he said clearly, repressed anger in his voice.

"Shall we look at the footage?" Triven asked, holding his

stare.

The viewscreen behind Triven and Sardok flickered to life.
On it was the footage of Ertic and Sebastian entering the ship.
The pair entered the ship slowly and passed by the
engineering crew, stopping to look at the large rotating bomb.
They continued into the ship and disappeared from view.

"Did you notice anything?" Triven asked with a saccharine
sweetness, as though he were selling weevils at a bread
convention.

"There was nothing to see. We entered, checked out the
main part of the ship and left," Ertic responded.

"Well, let's keep watching," Triven said, carefully stretching
each word as he sped up the footage.

After a few moments, the engineering crew left the ship,
quickly followed by the other inspection crews, until only Ertic
and Sebastian remained on board.

A short while later, they reappeared, running, with Ertic
carrying some kind of jug.

"What exactly, is that?" Sardok asked, as he froze the image
on the screen and looked carefully at it.

"It's a jug," Ertic responded, desperate to be anywhere else
at this point.

"Shall we continue?" Triven asked.

He was, of course, only asking as illusion to mask his intent.
Similar to a lumberjack asking if he should avoid cutting a
tree down while swinging an axe towards it, or a polar bear
asking a seal if it would like to close its eyes for a moment
while the polar bear promised absolutely not to eat it.

He had no intention of stopping. He intended on continuing
to watch in the way a banker would continue to bank, or a
Centarian Squelcher would continue to squelch.

*'The Centarian Squelchers are odd creatures, looking like a
cross between matted wet hair and roadkill. They live on the
edge of the mud swamps of Gringleflax, surviving by sifting
through the mud for small microbes to eat. This task*

continues for approximately two cycles as they get progressively fatter. During this period, they ingest relentlessly, feeding off the fetid muck of the swamp. Once they have ingested enough of the microbes, they release the enormous buildup of stored methane in one intense and focused burst. This propels them about two hundred feet in the air, elevating them from the mud and transferring them to the nearby grass, to begin the next part of their lifecycle as marketing executives.

Oddly the orifice used to exude the gas is the same one with which they communicate. The strangest thing in all of this is how prized they are in the world of marketing, perhaps putting back into the Universe many fold, that which they ingested for so long.'

Excerpt from: *The Universe is odd and so am I by Oodlebax the third.*

The video, now running at normal speed, showed Ertic as he ran towards the console by the Decimator with his tail wagging. He could clearly be seen taking the jug and placing it on the control panel near the Decimator, before both he and Sebastian quickly ran from the ship.

"Well, that was interesting," Triven said, an edge to his voice, this one serrated.

"What was in the container?" Sardok asked cautiously.

"And was that the console that controlled the shields?" Triven demanded.

Ertic just wanted to be back on Earth, curled up on the sofa, with his fur being gently massaged. He raised his hand to his head.

"Nothing that should have made any difference to the mission," he said with certainty.

"What was in the container?" Sardok asked again.

"Urine," Ertic said quietly.

A gentle silence descended on the room, a little like the calm

before the storm. This calm seemed to bring a family of ducks
to sit on some water and admire the oncoming storm, as the
clouds gathered in the distance.

Triven sat still, staring at Ertic with wide eyes. He was
trying to catch his breath, but his breath seemed to have been
training for the marathon, while the rest of him had been
distracted by the ducks.

"I'm sorry, I think I may have misunderstood," Sardok
began, "What was in the container?"

"Pee." Ertic repeated, this time a little more coherently.

Triven's breath still eluded him, and his skin was showing a
variety of colors rarely seen in polite company.

He finally managed to take a deep breath and exhaled,
shouting, "You put pee on the console?"

He then hyperventilated for another few seconds.

"No," Ertic said, a little perturbed, "I put pee in a jug."

Sardok sat watching Triven, wondering a little about his
health and the succession of command in times of crisis. Then
he watched Sub-Commander Ertic and tried to process his
urological tendencies.

"Whydidyouputpeeinajugontheconsole?" Triven practically
squealed.

"I think that is a very important question," Sardok echoed.
"We should probably focus in on that."

"On Earth I transformed into a dog," Ertic began.

A deep silence had descended upon the room as Ertic's voice
seemed to drown out the gentle sound of Sardok's breathing
and Triven's desperate rasping. The two guards watched on,
quiet confusion on their faces.

A look of intrigue sat on Artun's face, confident that it had
found the right resting place.

"Dogs have a habit, well a need," he continued, "they pee on
things to mark their territory. They pee on as much as they
can to tell others what belongs to them."

"Go on," Sardok said. Triven just sat there, an odd maroon
sort of color with his mouth open and his eyes wide.

"I have had difficulty since transforming back. Some of the innate mannerisms that come with being a dog are too ingrained to be ignored."

"So, you're still feeling these tendencies," Sardok asked.

"Yes," Ertic responded.

"So, it's a sort of mission injury," Sardok mused.

"You put pee in a jug compromising the mission," Triven said forcefully, now his breath had returned.

"There's no way the urine could have done that," Ertic responded.

"Let me paint you a scenario," Triven hissed. "The urine, your urine, flew about the room and destroyed the circuitry in the Decimator, after other parts of the room that were flying about had smashed it open because of the maneuvers of your pet human."

Ertic sat forward, his eyes no longer glancing down, and fixed Triven with a fiery stare.

"How do you explain the shields?" He said roundly. "Sure, the urine might have damaged the Decimator. It's almost impossible to believe, but let's work with that idea. Why were the shields down? The engineers were in there doing last–minute checks. They would have ensured proper readouts, checked the AI preparedness, and then disconnected the input consoles," Ertic said. "Someone sabotaged this and probably my mission, too."

"Assuming that the engineers remembered to disconnect the input console and didn't leave it open to sabotage," Triven threw the idea at him like a dagger.

"Even if they didn't, do you really think a little liquid would break through the waterproofing membrane? You could submerge the ship in water for a month and the console electrics would stay dry," Ertic said.

"What I see is this: a rogue officer and his pet human, assuming that's the correct order, arrive back from a mission where he was likely brainwashed just in time to see the fireworks. After gaining access to the ship that is due to deliver the Decimator, just at the point where all the other staff are busy or distracted. They then proceed to parts of the ship where they do not need to be and sabotage the shields, maybe through another input console, in another part of the ship. Then they return to the payload to sabotage it, by urinating on it, ensuring that it will not explode on contact. The reason you are expecting me to believe that you did this is because you *needed* to pee on it? Pathetic," he spat.

"Security, take Sub-Commander Ertic back to his holding cell in the brig and bring me that human. Don't think this is over *Sub-Commander*. We have a *lot* more to talk about," Triven finished, his voice almost choking on the words like a cheese grater, grating on some nuts.

Artun stood next to Ertic as he rose and began walking him back to the brig. They turned and left the interrogation room with Triven still foaming at the mouth.

"Had to pee on it, eh?" Artun commented.

"I couldn't help myself. The urge was overwhelming," Ertic responded quietly, his head down.

They walked in silence for a brief while.

"Did you get any further on the investigation?" Ertic asked eventually.

"It's still ongoing, although you should probably know that you're on the list of suspects," Artun responded.

Ertic raised his head and looked at him.

"He made some excellent points about timing," Artun said, looking straight back. "If it's any help, you're not that high on the list," he finished.

"Why not?" asked Ertic.

"There were a hundred other ways to sabotage that mission that didn't need you to pee on a huge bomb. Even as a cover, it may be the stupidest thing I've ever heard. A tenth level genius couldn't come up with a story that stupid. You're no fool, but you're no genius either," Artun said.

"How do you know?" Ertic asked, a little taken back.

"You tried to urinate on a huge bomb. A death machine. A

bomb capable of destroying a planet and all its moons, a bomb
that nobody knows just how unstable it is, and you tried to
pee on it. I really can't emphasize that point enough," Artun
said pointedly. "Also, you seem unhappy, actually unhappy,
not to be higher on my list of possible traitors because I've
categorized you as 'not a genius'," he paused for a moment,
observing him, "and then you asked me how I know you're not
a genius."

Artun's voice dropped a little, "these points are not
unrelated."

Artun took Ertic back to the holding cells.

"All right human, it's your turn," Artun said as Ertic
returned to the cell.

Chapter 23

Artun led Sebastian to the interrogation room.

"Is there anything I should be worried about?" He asked.

"Just tell them the truth and expand on it. They'll compare it with the Sub-Commander's account and, if they match, you're in a much safer place," Artun responded.

"And if they don't?" Sebastian asked.

"You don't want to go on that path," Artun said coldly.

He opened the door and Sebastian walked in. In front of Sebastian was a table with Triven and Sardok. He moved to the table and sat opposite them.

"Well then, human," Triven said calmly, "you flew the ship through an almost impossible course. I'm not sure there are many pilots in the systems that could have matched that. How did you do it?"

"I just played the game," Sebastian said. "I'm very good at it."

"How good?" Sardok asked curiously.

"I won a couple of competitions for it," Sebastian replied.

"What type of competitions?" Triven asked as he leant back slightly, getting more comfortable in his seat.

"There are local and national competitions. I won the local for the city. The next competition is the one where all the local champions battle it out," Sebastian said.

"Show me this game," Triven said carefully.

Sebastian reached into his pocket and felt for his phone. It was right next to the air freshener. He thought for a second. He was keeping the air freshener quiet unless they pressed him on it. After all, he'd gotten some alien stuff, and he wanted to keep it.

The way he saw it, there were only two possibilities. Either he was hallucinating and might have stolen someone's air freshener, or he'd just pulled off an amazing piece of flying and deserved a free air freshener. Also, he needed a shower, and the thing smelled of lemons, so he was doing everybody a favor either way. Although, at this point, he may well have been wandering the streets and just stuffed a pigeon in his pocket.

He pulled the phone out of his pocket and scanned his thumb. The game started up with the logo coming across the screen. Triven stared at it cautiously. It was a silhouette of a plane, piloted by a dog, with some arcade style writing that said, Scrappy Dog–Fighter II.

As the game started up, Triven saw that the controls were quite simple. The pad on the left controlled the left, right, forward and backward, while the one on the right controlled how the ship pointed in three–dimensional space. It started and Triven moved his fingers across the controls. As he did, the plane dashed about the screen, avoiding the incoming fire. This lasted only briefly until, while avoiding one attack, a duck blindsided him, destroying the plane and ending the game.

Triven watched the credits as the game closed down before placing the phone on the table.

"Tell me what else you have, human," Triven said.

Sebastian put his hands into his pockets and felt around. Damn, he really wanted the air freshener.

He pulled it out and placed it on the table. It rolled a little and reflected the light a little like a dry clay marble as it gently filled the air with a lemon smell.

"It's an air freshener," Sebastian said.

"Does your species actually have to carry an air freshener about with you," Sardok said, surprised and wondering how the creatures actually smelled.

Sebastian picked it back up and put it back in his pocket, glaring at Sardok as he did.

Suddenly, he remembered something else and put his hand into his inside jacket pocket, pulling out his self–help book.

He truly hated that book, and, as he was rapidly learning to dislike one of the people opposite him, he felt they should be introduced.

Triven picked it up and looked at the title.

"How to be the best you, and how I know you'll like it," Triven read the title aloud.

He turned the book and examined the information, and affirmation printed on the back. In the end, he put it down and looked at Sebastian grimly.

"Do you know I suspect Sub-Commander Ertic of being some kind of spy or saboteur?" he asked, as his left hand reached down the side of his chair and released a small clasp.

"No," Sebastian responded cautiously.

"Show me your hand," Triven demanded.

Sebastian lifted his hand across the table closing the space that separated him from Triven. He blinked and at a speed that belied his size and shape, Triven's right hand raced across the table and grabbed Sebastian's wrist, while his left flew across, thrusting a snake–like creature into Sebastian's hand.

Sebastian tried to pull his hand back, but it was held too tight, and, as he watched, the creature in his hand wrapped itself around his wrist, exposing a large stinger at the end that pointed straight at his palm.

Artun's eyes bulged as he quickly left the room.

"What the hell is that?" Sebastian asked.

"That is a Tellusian worm. Are you familiar with them?" Triven asked.

He noted the confusion on Sebastian's face. "I'm not surprised, very few people have even seen one, much less experienced it. There aren't many of them left on their home planet. There's only a few places they even live, and for some reason they don't really develop elsewhere."

"Number One," Sardok hissed. Triven ignored him.

"No, I haven't seen one before," replied Sebastian. He stared straight at Triven. "although ..." He stopped. He had been about to say that it looked like Triven's mother, but the creature tightened around his wrist as it made a hissing sound, its stinger hovering menacingly above Sebastian's palm.

"I see you understand," Triven said. "Let me tell you the rules. Pretty simple, really. If you lie, you die."

"Are you allowed to use this?" Sebastian demanded.

"Number One," Sardok hissed again.

"It's a grey area. We can use it on prisoners, but we can't use it on diplomats," Triven replied.

Triven looked at him.

"Are you really a diplomat?" he asked.

Sebastian remained silent as the creature on his wrist seemed to relax a little.

"I didn't really think so either," Triven said. "Let's start with a few easy ones. It will give the creature a chance to adapt to your neural eccentricities. Believe me, human, this is something that you want to happen successfully."

Sardok sat, staring at Triven uneasily.

"What is your name?" he began.

Sebastian was about to lie to him, but the Worm began swaying aggressively and hissing.

"Oh, be honest now," Triven said with an evil grin on his face.

In the hallway, Artun was inputting information into his communicator as fast as possible. After a few moments he heard a voice from the communicator.

"Chief of Security, Veltrid Sector Base, you're authentication code has been accepted."

"I need to speak with him," he said "Now!"

Quickly, a shorter, rounder man appeared on the screen with four round circles arranged horizontally on his sash two purple and two black. Artun began communicating rapidly.

"Where do you live?" Triven continued, he intended to get

the answers to every question he had for this creature.

In the hallway, Artun was reaching fever pitch and the person on the other end of the communications device was running. The minutes continued to pass as Triven's asked ever more questions.

"How did you meet Sub-Commander Ertic?".

At the other end, the communicator had been passed up the chain and was now being held by someone who was tall and gaunt, his angular face looking more than a little annoyed. On his chest was one horizontal green stripe and beneath it were another three round green circles in a horizontal line.

In the interrogation room the questions kept coming one after another.

"Who is this girl you speak of?"

Outside the room Artun quickly began explaining as the time seemed to pass rapidly. Inside the room, Triven continued his relentless questioning as he continued gathering information about the newcomer.

"What is this, and where does it come from?" Triven continued, holding the book in the air.

"It's from my job," Sebastian replied. "The pizza company gave self–help books out to everyone. It's supposed to make people improve themselves."

"Does it work?" Triven asked.

"I still work at a pizza restaurant, so, no, it's terrible. It just keeps talking garbage about quantum connection and mystic oneness. Visualize the future you want, and it'll be inevitable. You get the idea," Sebastian replied, watching the creature sway from side to side on his wrist.

Triven's eyes narrowed.

"And where do you work?" he asked.

"Alonso's Pizza Shack, Orchard lane." Sebastian replied, glaring at Triven.

Triven stood up and leaned across the desk and spread his arms to support his weight. He had all the information he needed now. He looked Sebastian dead in the eyes.

"Do you mean us harm, human?" he hissed.

The door burst open, and Artun appeared, holding out his communications device.

"Stop this," the voice on the other end shouted.

"Do you mean us harm?" Triven shouted at Sebastian.

"No," Sebastian replied. The creature hissed audibly while it contracted on his wrist, its stinger pulled back to strike.

Silence descended on the room as they all stared at it.

"Well, maybe you," Sebastian corrected himself, "but you suck. I really wouldn't mind if some harm came your way. Nobody else here, though."

The creature stopped hissing and visibly relaxed, its stinger retreating once more into its sheath.

Triven stood glaring at Sebastian, and Sebastian, still sitting, held his stare.

"Enough!" shouted the person on the screen. "Remove that creature."

Triven reached down and carefully removed the creature from Sebastian's wrist. He placed it in a small container and pushed down the lid.

"It appears you were telling the truth," Triven said, glaring at Sebastian.

"Consider it my gift to you," Sebastian replied grimly. "Let me know if you'd like me to expand on it," He said menacingly, as he raised himself up to face him.

"This is unacceptable behavior Number One," The person on the screen stated. "Under no circumstances are diplomats to be interrogated in this manner."

"He failed to identify himself as a diplomat, Sir," Triven replied, standing to attention.

"The first time we contact a new species, we afford them that status until they choose one among from their ranks," the voice replied testily. "But you know this. If we weren't otherwise engaged, I would have you in the brig and cleaning the waste processors for a month," the voice growled.

"Yes, Sir," Triven replied, still standing to attention. "At least now we are aware his intentions are not hostile."

"Don't test me, Number One," the voice at the other end said quietly.

Triven remained silent, his face hard.

"I hope we can put this incident behind us and move forward in a spirit of cooperation between our species," the voice at the end of the communicator said.

"Sure?" said Sebastian, not really certain what they expected of him. Seeing what looked like an opportunity, however, he said, "Does that mean that me and Ertic can get out of the brig?"

"Indeed, I am aware of the Sub-Commander's return," the person said, "I will place you both under the care of the Chief Security Officer, who will ensure that your immediate needs are met. For the moment, however, I must attend to my duties," he finished.

And with that, the person at the other end of the screen vanished, and the communicator was blank once more.

Triven glared at Artun. "Don't think I'll forget this in a hurry," he said as he turned and stormed from the room.

Sardok visibly relaxed as some form of color began to re–emerge on his ashen face. The tension leaving his body, left it looking more like a body, and less like a statue with anxiety issues and an itchy nose.

Artun just stood there a while, seemingly unfazed.

"We should go and pick up Ertic. A change of venue will do him good," he said.

Chapter 24

Triven stormed back to the bridge seething with repressed anger at the idea that a human, who was useless, dangerous or some combination of the two, was to be afforded the rights of an Ambassador.

If it were up to him, they would all be sitting in the brig.

One of the junior bridge logistics officers, a second lieutenant with orange scaled skin and marbled black stripes approached him.

"What is to be done with the Ambassador?" the junior officer asked.

"What do you mean?" he snapped.

The junior officer tensed slightly and held himself a little more upright and formal.

"Where is the Ambassador to stay on arrival?" the officer continued. "Security Chief Artun is dealing with his immediate needs, but you still need to arrange accommodation. It's just that the rules of first contact clearly state formal arrangements and reception are the responsibility of the ranking officer."

"I know what they state," Triven snapped. He paused for a moment, thinking.

"Tell me," he said suddenly curious, "what is your opinion?"

The junior officer paused. "Can I speak freely, Sir?"

"Please do," Triven replied gruffly.

"Why are they here now? I understand we got Sub-Commander Ertic back and I'm happy about that, but why did he bring a human? Why didn't the bomb go off and why were they the last on board the carrier ship?" he said.

Triven appeared to relax at the news that, at least some in

the crew, were smart enough to be suspicious.

"Have they provided us with a landing bay yet?" he asked.

"Yes, Sir," the officer responded. "They want us to proceed directly to the palace, General Fludge wants to speak to them himself."

Triven's brow furrowed.

He sat and thought a while as the junior officer waited, feeling a little more awkward by the second as the silence continued. After a short while the junior officer found his mind wandering back to his time as a young Borfanin in the swamp planet of Horfanz, when he won the district Floomjumping contest, before retiring for an early lunch.

The Floom is a large bird, like a hyper-chicken but five times taller, with the color of a setting sun. It's legs have a biological mechanism within them that allows them to store up massive amounts of energy that they can then use to both jump high into the air and to land safely. It has the look of a creature that has taken in far too much swamp gas, but to be fair, this is because it has. It travels wherever it wants to go in enormous jumps from its powerful legs, before descending gracefully and slowly, like a parachuting pot roast.

Flooms are simple creatures who love only puddles and jumping. When left to their own devices they will happily jump from puddle to puddle. This alone, however, means that they will never be left to their own devices as racing them is too much fun.

The Flooms have three weaknesses. The first is that they view everything else in the Universe as friendly. The second is that they taste like hyper-chicken. The third and arguably most serious weakness is that, as they are full of swamp gas, if you introduce them to fire, they will immediately explode, cooking themselves instantly and providing a ready-made meal.

They are often raced by people who don't want to carry their own food. However, they are so flammable that it is not

Excerpt from: *Flooms; Hyper-chickens more surprised cousin by Lartle Wonfondle.*

After an uncomfortable amount of time, Triven smiled and sat back in his chair, as if daring someone to ask.

The junior officer cleared his throat, "and err.." he began hoping that would be enough to prompt Triven to continue with his train of thought.

After another few brief moments, it became obvious he was going to need to ask properly.

"Excuse me, Sir," he began. "What should we do with the Ambassador?"

Triven looked at him curiously.

"Why don't we supply him with a full ceremonial guard," he said. "I think a full guard for all of his duties will show him the regard that we hold him in."

"What about his quarters, Sir?"

"Well, only the best will do for our esteemed Ambassador," Triven said thoughtfully. "Let him use the Emperor's quarters."

"But the Emperor…" the officer began.

"The Emperor will be busy until either the creature destroys the planet, or we destroy the creature. By now, anything of real importance will have been moved to a safe location," Triven snapped. "It is the most protected room in the entire palace. With an additional guard, our new 'Ambassador' can do nothing but build relations in a public setting."

He paused and smiled.

"After all, we wouldn't want him to experience less than the best hospitality we can provide now, would we?" Triven finished.

Triven sat back in his chair, feeling rather pleased at his plan to control the 'Ambassador'.

Chapter 25

As Artun and Sebastian approached the holding room, they heard a pop followed by a muffled high pitch whistling noise and a gagging sound.

The door to the room opened and a pipe leading to the food printer was spewing a stream of nauseating liquid out and over the table. There was a growing stench in the air that felt like you could cut it with a knife.

The guard, none too happy about having the liquid dripping from the food printer, or the smell that came with it, glowered at Sebastian with such ferocity that Artun took a step forward.

The guard backed down.

Artun looked about the room and took a few steps back into the corridor, unwilling to travel any farther into the foul-smelling place.

The door to the cells opened and Ertic stepped out.

"Oh, my..." he began as the air in the main part of the room hit him like a gentle spring breeze wrapped in a family transport.

His knees almost buckled, and he started to run for the exit. The guard joined him, running to their escape in the hallway.

Once outside in the hallway, the door closed and Ertic dry heaved a few times before wiping the tears from his eyes.

"They're assigned to me now. Go breathe some fresh air," Artun said to the guard.

"I haven't smelled anything like that since training," Ertic said, as the three of them moved quickly away from the room.

"What happened in training?" Artun asked, shocked that anybody could have smelt something so horrendous before.

"One intern broke up with his girlfriend, got drunk and reprogrammed a food printer to print out the ass end of a Kallaxian murder–skunk and left it on repeat. By morning, we had an entire room jammed full of thousands of them. The trainers contacted us over the communicators, from thirty miles away, and ordered us to do a clean-up. Turns out the top stripes had already evacuated, and from the smell, so had the asses of the skunks," Ertic said.

He shuddered as he recalled it. "We threw everything, the machine, the skunk–butts, the building and some other nearby buildings into a huge open cesspit and set it on fire. Then we moved the camp to another continent," Ertic replied, his eyes still a little glazed, "But we made sure not to set it on fire until the wind would help the stripes get the best of what the skunks could give. The only ones happy about any of it were those little toilet robots. The were going mental, don't think I've ever seen them look so happy."

Artun looked closely at Ertic and decided he still appeared a little disorientated.

Ertic was looking at Sebastian. "Use the toilet while I was being interrogated, did you?" he asked, wincing. "I don't think that the system recognized your gut bacteria."

"Let me know the next time you need to go to the toilet," Artun said to Sebastian. "We need to get a reading on your gut bacteria and excretions. The effects are unusually extreme. We're just lucky that the processors are localized and don't interconnect."

"Follow me," Artun said, leading Sebastian and Ertic down the hallway, as the guard, who had now removed his jacket to escape the lingering smell, started vomiting in the hallway.

As they moved along the hallway, a toilet bot, small and rounded, like a little white bollard on wheels with two arms and a visor, rushed to enter the room and gasped, which was no mean feat for a robot. It was overjoyed at the scale of the clean–up required. It began to hum happily, as it enthusiastically waved its toilet brush and rushed to attack the problem.

Artun turned and looked back with pity at the guard, then he looked with some suspicion at Sebastian.

"Something is deeply wrong with you, human," he muttered, wondering what it was that actually lived in Sebastian's intestines and whether it posed a ship–wide threat.

Sebastian shrugged, a little embarrassed.

"What happened?" Ertic asked, as his head cleared, and he regained his senses once more.

"Triven was relieved of the need to deal with you personally. I'm responsible for you now," Artun responded.

"I like the sound of that, but it doesn't cover the reason," Ertic replied, wondering what had prompted this.

"His senior wasn't a big fan of the idea that Triven wanted to use the Tellusian Worm on the Ambassador here," Artun said, gesturing towards Sebastian.

"He did what? Where did he even get one?" Ertic growled.

"Don't worry about it. I think the higher ups will have a few more things to say about it when we get back," Artun said. "At least after we stop the creature, anyway. Triven seemed quite fixated on the idea that the human meant us harm."

"And he used the Tellusian?" Ertic asked.

"Yes, seems he's not a big fan of Triven, but the rest of us should be ok," Artun said, grinning.

Ertic looked over at Sebastian. "That should never have been allowed. Still, it seems like you could join about half the crew now," he said.

"He's one of us," Artun said with a chuckle.

His grin vanished for a moment.

"We really need to map his gut bacteria," he said, a seriousness to his voice.

Chapter 26

Artun and Sebastian sat in the diplomatic quarters as the ship glided deftly towards the planet. It moved like a leviathan skipping silently through space, a silver bullet that seemed to bend space about it as it moved. To an observer outside of its shielding, it looked like a hairy mango swimming backward, embroiled in a philosophical dilemma.

'In the early days of the Empire, two competing scientific teams developed slightly different designs of superluminal drives. The first generated a rounded shape about the ship, looking rather like a Fedoran Plum. The second created a more elongated shape like a Leritan Mango. Every increase in the speed of the vessels created an increase in the number of filaments visible, stretching out from the shape as it travelled, giving the appearance of hair.

Eventually the two warring teams were able to bury their differences, after they sent the funding council into space. Each of the groups were finally able to take pride in the achievements of the other.

This newfound respect led to the now popular greeting in the scientific community, "May your plums be as hairy as my mangos."

The funding council, however, has not yet been located, and it is not believed that anybody is currently looking.'

Excerpt from: A history of the scientific wars - when knowledge kills: Kromatin, P. Bin.

Sebastian stood by the viewport in the diplomatic quarters

and looked through the window. Outside was the deepest black. No stars or light of any kind shone through.

"Where are the stars?" he asked.

Ertic looked up at him, confusion briefly crossing his face. Then he appeared to relax a little.

"The stars are still out there in the universe, it's just that we're not," he said. "We're sitting slightly outside the Universe. The bubbles surrounding the ship bend light around us."

"That's a shame," Sebastian said. It added a little more weight to the idea that this was all just some kind of hallucination.

"The ship travels faster than light. It needs the bubbles to make that happen," Ertic said. "Even if we could travel that fast without them, the energy from the light would build up on the ship's hull and melt it like a giant laser."

"Would've been nice to see the stars, though," Sebastian said thoughtfully.

"Maybe later, human."

"What are we going to do now?" Sebastian asked, curious about the next step.

"We go back to help them face the creature," Ertic said. "I don't know if it's even possible to stop it though. We'll just have to help with the final evacuation and hold it off for as long as possible. We'll likely try to counter–attack. Any extra time we can buy is worth the price." Ertic paused staring into the black of the window.

Slowly, the ship shuddered.

"It seems we might be here, Earthman," he said.

"Already?" Sebastian replied.

"Faster than light travel," Ertic said, a smile returning to his face briefly. The darkness that surrounded the ship was fading from the windows, dissipating, as a planet started to come into view. It was blue, green and silver with colorful rings stretching out around it. It was easy to make out vast cities gleaming in the light from the two alien stars.

Sebastian moved to the window in awe of the sight that awaited him. Huge swathes of the planet were clearly developed, and other sections seemed almost like huge preserves. An alien sea glittered, reflecting the binary system as the ship grew closer.

He put his hand out and touched the window. As he made contact, his hand slipped over the surface as if there were nothing to feel, just a smooth frictionless plate.

He disliked the feeling. It was like trying to hold on to a slippery wet eel that was oddly dry. He touched the wall, and it had the same odd feel to it. He subconsciously wiped his hand on his jacket–as if it were wet or sticky.

Slowly the ship descended. The clouds beneath them honed into view, bright and fluffy, floating as if completely unaware that a giant space slug was on an imminent schedule to introduce itself.

On the horizon, mountain tops thrust through the clouds like giant meerkats, poking their heads up to check for danger. The ship continued on its path; the clouds parting as it slowly descended through them.

The mountains also seemed to be blissfully unaware of the giant space slug, or at least they didn't dive into their burrows.

The clouds hung with a soft pink hue as though a gentle candy floss had ascended to the sky.

"The clouds are pink," Sebastian gasped as the ship descended through them.

Ertic nodded lightly, watching the window deep in his own thoughts.

"It's not a good sign."

"You don't always have pink clouds?"

Artun gave him a disapproving look.

"Clouds are supposed to be white and grey…" he began.

"Makes sense." Sebastian said.

"…with hints of blood red and gold. I don't even know what this is," he said, gesturing outside. "Looks like the color you'd find in an interior designer's hat collection. I mean really, what's wrong with blood red and gold?" he asked of no one in particular. "Was it designed by an intern? Cloud design is a basic part of weather management. Whose idea was this?" he muttered.

The ship continued its descent, now level with the largest of the skyscrapers, monolithic structures that looked as though someone had planted giant silver and glass carrots upside down.

Transports zipped about the city, as other transports lifted off to fly between the buildings. Larger transport crafts were located about the city. Streams of smaller ships carrying people to be evacuated flowed towards them. Rushing around, barely visible from the ship, were a few lone individuals, but most pathways were empty, as everyone was making their way towards the larger transports to leave.

All around there were ships rising into the sky of different sizes and shapes, carrying people to safe havens off world.

Out the viewport Sebastian and Ertic could see their destination was almost upon them: a giant floating city that hovered above the water at the edge of the land, where the city beneath ended.

Roadways rose from around the city to reach it. The once perfectly maintained lawns that covered the floating city were now littered with the marks from the landing gear of a hundred ships as more continuously arrived and took off again a short time later. They were like bees moving about their business, with the lawns holding only the memory of their once pristine majesty.

This was the site from where the entire Callaxian Empire was controlled. Sprawling buildings dotted the landscape, their density such that each attached to the next by corridors or walkways forming a massive complex across the top of the floating city. In the gaps between the buildings and walkways were large swathes of pockmarked lawn, bushes and paths.

The clouds continued on their way, as did the mountains

and the skyscrapers, as the ship descended. They continued inexorably towards one of the few remaining immaculate sections of lawn on the floating city, clearly with the intent of remedying its presentation.

As the ship approached its destination Triven's voice sounded over the intercom. "Upon arrival, aid with any tasks required until the hangars with the ships arrive from the base. Then those pilots, whose ships are still in service, can rejoin their ships and aid with the defense. The hangars that survive the trip will relocate and reform about the floating city. Expect them to arrive soon."

Slowly the ship moved until it was hovering above an immaculate section of lawn just in front of the sprawling palace. The reflected copper light from the roof of the building gave a truly regal appearance. The ship carefully extended its legs ready to plant itself down gently in its majestic surroundings.

It touched down in a way that sounded like a manatee passing gas. The extended legs of the ship splarped into the short damp grass and pushed their way into the soft mud beneath.

The ramp extended majestically, touching and then embedding itself into the ground. As it did this, it made a 'ribbety' sound, reminiscent of a chorus of excited frogs strapped to a cathedral pipe organ.

The senior members of the crew emerged rapidly from the ship, standing to the sides as Triven powered down the ramp. They saluted him as he passed and he ignored them, basking in his perceived importance.

He made his way up the lawn towards one entrance to the main complex. Two officers descended from the main building to escort Triven back towards it. He stopped and saluted them as they got close. Then they turned and escorted him towards the structure.

A squad of heavily armed soldiers in full regalia, wearing long blue coats with polished brass–colored buttons, thick white belts and red trousers, marched in formation down from the entrance to the citadel towards the bottom of the ship's ramp. The thick soles of their knee–high black boots pounded rhythmically on the soft ground while they slapped their chests with their rifles.

Each soldier wore a large white hat with a strange red, feathery, adornment that seemed to stretch a foot or more into the air, before crashing back down across their face, like an errant, feathery, waterfall.

This was the most exciting thing to happen to the ceremonial guard since they had been requested to increase the amount of acrobatics in their routine, from none to some with only twenty minutes notice.

Nobody had believed they could make a giant tower nine people high. Not the person on the base of the tower and even less the person at the top. The display that followed will certainly never be forgotten by those who witnessed it. Despite all the therapy, those who participated in it, will also never forget.

The person that was on the base of the tower remains three inches shorter than their uniform size. By sheer coincidence this is the same amount that the arms of the person on top of the tower had grown, from refusing to let go of the roof beams for a full two and a half hours.

The irony of this is that the soldier on top of the tower was a Laternian, whose cartilaginous bones show they are descended from fish, yet he is now nicknamed the Laternian Cat.

The person that was on the base of the tower is now nicknamed dumpy.

All the others in the tower suffered a multitude of injuries, from broken bones, to regret about wearing the pointed helmets. The thirty seconds it stood for though, still brings pride to the regiment.

The ceremonial guard were nothing if not determined to succeed in their duty.

As Sebastian, Ertic and Artun started to exit the ship, a high–ranking officer in full regalia marched up the ramp. He approached Sebastian and gave him a salute, which in this case seemed to be as much a battle to move aside the enormous plumage that had draped across his face, as it was to show respect to an honored guest.

"As the Senior most diplomat from Earth to visit, you will be given a full guard to accompany you to your quarters during your stay," he stated after his impressive salute.

Sebastian looked at the ceremonial guard of twelve soldiers.

"And, er, do you also come into the quarters…?" he asked hesitantly, unsure of the logistics of the operation and very much hoping the answer would be a strong no.

"No, Sir," the soldier responded, his plumage priming for flight. "A small guard shall remain outside at all times to show you the full respect accorded to your position, and to ensure your safety."

The feathers shifted suddenly to the side as though their original owner was watching for his response.

Sebastian watched it as if returning its gaze, almost hypnotized by its uselessness atop a military garb.

"That will be all," Ertic said in an authoritative voice.

The officer led them to the base of the ramp where the rest of the ceremonial guard then assembled behind them. The officer at the front led them, as they made their way from the ship and across the once manicured lawn that stretched to the front of the palace. As they walked, it looked as if the feathered creature atop the officer's hat may at any moment escape, yet somehow, despite all hope, was kept there by an invisible force.

They continued towards the prearranged accommodation as the décor on his hat bounced about as though a disoriented squirrel covered in treacle, had taken refuge in a burlesque club, and was now desperately seeking its nuts.

They approached a beautifully ornate residence that stood near the center of the complex. Intricate statues seemed to line the walls guarding the windows. The walls were themselves adorned with carvings telling stories of the history of the Callaxians. The roof had a polished copper tone to it, reflecting the light and filling the courtyard with a warm, welcoming glow.

They came to a dramatic stop in front of a vast and impressive carved wooden door. It seemed as tall as it was wide and was covered in the most intricate, delicate details, ranging from flowers floating in a sea of starlight to some kind of creature traversing a grassland. All–in–all, it was an impressive carving.

This was no accident as it had taken five of the planet's most skilled craftsmen four months to carve it, from the base of a single, now extinct tree, and another two months to fill the inlay and varnish it. It was a masterpiece.

"This will be your quarters during your stay," the officer said with an air of authority.

"This can't be right," Artun stated in a matter–of–fact manner. "This is the Emperor's personal suite."

"The orders come straight from your Number One, Sir," the officer replied with certainty. His dancing feather squirrel suddenly motionless and looking dangerous.

The officer raised his hand to his ear, listening to a communication.

"They're ready to talk with you both now. You need to go to the control room."

"And him?" Ertic gestured towards Sebastian.

"It would be best if the Ambassador remained here," the officer responded. The feathered squirrel gyrated with gravitas.

"Don't worry," Sebastian said. "I could use a chance to process this."

Ertic visibly tensed as a guard stepped forward and opened the door. Sebastian entered the room.

The door closed silently behind him as the first two guards took up their positions on either side of it. The remaining guards marched away in unison; their ceremonial duties completed.

Ertic and Artun made their way to the control room.

Chapter 27

The control room bustled with life, filled with different groups, gathered about different stations. Each was focused on a singular task, working to either safely evacuate people, collect and save key material, coordinate the ships, ration the supplies and fuel, and muster the troops for a counterattack. The sense of purpose was breathtaking.

Ertic walked in with Artun at his side and felt immediately at home. It had been some time since he had stood here, and it felt like it was welcoming him back.

They moved between the groups as the groups seemed to dance about each other, each vying to achieve their directive as effectively as possible.

In the center of the room, on a floating chair above an elevated platform, sat a general with a thin silver band wrapped about his head.

As they made their way through the room, the center chair descended slowly to the platform. The general was addressing two others, Triven and a small, slightly rotund individual also wearing the rank of a general. The three talked in an animated manner.

They navigated through the person sized ant farm as it bustled about them. The maelstrom of ants serving their collective mission.

As they approached the chair, the small, rotund man turned to greet them.

Both Artun and Ertic stopped and hit their arm across their chest in a sign of respect.

"Gentlemen," he began, "we must discuss this quickly. This is obviously in addition to the meeting that you have already had with Number One." He gave Triven a sharp look. "As you can appreciate, we have little time. Number One, you are expected to sit in on the meeting."

"I believe I may be more useful mounting the defence …" Triven began.

The short, rotund man waved him off with a motion of his hand. "Given your recent actions, I wouldn't push this," He snapped.

Triven looked more than a little irritated.

"Order your Second in Command to relocate your troops to sectors three, four, and nine. They will benefit from the extra assistance to load the ships. Your Second Officer can help with the supply lines here in main control. Your bridge officers will also be of use here. Allocate your medical staff to our medical bay. They can relieve some of the staff who are already there."

Triven muttered the commands into a communicator.

"As you can see," the rotund man said, gesticulating about, "We're in the middle of evacuating, supplying and creating a counter offensive. I am General Fludge. We must talk immediately. I need to hear if there's anything we could use to aid in the capital's defense. The transportation technology is risky, but we have enough volunteers and energy left for a couple of trips, if it's worth the risk."

"You're wasting time we don't have. There's nothing we can use on the human's planet," Triven spat.

"I'm wasting time I shouldn't have to," Fludge replied, looking hard at Triven.

Fludge turned and made his way to a door at the back edge of the room that was flanked by guards, followed by Ertic, Artun and Triven. As he arrived, a guard opened it for him and all four of them walked through.

They entered a large room with ten Chief Generals and two vice commanders gathered about the ends of a long table that was off to one side of the room. The Chief Generals were sitting at either end of the table in groups of five, recognizable by a horizontal line on top of three circles that sat horizontally on their sashes. On the one end was the intelligence group with their purple colors and on the other end was the transport group with their green colors. The sixth member of each group, a Vice Commander, was working with them, moving about the group from member to member. They were all deeply focused on viewscreens showing on the tables surface, occasionally raising their head to check with their nearby colleagues before continuing.

Artun recognized the officer he had talked to on the screen working in the intelligence group.

General Fludge continued through this first room, opened a door on the far wall and moved into a second smaller room that was attached to it.

He sat down on a chair next to a smaller light green table and motioned for the others to do the same at the chairs closest to him. The room was twenty foot long and fifteen foot wide. It had no viewscreens or technology within it. There were no windows, and the two-tone blue carpet was soft and functional underfoot.

Ertic and Artun sat opposite him, and Triven followed.

"We have a very limited time. We are now in a secure meeting station. I need to know what is on that planet that we can use," Fludge stated.

"Really not the time," Triven hissed.

"First the report. Tell me what we can use," the General said levelly.

"Walls," Triven snorted. "Just bloody walls, a race so stupid they think aliens turn up and build walls."

General Fludge shot Triven a look that clearly made him uncomfortable. "This is a direct order from the Emperor. After your previous effort, I suggest you comply," he said clearly and coldly.

"I'm afraid he's right Sir. They are an undeveloped species," Ertic began. "They've gotten as far as nuclear weapons."

"Ah, a planetary defense network," Fludge said approvingly.

"Unfortunately not, Sir."

"Then what are they doing with them?" General Fludge asked, now confused.

"They point them at each other, and then refuse to talk about it."

"What?" Fludge said, clearly shocked. "Why? Don't they know how dangerous they are?"

"It's called a nuclear deterrent," Ertic said.

"Who are they deterring?"

"Themselves," Ertic responded.

"What from?"

"Building nuclear weapons," Ertic replied.

"Then why did they build them…" General Fludge trailed off, looking thoughtful for a moment. He focused back on the conversation, hoping that perhaps there may be a positive outlook to this clearly insane approach. "Is it working?" He asked.

"Not really, I'm afraid. They keep building more," Ertic said.

"Do they have impulse control problems?" Artun asked.

"So, how does this deterrent work, exactly?" Fludge asked carefully, trying to make sense of the situation.

"Their civilizations build nuclear weapons so that they don't get invaded by other civilizations that already have them. If they don't have them then other countries will invade them and take their things. Normally oil, but they do like shiny stones, gold, silver and iridium. If your country has those and you don't have nuclear weapons, then you will either be invaded, or they'll manufacture a situation they need to 'help you with' and you end up with a houseguest that you just can't get rid of."

"So, they build them to keep their civilization safe from other civilizations that have nuclear weapons?" Fludge asked.

"That's correct, and then, if they have them, they are elevated to a sort of 'preferred civilization' status. It's like a club. Nobody invades them anymore and they can threaten to invade other countries. If they need to exercise their armies at any point, they can send them to a third country that doesn't have nuclear weapons to prop up one side of it politically, while another nuclear armed country props up the other side. It creates a sort of 'safe space'. Then they can exercise their armies and tactics in a location with no nuclear weapons. It's a popular pastime when their weapons are getting a bit dated, and they want their population to buy them the shiny new ones. If the other country doesn't want to engage, then they just keep punching them until they change their mind." Ertic said. "They both pretend not to be there while the third country gets destroyed. Then they trade the pieces as a way to funnel more money about."

"So how does the nuclear deterrent work between the countries that have them if there is a confrontation?" Fludge asked.

"Well," Ertic began, "The theory is if any country with nuclear weapons uses one, some other country with nuclear weapons, who doesn't like the first country, gets to destroy the planet."

"That's the stupidest thing I've ever heard," Artun stated.

"Do they have enough nuclear weapons to destroy the planet?" Fludge asked.

"At least a hundred and twenty times over," Ertic replied, "They exploded over five hundred of them in their own atmosphere over a thirty–year period, I'm not convinced they didn't drop their own temperature by half a degree while flirting with a nuclear winter."

"They sound unfeasibly stupid," Artun muttered. "It's not a joke is it, like that time Emperor Hafartus the Third mutated a planet of tiny lizards to grow stun lasers and then gave it to his cousin for a wedding gift?"

"No," said Ertic.

"And their government type?" he asked.

"It's a sort of unaccountable democracy," Ertic answered.

"How is it unaccountable?" he asked.

"Many of their countries use the idea that the power of their politicians should be held in check by the legal process, and their press," Ertic began.

"That sounds reasonable, what happened?" the General asked.

"Rather than keeping them separate, they got politicians who were lawyers. So instead of being held accountable, they just don't answer questions. That way they're not technically lying, not technically breaking laws and thereby avoid any and all legal accountability."

"And their press?"

"Owned by the people who give the politicians money. The politicians are lawyers so they know what they can accept, and how they can accept it, without quite breaking the letter of the law, so they can pretty much do what they want."

"They actually vote for this?" he asked, incredulity clear in his voice. He looked a little disappointed.

The great philosopher Oolephant the 12th of the Umpratta once said that there are two ideas of democracy and that one can only understand how democracy actually works if one understands both perspectives.

The first idea of democracy is that of the people being governed–they believe that democracy exists to underscore the will of the people, to enable the voiceless to speak and be heard and to protect them in times of crisis.

The second idea of democracy is that of the government and, in particular, of politicians–they believe that democracy exists so that they can make money and more rules. These rules are necessary to restrict the impact of the governed who really need to shut up and let the smart people talk. These rules are best implemented during a time of crisis.

The most important act of any democracy from the point of the politician is to implement a crisis and bring in new rules to keep the population quiet.

The most important act of any democracy from the point of

those being governed is to say, 'hang on a minute—where did this new crisis come from and why is it that everything the politicians and the government do makes things worse?'

The rest of the conversation between the politicians and the people then depends on the type of democracy that dominates.

In a type 1 democracy it often goes like this: the politicians will simply respond, 'Oh, make it better, yes, we hadn't thought about that, please don't vote against us.'

In a type 2 democracy it goes like this: the politicians will say 'I don't think so.' The people will then reply with one or more of the following responses: 'Ouch, stop hitting me, I just asked you to do your job.... Why am I now unemployed? Why does my bank account not work? Where did all these extra rules come from? Didn't I have a house? Why can't I vote anymore?' And of course, the all-time classic, 'so I just need to sign this piece of paper?'

The only way to tell what type of democracy one is currently in, is to count the number and rate of crisis occurring. This is important in preventing a type 1 democracy from becoming a type 2, as, in the absence of guiding principles, the rules themselves become the principal guidance, and those who control the rules, control the guidance.

> Excerpt from: *Democracies don't work, now I can't work, I shouldn't have signed the paper, by Hardwoon Shappro, Leader of the opposition.*

"They can vote for their pick of either of two sets of lawyers. This is really the option to pick which ones will get the richest." He paused. "It's not a well thought out system. If they get a group so incompetent as to launch nuclear weapons and destroy the planet, then these politician–lawyers will be the only people with guaranteed access to shelters and food, while everyone else dies in the resulting nuclear confrontation," Ertic responded.

"Eurgh!" Artun said, sounding disgusted.

"What about the walls?" Fludge asked hopefully, remembering Triven's comment previously.

Ertic sighed, "There is some evidence of possible advanced intelligence that created large structures."

"Including walls," said Triven derisively.

"And walls," continued Ertic, "of a very precise nature, using very large stones."

"They built walls?" said the General, clearly losing hope.

"That's right," said Ertic, "and nobody remaining on Earth really knows how they did it."

"Nobody knows how they built walls," Fludge repeated, rubbing his head with his hands.

Fludge removed his hands from the side of his head and sat back in his chair. "So, they had the technology to build walls and now they've lost it, or at the very least are confused by it. On top of this, they're holding themselves hostage by pointing nuclear weapons at themselves, because their political classes are severely compromised lawyers who want extortion money," he said, summing it up. "How have they even survived this long?" He paused. "I fear that this is not the game changer we were hoping for."

"Maybe we could get them to join forces with the enemy," Artun said optimistically.

"It seems unlikely that an impervious giant space slug carries much weight in the diplomatic sense." the General said, his voice tailing off as if entertaining the idea.

"Alright, if that is all gentlemen, I'll report this up the chain." He paused. "I doubt anybody will be pleased," he added.

"I'll have you escorted back to the human. Where is he now?" he asked, standing up.

"The Emperor's quarters," came the response from Ertic.

The general froze. "What in the hell is he doing in the Emperor's quarters?" he demanded with an edge to his voice.

Triven looked at him. "He appeared just before the mission, and he was on the ship before the Decimator failed to work.

One of those alone would make him suspicious. So, tell me, where would you put an unknown quantity where he's protected and well looked after, without possibly compromising the entire response effort?" Triven looked at him hard. "Especially when he has received the full rights and protections of a diplomat?"

Triven looked like he was daring him to respond.

The general looked back at him just as hard. "He will stay there for the moment, only because we can't spare the time to deal with your mess. Once this has been resolved, you will explain yourself directly to the Vice Commander."

General Fludge appeared to calm down a little. "Number One, you can report to active duty."

"About time," Triven muttered, storming out of the room.

"Chief Security Officer," General Fludge said looking at Artun, "you can join the security in the command room - help with anything that people need help with, even moving things. The more security there to help the better. You already have security clearance. We can empty out faster and we're ready if anybody panics."

"Yes, Sir," Artun responded.

Chapter 28

Sebastian looked about the room, the opulent furnishings strewn about the area gave the impression of a catalogue photo shoot at an opulent French chateau. Now and then, as he cast his eye about, he saw objects utterly foreign to him. A chair with one leg that seemed to sway gently from side to side, a flat levitating mirror that floated above a table, slowly lifting and falling a few inches at a time, as though it was breathing.

He found himself fascinated by the place as he moved about it, touching everything, just trying to take it all in. There was a smoothly polished wooden chair treated with what seemed to be varnish but when he touched it, he could almost feel it returning his grip, as though shaking hands. It was a world away from the engineered feel of the spaceship with its artificial walls.

Wherever he looked was almost magical.

In the corner, he saw a small plant that was swaying in time with the one–legged chair. He watched it hypnotized by its motion and slowly reached out to touch its petals, rapidly pulling his hand back as it tried to bite him.

Taken aback, and still rather convinced that this was likely a hallucination, he distracted it with his left hand and then, as it carefully moved forward to bite his finger, he tapped it lightly from behind with his other hand.

The plant stopped, shook its flower petals, pulled back gently and then tried to jump out if its pot to attack him. Sebastian let out a scream as he fell backward, landing on the floor and the plant fell forward, landing between his legs, with red soil spilling about its base.

It sat there ferociously trying to attack him but thankfully held back by its heavy pot, that now lay on its side, on the floor.

That's another indicator that this is just a bad trip, he thought to himself, eyeing it warily as he backed away.

The plant jammed its flowery head into the floor and pushed the pot upright. It continued to watch him as he walked on through the room, touching random objects.

He left the room and moved farther into the complex. There were paintings adorning the wall and plush, thick carpeting that continued throughout every corner of the place.

There were a few pieces about that didn't seem to fit. Odd eyesores that just took away from the majesty of the visual impact.

Sebastian looked at one such piece, a squat, square stool about four feet across, that just took away from the overall impression. As he did, he noticed an old painting on the wall nearby that showed a small man in full regalia with his foot on it, holding a scepter and wearing a crown.

He went over and sat on it to see what was so special about it. It was quite comfortable. He bounced up and down on it gently, trying to assess its suitability for royal buttocks.

As he did, something gave an audible click.

Sebastian shuffled on it gingerly, hoping that he hadn't damaged it with his own, less than regal, behind. It didn't feel loose or weak.

He leaned over and tried to look a little closer. Near the top of one leg, a little catch had popped out. It was beautifully crafted and would have been invisible, had it remained closed.

Sebastian struggled to look at it clearly. It sat awkwardly beneath the muffin top shape of the padded surface.

"Dammit," he muttered, struggling to see it better.

He stood up for a better view and lowered himself to be closer to it. As he did so, the front edge of the cushioned top slowly raised itself up, as though hinged at the rear, and he found himself looking inside the stool. But where the inside should have been, there was a staircase descending into the floor.

Sebastian stepped back and looked under the stool.

He could see clearly under it as if it were just a normal stool. It had four legs and a gap of about a foot between the base of the top and the floor. There was definitely not a staircase. He put his hand under it and waved it around to be sure there were no mirrors.

There was nothing there.

He sat up again and looked suspiciously down the staircase once more.

It was still there, harassing his understanding of three-dimensional space, as were the stairs, which had gone beyond harassing his understanding and had moved on to bullying it.

He looked under the stool again, deeply disbelieving of what he saw.

Glancing across the top of the stool he saw an object that looked like a bathrobe hanging on the wall.

Sebastian got up and walked over to it, and, after carefully and delicately removing it from the wall, walked back to the staircase that stretched down into the stool. He held onto one side of the robe and threw the rest of it into the hole. Then he pulled it back out again.

It was still in one piece and seemed undamaged.

He reached down and slipped off his shoe and knelt down next to the stool. He held the shoe in his right hand and steadied himself with his left against the edge of the stool. Sebastian tentatively lowered the front of the shoe into the hole until he could kick the surface of the top step with it. Then he pulled his shoe out and felt it.

It felt normal.

He looked at his foot, sitting at the end of his leg, wrapped in a sock.

He wiggled his toes.

They wiggled back.

Then he stood up and put his toes inside the hole.

He wiggled his toes again.

They wiggled back once more.

Sebastian put his shoe back on his foot.

"Why not?" he said under his breath and carefully put a foot inside the hole and gingerly placed it onto the top step.

Nothing untoward occurred.

He pulled his foot back out again and poked at it.

All seemed well.

He did it again, and this time followed it with his other foot. He paused and looked down at his feet. He wiggled both sets of toes and shook his knees a little for good measure. Everything seemed to remain functional, he started carefully down the stairs.

About half–way down, when his stomach was level with the entrance, he reached over the edge of the stool and ran his hand through where his body should have been.

"Oh God, I think the drugs are kicking in again," he muttered, a cold sweat forming on his brow.

He stood up straight once more, and slowly, carefully, looking into the dark staircase, followed the stairs down into the blackness.

He held his breath and as his head moved below the top level of the stool, the dark stairway he was descending was transformed into a well–lit, rather majestic, polished white marble staircase. He stumbled down the last few stairs and, continuing his stumble through a doorway, found himself standing on a large, polished stone floor, in a polished white marble room.

It seemed to stretch for hundreds of meters in each direction. The floor was a marbled white, as were the walls and the enormous fifty-foot-high ceiling. In the center of this enormous room was an enormous fireplace, open on all sides. The flames danced all along its surface, their orange and yellow light casting a warm glow into the room. It was so large that it could host a hundred medieval banquets full of wine and debauchery in near unison and a gleaming finish so clean, that it wouldn't even host a renaissance fair.

Near to the fireplace sat an impossibly large sofa.

Lying back on the sofa was a small thin man with perfect light brown hair, a perfect mustache, neither garish nor gauche, wearing a smoking jacket and some white trousers.

As Sebastian entered, he sat up and looked at him quizzically.

"And who might you be?" he asked in a surprised tone.

He got up from the sofa and moved toward Sebastian with a speed that was difficult to reconcile with his frame.

Sebastian took a step back in surprise.

"Err, Sebastian," he said.

"And now for my second question," he began, "what are you doing here?" He said, motioning around the room.

"I just walked down a staircase in a stool," Sebastian said, feeling rather silly that the sentence he used even created a realistic interpretation of events.

The man looked at the side of Sebastian's head and saw the reality modifier sitting on his temple.

"What do you do here?" Sebastian asked, looking about the room, "and also, where is here and what's happening? "

The man thought for a while.

"This is the lounge of the research department, and I am the chief engineer," he said grandly.

Sebastian had met a few engineers from the university and knew there was nothing they loved more than to discuss engineering.

"So, what are you working on," he asked, looking around the room, which, apart from a collection of doorways that lined the distant walls, was completely empty aside from the fire and the sofa.

"Interstellar travel," the man said, "but this really isn't a time to discuss it. We're under attack you know," he said looking thoughtful.

"I'd heard," Sebastian replied. "Some kind of giant slug..?" he asked, hoping for a little more information.

"In a manner of speaking. It's an ancient creature, as dumb as a box of rocks," the engineer responded. "I have to be available should the Emperor require my services, so I'm afraid I must ask you to leave. I can't imagine he'd be too pleased to know you found your way in." He paused. "How did you find your way in?" he asked.

"I've been told to stay in his accommodation. I think they're trying to figure out what to do with me," Sebastian replied.

"Ah, so you're in his room rifling through his stuff then? I wouldn't want to get found doing that. I think it's time to go now, don't you?" he asked, although something about the way he said it made Sebastian feel it wasn't really a question.

Sebastian looked around once more. Something just seemed out of place, beyond the portal, the fire, the sofa and the odd state of his brain. Something just didn't seem to fit.

"Thanks," he said, and, looking about once more, he made his way back up the stairs to the Emperor's quarters and closed the stool.

Chapter 29

Ertic moved quickly through the courtyards towards the Emperor's residence, the air hummed with the motion of ships darting backward and forward, attempting to complete the evacuation before the creature's imminent arrival.

He approached the magnificent entrance door that was flanked by the two large guards. They opened the door for him, and he walked inside. The room he now stood in was every bit as uselessly opulent as he had imagined it would be. So many things that nobody actually needed. It looked like someone had gone impulse shopping at a medieval flea market and bought everything that was most likely to actually have fleas. From the looks of the purchases, they had likely done this with someone else's credit card.

There was a picture of the Emperor adorning one of the walls.

Ertic shook his head. As much as he was loyal, the idea that there was a picture of the Emperor in the Emperor's own quarters seemed a little ridiculous.

He looked about the oversized quarters and eventually found Sebastian. He was just starting to sit on the plinth of a fertility inducer, in the third room that he looked in.

He cleared his throat and Sebastian looked up, a little startled, trying to get comfortable.

"I know it looks like some kind of designer chair. It's not," Ertic said. "If you sit on it for too long, there's a strong risk, it'll badly affect your posture for the next three hours."

Sebastian jumped up and looked suspiciously at the chair he had been sitting on.

"What do you mean?" He asked quickly.

Ertic chuckled. "Don't worry about it human, just don't sit there."

"What happened with the meeting?" Sebastian asked as Ertic walked towards a raised cube, pushed on it and waited for a chair to form.

"Same as before," Ertic responded, starting to mimic his earlier conversations. "What's on Earth? - *not much*, - is there anything that could help? - *no*, - Are there any weapons - *no*, advanced civilization that can help - *no*, walls - *yes*, you get the idea."

"Walls?"

"Yep, big old walls and pyramids but no aliens or advanced weapons."

"Oh," said Sebastian sadly. He had been hoping for some information that would tell him more about what was happening outside of the apartment.

Ertic took off his personal communications device and turned it over in his hands, looking at it carefully.

"What is it?" Sebastian asked.

"There are two things I don't understand," Ertic said. "Why did this thing stop working when I arrived on Earth?"

He paused, inspecting it and changing its position relative to the light coming through the window.

"What's the second thing?" Sebastian asked after a few moments.

"Why did it start working again?" he replied.

"Can't you ask someone to look at it?" Sebastian asked helpfully.

"They're all a little too busy at the moment," Ertic replied. "This is a very low priority."

"I know a guy," Sebastian said.

Ertic looked at him as though he had just grown antennae.

"I don't think that anybody on Earth can help us with this," he responded. "Not least given how far away it is," he added, his voice softening.

"Not from Earth," Sebastian retorted. "The Chief Engineer,

he's in the large footstool."

Ertic watched him closely. "This place is really rather similar to Earth, human. People are about the same size and things take up about the same amount of space. They tend not to live in footstools." Ertic worried that perhaps the human had seen a little too much, too quickly.

He looked at Sebastian a little more sadly.

"I'm not sure what's happening," he added with a touch of worry in his voice, "but, rest assured, that there isn't a chief engineer in the footstool."

"Yes, there is, I'll prove it," Sebastian spouted and walked to the stool.

Ertic was getting concerned now, he wondered if the strain of coming into contact with an alien civilization may actually have broken his poor primate's mind. It was a lot to process.

Ertic watched him as Sebastian stood next to the stool and then sat down on it, before standing up and trying this again, multiple times with increasing enthusiasm.

Sebastian stopped standing up and sitting down and started bouncing about the top of the stool as though it was a 1980s space hopper, jumping all around it like a man possessed.

Sebastian heard a click and looked down to see that the little lock had released.

"Prepare to be impressed," he said confidently, watching as Ertic's face turned from a sort of curious pity to surprise, as the top lifted back to show a portal opening that led to some stairs.

"What the...?" Ertic began.

"Want to meet the Chief Engineer?" Sebastian asked proudly.

Chapter 30

The Chief Engineer sat on top of his oversized sofa and stretched out in front of the large roaring fire. He was relaxing, enjoying the warmth radiating from the hearth when Sebastian and Ertic walked down the stairs.

"Well, we are busy today," he murmured, sitting up and placing what looked like a flaming martini on the floor.

He walked over to greet them.

Ertic stood, stuck to the floor, watching with wide eyes as the Chief Engineer approached.

Sebastian looked up. "Hello," he said.

"Indeed," replied the Chief Engineer.

Sebastian looked past the engineer to the martini on the ground. The scaling of everything just seemed to be off. From where he was standing, it looked about five feet tall. He wondered if he was having some kind of brain stutter.

Ertic remained rooted to the spot.

"Err," began Sebastian, "This is the Chief Engineer. "

"Don't think it is," muttered Ertic quietly.

"No, it is," Sebastian answered.

"Oh yes, that's me," said the Chief Engineer with what looked like a grin crossing his mouth.

"Nope," Ertic continued, again quietly, "how would he hold a screwdriver?"

"What do you mean?" Sebastian asked He felt like he was missing something.

"Engineers build things, they fix things," Ertic continued.

"Sure do," the Chief Engineer agreed.

"How does he hold a screwdriver?" Ertic repeated. "Can't hold a screwdriver when you have paws three feet wide."

"Rude," said the Chief Engineer rather matter–of–factly.

Sebastian was feeling thoroughly lost and was trying to make sense of the conversation when Ertic carefully reached across and tapped on the reality modifier on the side of Sebastian's head.

As he did so, the rather gaunt man who had until recently been holding the flaming martini transformed into a dragon with scales of gold tinged with blue. It was thirty feet long, wings folded gracefully along its back, and it's paws were indeed about three feet wide. The flaming martini on the ground, however, remained unchanged.

Sebastian took a step back. "A dragon," he muttered, "A dragon," he said again, this time a little louder. "You have dragons?" he said excitedly, now this was a hallucination he could get behind. As a child he had been obsessed with them. He'd had a hoard of marbles and he pretended to be a dragon, running about and breathing fire on things.

Now, here in front of him, was an actual dragon. It was breathtaking.

The dragon cleared its throat.

"I hope, that when you say dragon, you are not referring to me," it said sternly.

"Aren't you a dragon?" Sebastian asked, pretty sure he was looking at a dragon. He looked at it again, scales - check, huge lizard - check, wings folded back - check, general dragon–ness - check.

"How can I be a dragon? They're tiny creatures that live in ponds, they're like the wyrms that live in damp soil but with eyes and little feet as well." It cleared its throat and raised itself high, "I am a Newt!" the creature said in a voice that bellowed, its chest swelling with pride.

Sebastian looked at the creature as the light reflected from its scales majestically and its voice seemed to fill the immense room in which they were currently located. It seemed almost to grow, its magnificence matching that of the room.

"Why are you hiding in a stool?" Sebastian asked. There

were several hundred questions that seemed to present themselves at this point, but he just couldn't wrap his head around how a thirty-foot dragon could have gotten into the room and why it would then hide there. Certainly, the room was large enough, but there was no way the dragon could have made it through the entrance.

"Really?" it said sounding a little exasperated, "for a start I do not hide, the Emperor asked me to wait here and in case you're thinking of asking me how I fit in the hole… well," it said looking a little more critically at him, "there is more than one entrance, and, at a risk of repeating myself, rude."

The dragon turned and made its way back to the sofa. It sat once more upon it, stretched itself out and reached down for its martini.

Sebastian reached up and turned on the reality modifier on the side of his head once more. As he did so, the large, majestic dragon was again replaced by a dapper man in his mid-thirties who looked at him and poignantly raised an eyebrow.

"I've heard of these creatures," Ertic said, looking at the Newt on the sofa. "They're said to span multiple dimensions. They can even jump through large sections of space in an instant. I didn't think that they even existed, just legends and folklore."

"You know, if someone's in the same room as you, you should really refer to them by their name. Just common courtesy really," the Newt said calmly.

Sebastian walked over to him confidently, the reality distortion field keeping his mind from confronting the overwhelming danger he would be in, if the creature were to be riled.

"We clearly got off on the wrong foot," he began, "I'm Sebastian."

"I'm Garrat," the gaunt man said as he stepped down from the sofa to meet him.

Sebastian extended his hand, as did Garrat. The reality

distortion field allowed Sebastian to watch two hands shaking, but he could sense the enormity of the creature being hidden from him.

Garrat seemed far more relaxed by the polite interaction.

"And you are?" he asked, motioning to Ertic.

"Ertic." Came the reply.

"Delighted to meet you," the Newt responded.

"Likewise," Ertic muttered, still feeling very confused.

"Now," began Garrat, "at the risk of appearing rude myself, what brings you back here and this time with a friend?"

"I'm not sure if you can help, given the questions over your engineering credentials," Sebastian said.

Garrat sighed, "You know, if you don't ask, you'll never find out."

"Alright," began Sebastian, "we were just transported through a gateway of some type or another here because Ertic's device started working again. We need to know why it stopped, and then why it started again. If you're an engineer, we thought maybe you could help. Apparently, we're low priority at the moment."

Garrat's head swiveled to meet Ertic's gaze. "Do you have the device now?" he asked intently.

Ertic lifted his sleeve to show it and then paused, looking quite uncertain.

"Oh please," Garrat protested, "do you really think my interests and your Emperor's don't align? I'm apparently living in a palatial setting hidden in his stool."

Ertic took it off and handed it to Garrat. "Can you figure out what's wrong with it?" He asked. "It might just be badly made. All of them stopped working, so it's probably just a poor design," he continued.

"Give it to me," Garrat demanded gruffly.

"A poor design," he muttered. "This may be one of the most advanced and carefully crafted pieces of technology your species has ever seen. If you broke it, it's on you."

"How do you know about it? I thought they developed it in

absolute secrecy," Ertic asked, curious how this creature seemed to be so confident in his knowledge of the device.

"Who do you think built it?" Garrat replied.

"But how…?" Ertic trailed off as he asked, looking at Garrat's huge paws.

"R," began the newt ominously.

"U," he moved closer.

"D," at this point, he was only a foot away, and Ertic stood transfixed to his spot.

"E," finished the Newt, now only a few inches away. He snorted some air out through his nose.

Sebastian's perception altering device did not show him the sight of a mildly disgruntled Newt. Rather, it showed a gaunt socialite moving closer and closer to the Sub-Commander, until he was only inches away. It was only noticeable that something was amiss when Garrat snorted and instantly Ertic looked like a weatherman staring down a hurricane and thinking about his medical coverage.

"Now if you don't mind," Garrat said, stepping back and gesturing at the device.

"Sure," Ertic said, a little uncertain, and then passed it to him.

Ertic watched intently as the Newt looked into the device, layer upon layer seemed to strip away and magnify, reorient and peel back more.

"How are you doing that?" he asked.

Sebastian's reality modifier could only translate it for his brain as an image of Garrat staring at the device and puffing and unpuffing his cheeks.

Sebastian looked at Ertic, confused.

Garrat seemed to Ertic almost to smile.

To Sebastian, Garrat now had a crazy person grin while staring intently at the device and flaring his nostrils.

Garrat kept looking at the device, peeling back complexity after complexity, magnifying it and examining each component.

"If you can manipulate the dimensions, then everything else is easy," he said slyly.

As he examined it circuit by circuit, he seemed continually pleased with his creation, right until he found a circuit with a clear break in it. Across the circuit lay a tiny cubic robot.

Garrat paused and stared at it. He reached into the device and turned it with his hand. "A nanite," he spat. "Someone sabotaged this."

He sat back, a look of intense anger on his face. "You need to inform the Emperor."

"Us?" Sebastian asked.

"I am a Newt, a creature of legend, not an errand boy. One of you will have to approach him with the information."

"There's no way to reach him at the moment. He's rather busy with the defense of the planet," Ertic responded.

"If you don't reach him, the defense may already be over. Someone sabotaged this, and likely the others to prevent their return, only higher–level officers could have had access. If there is someone working against us from the inside, we don't know what else they may have already sabotaged. Without this information, we can't even begin to understand how much trouble we're in." the Newt stated abruptly.

"How can we even reach him?" Ertic asked.

Garrat looked at him with an amused grin. "More than one entrance," he said, "but you'll need the password and traditional Newt greeting. It's the only way to tell that you're there on my behalf. Also, and this is really important, you may not like it, but you have to go in naked to show you don't have any concealed weapons."

Chapter 31

The Emperor sat at the table with four of his seven Commanders. His uniform was the same light-yellow with a red stripe descending over his shoulder, but it was a variation on the original design. This was to accommodate his slightly short, plump figure. He had two horizontal stripes on his sash. The top one was a grey stripe, and the bottom was a red one. The grey stripe had been his own design.

The troops and Strategy Commander, a burly blue individual with a wide chest, two horizontal red stripes on his uniform and a deep voice leaned forward. "The civilian population has been evacuated. Most of the Ambassadors have now left. We've been allowing ships to land and take off from the lawn because of the number of extra ships in the area filling all the hangars and the speed of access from command. We've also allowed the arrival of hangars from off world to aid in the defense. The explosion created by the ship carrying the Decimator cleared a large amount of the surrounding meteoroids from the edge of the creature. We have active troops in the air attacking it non–stop. As expected though, it's having no noticeable effect." He finished.

"Most of the population have been transported off world to the colonies," the Transportation Commander began, a thin individual with piercing eyes. He wore two horrific puce colored stripes on his sash which contrasted with his blue skin tones. "We should be on a skeleton staff shortly, with enough ships remaining to complete the full evacuation in the event of any problems with the floating city. The floating city itself is primed to leave at any time."

"If it leaves, it leaves last," the Emperor stated, "and the supply ships for the colonies?"

"The supply ships have now departed. The colonies are fully stocked and ready to move to a decentralized model until we can regroup. We also sent two supply ships with the delegations from the inner planets of the Stromada system..." began the Logistics and Communications Commander, a green woman with mid-length hair sporting the two yellow stripes on her sash before trailing off as she watched Ertic enter from a side door.

He was naked with his arms spread wide, as though he had joined a cult and was now seeking to hug an invisible hippo. This had been important, according to Garrat, as it would show he wasn't armed or a danger.

"What the ..." the Science and Research Commander began, a mostly thin male with a soft belly that was a little too large about his waist, his blue skin highlighting his wide eyes and his mouth now open in surprise, two blue stripes on his sash complimenting his skin tone. The Transportation Commander and the Logistics Commander sat watching, their mouths agape, confusion on their faces. The Troop Commander took out a weapon and placed it meaningfully on the table. After a moment the Logistics, Science and Transportation Commanders had all pulled out weapons and held them pointed at Ertic.

"Naboon anarta bee–an," he said in a loud clear voice, before he jumped up and down once, his tail bouncing behind him.

The Emperor, his eyes wide, stood up and walked towards Ertic. "Put your weapons down and continue with your work," he muttered angrily.

He guided Ertic back into the room from which he had come and towards the portal, his face quivering with anger.

He stormed through the portal and arrived in Garret's palatial room on the other side of the fireplace.

"Naboon anarta bee–an!" he roared.

"He said it, he said it," Garrat chuckled, so beside himself with glee that he could barely sit still.

"What does it mean?" Sebastian asked.

"Your shirt is as ugly as your sister," the Emperor growled. Garrat began to laugh.

"Why didn't the translators just translate it?" Sebastian asked.

"I'm guessing the language is too ancient. It's not recorded in the database, and it has no similarities to the recorded languages," Ertic responded, glaring at the Newt as he started to get dressed.

"What in the hell was that about?" The Emperor demanded.

"And he was still naked?" The Newt asked, his eyes wide, his breath held in anticipation.

"And jumping," shouted the Emperor.

Garrat roared with laughter, tears forming in his eyes.

"Was there..." he began, struggling to breathe before finally muttering, "Was there anybody else there?"

"Four of the seven Commanders of the Union," the Emperor growled "In an official briefing!" he roared.

Garrat rolled about on the floor, laughing and writhing, before sitting up, looking at the Emperor and falling down laughing again, kicking his legs in the air. From Sebastian's perspective he was rolling about on the giant sofa holding his stomach and laughing hard.

"Do you really think that now is the best time?" the Emperor hissed through clenched teeth. "I hate to remind you of the danger we're in."

Garrat composed himself.

"He said I had fat paws," Garrat said self–consciously.

"You do have fat paws," hissed the Emperor.

"Well, you have a fat ass," the Newt shot back, before continuing to chuckle about the event.

"Dammit Garrat, what do you want?" the Emperor demanded.

Garrat composed himself while the Emperor stewed. He took a couple of deep breaths and finished calming down. "Someone sabotaged them," he said finally.

"What was sabotaged?" The Emperor asked, his attention now fully engaged.

"The troops that you sent off to other worlds to find useful technology. Somebody sabotaged their tracking devices," Garrat said.

The Emperor took a deep breath, his eyes gleaming. "Are you sure?" he demanded.

"A single nanite," Garrat responded, "took out a small connection in the command circuit. This one," he motioned towards Ertic's tracking device, "only started working because the defunct nanite ended up bridging the gap," Garrat finished.

"That was lucky," the Emperor said, watching Ertic carefully.

"Indeed," Garrat said, "Upon examining it, it just separated. It was only being held there by the magnetic field created by the small electric current in the bridged circuit. When that reduced, it fell off. You were lucky that you got him back when you did, otherwise it would never have happened."

The Emperor seemed to relax with that information.

"We still have a problem though," said Garrat. "We don't know how deep the rot goes. If they were close enough to sabotage the devices, what other damage has been done, or traps set."

The Emperor grew tense again. "We have no way of knowing who's responsible."

"We can trace back the personnel involved, one at a time, interview them, see if we can narrow down the pool," Garrat responded. "Until then, everything needs to be questioned."

"We don't know who we can trust," the Emperor said ominously, pulling out a small stool from under the sofa and sitting down to think.

"If there are sleeper cells here, we don't know how they communicate," he began. "We need to restrict communication between the different departments and tasks to ensure that there is a minimum of collaboration between the teams."

"Is that even possible at this point?" Ertic asked.

The Emperor looked at him carefully. "Each of the groups has clearly defined tasks. It should be possible for them to focus on them with a minimum of contact. If we can control the contact, then it becomes possible to limit the communications."

"How can we do that?" Ertic asked.

The Emperor thought for a while and then looked at Sebastian and smiled.

Garrat grinned, "That could work," he said.

Sebastian watched them suspiciously, "What could work?" he asked.

"We're going to set you up as the coordinator between divisions while we try to find out who our traitors are," the Emperor said.

"What does that mean?" Sebastian enquired.

"In the command center, someone sits in the center and makes any decisions that are time sensitive with the full authority of the Emperor," Ertic said.

"That sounds like a technical job," Sebastian said. "I don't really think I'm qualified."

"Nonsense," replied the Emperor. "I'll set it up to restrict communication between groups. This will pressure anybody without our best interests in mind to either present themselves through their actions or run for cover for fear of discovery."

"So, what does that mean?" asked Sebastian.

"They need a figurehead," replied Ertic. "Someone to sit in the chair, nothing more. If it makes it any easier, just assume that you're still on drugs waiting for them to wear off and somebody's giving you a nice place to sit," he added.

The Emperor gave Ertic a rather odd look.

'There are three types of people who can end up as a figurehead. A moron who knows they are a moron, a smart person who everyone thought was a moron and a moron who

believes they are smart.

A figurehead is an individual who takes responsibility while others make decisions. Figureheads often view themselves as responsible and powerful people. This dichotomy is why it is important to have morons who know they are morons in figurehead positions. They will rely on the surrounding systems to guide them through their decision making. A true figurehead endures the greatest potential danger for the least reward and is often unaware of it. This is because the important people are nice to them as long as they're doing what they're told.

If a smart person ends up as a figurehead, they can be very dangerous. They will first attempt to ensure that they are not expendable. It starts as they gather the secrets of others to protect themselves. Then they use the surrounding systems to leverage those secrets and achieve their goals, placing people loyal to them into positions of power.

A smart person is limited by the structures in place around them, they will attempt to create dynastic rule and slowly change the systems to favor themselves, their children and their friends. They will, however, ensure that all those in proximity around them are either morons or have their self–interest met.

The most dangerous person to have as a figurehead is a moron who thinks they are smart. They will take control and destroy all the systems that have been carefully created to sustain the society and limit their power. They will then constantly pat themselves on the back for doing a good job. They will not understand why their power was being limited and will act out like a toddler who lost its toys.

A moron who believes they are smart will not lie. They will not have to. This is because they are convinced that they fully understand the problems that they intend to address. They will dismiss any attempt to enlighten them as some form of attack. Only by letting them talk does their stupidity become clear. However, this will not distinguish them from a moron *who knows they are a moron.*

The best way to tell if you have a moron in power who thinks they are smart, and not just a regular moron, is to watch the systems that exist to restrict or criticize their power, such as the press or the judiciary. If these systems do nothing, then you have a moron who thinks they are smart.

This is for two reasons: Firstly, because a moron who thinks they are smart has no idea what they need. They will destroy any systems they believe oppose them, whether they need them or not. Secondly, it is because all the systems designed to limit their power are run by people who will make every effort to meet their own self-interest. Their motivation is to continue to be paid and receive their perks while staying under the radar.

The systems must buckle to the whims of the figurehead otherwise the majority will become aware of how much direct power is managed elsewhere.

Once one of these delusional morons is in power, all control mechanisms will bend over backward and work very hard not to be noticed and avoid doing the only job they were ever designed for.

If the moron is truly dangerous, then the control mechanisms will stand on the sidelines and actively cheer the burning of their civilization, while those in the shadows consolidate power ready to take advantage of the money that will be spent when the society is rebuilt.'

Excerpt from: *In praise of Morons, a guide to politics, by Kloomfam Degrokka*

The Emperor thought for a second, and then disappeared back in the direction of the doorway that led to the briefing room. He reappeared a minute later in Garrat's lair, holding a round silver band in his hand.

"Is that necessary?" Ertic asked.

"You already know that it is," the Emperor replied.

"What is it?" Sebastian asked.

"Think of it as a means to encourage loyalty," the Emperor replied. "When someone acts as a coordinator, they wear one,"

"What does it do?" Sebastian inquired, slightly concerned.

"As long as you're acting with the best interests of the people in mind, then it does nothing," the Emperor replied.

"Otherwise?" Sebastian asked rather weakly.

"It reminds you of your duty," the Emperor responded. "Don't worry about it. As long as you're working for the betterment of the Empire, or in your case, the people in that room, then it will do absolutely nothing. To a greater or lesser extent, it really works on interpreting your intentions," he added.

"And why do I want to wear it?" Sebastian asked.

"Because" said Ertic, "there are only two possibilities. One this is real, and we need you to, and if you don't, there's a very real chance we could all die, you, me, the Emperor, Garrat, everybody outside, you get the idea. And behind door number two, this is a hallucination, and it doesn't matter. You get somewhere to sit and maybe some kind of hot drink, while the nice man gives you a hat."

"That seems fair," Sebastian replied.

"As an incentive human," the Emperor added, "You will be well rewarded for your service."

The Emperor took out what looked like a plastic square from inside his clothing and put it into Sebastian's hand.

"I feel we've struck a deal," the Emperor said, "but let's be clear you have only these tasks–finish the evacuation as best as possible and attack the creature. All groups communicate through you if they must communicate at all. Can you conform to this without deviation?"

"Evacuate, attack and separate the groups. I can do that." Sebastian replied, his head swimming.

"How will you inform the crew without raising concerns?" asked Garrat.

"Leave that to me," the Emperor responded. "While our

human maintains the status quo in the operations room, we shall find our mole."

The Emperor looked at Garrat.

"What are the chances of a transport corridor to the conference room? I want you involved in the process, and it would be good to be able to move quickly between the conference room and the control room."

"We already have the corridor from my residence here to the conference room," Garrat nodded in the direction of the stairs that the Emperor had just returned from. "That should allow me to be involved with the proceedings there. That will have to do unless you want to deal with the repercussions from a new corridor. I can't shield its creation on that time frame. You'll have to hide my involvement in there," Garrat replied.

"We'll turn up the reality control settings throughout the room. Everybody inside the room will see an illusion when they look at you," the Emperor replied.

"But how do you know someone else hasn't done that already?" Ertic asked. "The entire place could be covered in sections where the reality control field has been activated. We could have them all over the control room just blending in. They could even masquerade as us," he said poignantly.

"I'm unaffected by them. I will only see what's in the room as it is," Garrat said.

"If the rest of us can have our reality affected, then how can we be sure that we're us?" Sebastian asked.

"I will give you some information that nobody else knows," the Emperor replied. "My middle name is Bertelmenflidgemantham."

"I'm sorry, could you repeat that?" Sebastian asked.

"Bertelmenflidgemanthum," the Emperor said with gravitas.

"Can we call you Bertie?" Sebastian asked. "I just don't think that I can really use that one effectively."

The Emperor looked a little crestfallen.

"Good idea human," he replied. "This way my middle name

remains hidden to all but those in this room and we can use the sobriquet 'Bertie' if our identity needs to be confirmed," he paused, "although I would have preferred Bertlemas," he said quietly.

"Bertie it is then," Garrat said with a grin.

"That won't cover all of us," Ertic said quickly, "we each need to share something that nobody knows. That way, we can ensure that we are who we claim."

"I dance very well," said Garrat.

A pause ensued, along with a few disbelieving glances.

"Well I do," said Garrat, a little hurt.

"I like the smell of fast food," Ertic said.

"What's that, food that runs?" the Emperor looked at him with a little disgust. "You do kill it first, don't you?" he asked.

"It's not alive," Ertic responded.

"Then how does it run?" Garrat asked, genuinely curious.

"It doesn't matter. It's an Earth thing," Ertic responded.

"I think I'm on drugs," Sebastian said.

"Something nobody else knows, quickly," Ertic said shortly.

"My favorite number is seven," Sebastian said.

"That'll do," said the Emperor, "we're ready."

They made their way through Garrat's residence and out through the Emperor's quarters to save time.

Chapter 32

Bertie, Sebastian, and Ertic made their way towards the center of the command room. As the Emperor entered, everyone in the room stood to acknowledge him.

He motioned for them to continue.

The group continued to the center of the room as the General in charge lowered his chair to the platform. The Emperor removed him from the chair and, after carefully studying the control panel on the arm of the chair, he placed his finger on a small blue button nestled in a sea of small blue buttons.

The Emperor began to talk, and his voice carried effortlessly throughout the room. "In order to maximize efficiency from this point on, we will focus only on our own units to complete the assigned tasks. All tasks are to be agreed by each team, prioritized and then performed as quickly as possible. Once completed, evacuate your groups. Move as a unit. For the next period, the human will oversee the operations. He brings with him unusual but effective combat knowledge from his home planet. You will follow his orders without question."

He paused and looked about, "Each group will meet briefly after they finish. This is to be performed with the supervising officers immediately upon completion of the tasks and the report is to be logged. This approach will allow as much clarity as possible in the successful completion of our separate missions."

"Raise the privacy levels about each of the stations," he commanded.

About each station, a small partition wall slowly raised to about the height of the people standing there.

"You know where to sit," he said to Sebastian as he stood up and motioned him to the chair. Bertie placed the band on top of Sebastian's head.

Sebastian sat atop the chair and waited for questions to come.

Bertie looked about the room. It seemed everyone had taken the switch in stride as they continued working on their tasks. He turned to the General, who had been controlling the command room.

"Rejoin your unit and help them complete their remaining tasks," he said clearly.

"My unit's already completed their tasks and moved off world."

"Find another task to be completed and join it. Then rejoin your team after completion," the Emperor replied.

The General headed off to join in with the first incomplete task he came across, and ended up with the rather less impressive task of changing the colors on the lights to reflect the level of danger that they were all in.

It seemed, however, the groups were very comfortable working independently, each focused on their own missions.

Bertie looked around and nodded to himself, pleased with the progress.

"I'd like to bring Artun in on this," Ertic said to the Emperor motioning towards Artun, who was working with one of the groups.

"Alright but be fast. We're beginning immediately," he replied.

Ertic looked over at Artun who was helping the group to pack their equipment. He looked up and Ertic motioned to him to come over.

The Emperor looked at Ertic. "We will take over the conference room in building B," he paused meaningfully, "In case you don't remember it, it's the one in which you were naked."

He walked through the room to the door. The royal guards

arrived, out of breath. They had run across the courtyards to join the Emperor after he had appeared emerging from his accommodation, rather than the conference room which he had entered. They arrived just as he reached the door and fell into place behind him, panting. They followed him as he moved quickly towards what was to be their operations center.

Ertic looked back over at Artun and saw he was traversing the room, carefully watching the people as he did. However, now the privacy barriers were up, it was difficult to see anyone properly.

Any groups of spies here were effectively neutralized from communicating.

Chapter 33

Artun waited outside the room with the personal guard and the seven Commanders of the Union.

To begin, Bertlemas called his personal guard and had them all place a band on their head. Then they recited their oath of loyalty. Every single one passed, even the one he suspected of stealing his yogurt.

Performing the tasks as rapidly as he could, he sent them out of the room and called in the seven Commanders.

Each of the Commanders headed one branch of the military union. For this part, though, he needed to have Garrat present. As much as the Newt could frustrate, he had a depth of knowledge on the political that was unbridled, and he was unaffected by reality distortion fields. He turned on the reality distortion field and set it to maximum to hide the Newt from the Commanders, then they entered and sat down.

Garrat placed his head and neck through the portal to examine the commanders. They seemed to be as they truly were, a little soft about the middle, but absolutely focused on the task at hand. To the Commanders, however, the distortion field could not easily deal with normalizing the neck and head of a thirty-foot Newt appearing through the portal. This reduced Garrat to a floating head that eerily bounced about like a lost moth.

The Commanders watched him with a mix of surprise and wariness.

"Why is there a floating head watching us?" the Troops and Strategy Commander asked.

"I am a floating head," Garrat said with pomposity as he bounced about above the portal.

"Not helpful," Bertlemas hissed.

The Intelligence Commander watched him closely. "First, a naked individual arrived at a restricted meeting and now a floating head," he watched him intently. "Something you'd like to share?"

"The floating head is a key advisor. He has unrivaled expertise, and he is unaffected by reality distortion fields. Because of this he can verify the identity of everyone in the room," the Emperor responded.

"They are exactly as they appear," Garrat stated with a grandiosity that now seemed to overflow, "overfed and over important."

"This is ridiculous," the Troops and Strategy Commander stated gruffly. "This is not the time for you to lose it." He said abruptly to the Emperor.

"He is here," said the Emperor quietly, "because he is the only known survivor of Regelmass 9."

The room fell silent.

"I thought everyone vanished along with the entire planet." said the Science Commander.

"Not everyone," said the floating head.

"Why is he here?" asked the Transport Commander.

"I am here to impart wisdom," said the floating head in his most pompous voice.

"He can be very insightful, although he is not always helpful," Bertlemas muttered.

"Is that his real form?" asked the Intelligence Commander.

"No," replied the Emperor.

"Can't imagine there are many creatures out there that could survive a planetary scale catastrophe," the Troops and Strategy Commander began, "and now, here you are," he said suggestively.

"Indeed." Garrat responded.

"We need to verify everyone's identity." the Emperor stated.

The Engineering Commander adjusted himself in his chair and leaned forward watching the Emperor, "Why do you need to verify our identity?" he asked.

"We have an immediate problem," Bertlemas began, his voice serious. "Someone sabotaged the technology for the Diplomatic Gateway Program."

"What do you mean?" demanded the Science Commander. He leaned forward intently in his seat. "That isn't possible."

"There was an intentional introduction of nanites, at most a couple per device, enough to get in there and immobilize the tech but not enough the be detected," Bertlemas said.

"How can you be sure?" asked the Security Commander, a thin yet muscular green individual, with a championship level moustache, who was deeply engaged with the idea that there could be a traitor among them.

The Emperor motioned towards the disembodied head, "He can be very insightful."

"And we're supposed to take his word for it?" demanded the Intelligence Commander.

"He was the one who designed and built the technology and developed the program to establish diplomatic relations," the Emperor responded.

"If there's a spy among our ranks with that level of access there may be no way to quantify the damage done," stated the Transport Commander, aware that even a slight glitch at this point could be disastrous.

"That's why everybody here, including myself, must recite the oath wearing a loyalty ring. If anybody with our level of clearance were acting against the Empire, then the game is already over," the Emperor said. "We all need to know where we stand."

He reached down and put a pile of eight rings in the center of the table. "Each of you take one at random and I'll take the one that remains, that way you know I've used a real one," he said.

Each of the Chief Generals took a ring at random and put it on their heads. The Emperor reached across and took the remaining loyalty ring and placed it on his own head.

The Emperor nodded and then in unison the seven
commanders of the forces and the Emperor recited the oath of
allegiance to the Empire.

All passed with no issues.

"How do we know the rings all work?" asked the Intelligence
Commander.

"Imagine doing something to harm the Empire." The
Emperor said.

Immediately all of them, including the Emperor grimaced
with the sudden discomfort of the ring.

They recovered quickly. The Troop Commander turned to
the Transport Commander "What did you think of to harm
the Empire?" he asked.

"Well," the Transport Commander began "Ouch, Dammit"
he muttered, glaring at the Troop Commander who was
chuckling.

"We don't have time for this," the Emperor stated, taking off
the loyalty ring and placing it in the middle of the table once
more, as the others did the same.

"We still have a problem," said the Intelligence Commander.
"Even if it's not at our level, there are many other issues that
could occur if the traitor has any reasonable level of
clearance."

"Agreed," said the Emperor. "At the moment any group
completing its assigned task meets with the commanding
officer on finishing. A limited full report will be completed by
the troops. In the report I have placed a small section to allow
the troops to report anything that surprised them over the
past year, any unusual behavior, or events that piqued their
interest. Any damage already done will have to wait, we
cannot pause our response and preparation. The creature is
almost upon us, but we may get lucky with the reports. It isn't
possible for us to check everybody on the base, we don't have
anywhere near the time, and we don't want to risk any panic.
We have no way to tell what's been sabotaged."

"Is that what happened to the Decimator?" asked the

Science Commander.

"No," the Emperor replied. "That was beyond sabotage. We may never know why that failed, but fail it did, bringing us here. Commanders, continue in your duties. Keep me informed of any leads. Anything, no matter how small, if it is out of place, may help us. I will assemble a task force to categorize discrepancies."

"I heard a rumor that one of the officers may have peed on it. Please tell me that isn't true," said the Logistics and Communications Commander.

"That wouldn't have affected it," said the Emperor curtly. "It's an interstellar bomb designed so that it could be placed at the bottom of the ocean or the center of a planet. That would have done nothing. Go about your business and keep me posted."

"So, someone did urinate on it?" asked the Intelligence Commander, looking confused.

"We can discuss this later," said the Emperor.

"This wasn't the one who was wandering around naked, was it?" asked the Logistics and Communications Commander.

"GO!" commanded the Emperor.

The commanders stood up and left the room. Bertlemas turned to the floating head.

"You know, I think the Commanders are getting dumber," Garrat said.

"We need to start," said the Emperor as he turned to face Ertic. "Get your friend in here."

Ertic quickly brought Artun inside.

The Emperor gave him the headband and had him recite the oath.

Artun passed with no difficulties.

"Do you know why we're here?" the Emperor asked.

"You think there's a spy in the system working against us?" Artun responded.

"Exactly. Ertic suggested you join us, and as you're a Head of Security I agree with him," the Emperor said, nodding to

Ertic. "We're going to find the traitor," he said with certainty.

"If we're bringing him in, he'll need to know our secrets." Ertic said "I like the smell of fast food, the human's favorite number is seven," he began.

"Why is the food still moving?" Artun asked, concerned.

"We don't have time," interrupted the Emperor, "my middle name is Bertelmenflidgemanthum. You may use the name Bertie, or Bertlemas. I prefer Bertlemas." He said levelly.

"Computer, for ten seconds bring down the reality distortion field in the room," the Emperor commanded.

"I dance very well," said Garrat, who was now behind Artun, no longer a floating head.

Artun turned and nearly fell over when he saw the head and neck of a thirty-foot Newt sticking through the portal.

Garrat pulled back and then put his paw through the portal to shake Artun's hand.

"I'm the Chief Engineer," he said.

Artun looked at Garrat's massive paws. "But how..." he began.

"Don't even," muttered the Newt from inside the portal.

Artun reached out and cautiously shook his paw.

"Now tell us something about yourself nobody knows, and we can begin. This way we can always check identity," the Emperor said.

Artun paused.

"Quickly," urged the Emperor.

"I like the doctor, Selim." Artun said quietly.

Ertic reached over and put his hand on his friend's shoulder.

"Now we can begin." said the Emperor with purpose.

Chapter 34

Sebastian sat on the chair in the middle of the operations room. He had decided against elevating it as he wasn't sure he could get it back down again. Now he was just waiting to be called on to dispense wisdom and allow groups to talk to each other.

This was without doubt one of the easier jobs that he had done. One by one, groups would appear, ask for permission to talk, and then leave. There were no customer complaints or questions about pizza deals.

Sardok had already asked if he could inform the crew that the attack ships had arrived, and now Sebastian was waiting for the troops to come in to ask to join the attack on the creature.

Things were worrying Sebastian. This didn't feel like a hallucination. He had never had one, but he assumed it would be like some kind of intense dream. When he said it in his head it certainly sounded like some sort of fever induced dream, but it felt real. So real, in fact, he was genuinely becoming concerned about the effects of any commands he might give, and the number of people they could adversely impact.

Slowly, the command room was emptying as the groups finished their tasks. Sardok and the officers that he had been working with had just finished and had begun to leave. As each group completed their respective tasks, they would send the leader of the group to be interviewed. Then the group would all leave the room at the same time, then separate to either resume their duties in a different location, board a ship to leave, or report to be reassigned.

Sebastian reached up and tried to remove the band from his head, but it stuck fast. The mere action of trying to remove it caused a sharp pain inside his head.

From the main entrance to the room, a group of well-dressed soldiers entered, some of their uniforms sporting small sets of vertical red lines, while others had green ones. They walked smartly up to the command chair. The one with the three vertical lines was the same Flight Sergeant that he had met earlier. The soldiers stopped and gave what Sebastian assumed was a salute and then stood firmly in front of him.

"Squadron Gamma–Nine from Veltrid Sector seeking permission to engage the enemy to slow it down, Sir," the Flight Sergeant said gruffly, three vertical green stripes on his sash.

Sebastian looked at him and felt his stomach sink. If he gave this order, if this was real then the people in front of him may well be about to die, but it could buy time for the last remaining people to escape into space.

"Seeking permission to engage the enemy, Sir!" he said again, this time more forcefully.

Sebastian looked at him and his squadron and felt the weight of the decision resting on his shoulders.

"We cannot continue without authorization, Sir!" he stated, once more, clearly frustrated.

The band was feeling decidedly uncomfortable on Sebastian's head.

He looked at the group once more, aware that they believed they had a chance.

Sebastian looked at him levelly. If he gave the order, then they may never return, but it may benefit the remaining people, which was probably why the band had started to feel more uncomfortable.

He had to know.

"Do you think you can pull it off?" he asked, watching him closely.

Slowly, the talking about the pockets of the room closest to the command chair subsided, some eyes started to peek over their partitions. Quickly the silence spread as others in the room gained the sense that something meaningful was happening. Soon everyone in the room stopped to watch his reaction.

The soldier set his jaw and stood straight, returning Sebastian's gaze.

"Whatever it takes," he said, in a strong, firm voice.

"Then do it." Sebastian stated. The soldier turned and left the room with his crew. Sebastian watched them depart.

He dearly hoped he was hallucinating. Quickly the room returned to its previous levels of activity.

"Course to intercept now programmed and uploaded to the attack craft," came a voice from what Sebastian guessed must have been the navigation section.

After a few moments, Triven entered from a different door and approached the chair.

"Listen up, human," he began, clearly uncomfortable with the new power dynamic between them, "my squadron is fighting against that creature up there. I want to accompany them to engage with it. As their commanding officer, I deserve the right to fly with my soldiers to meet the threat head on."

Sebastian looked at Triven and thought about the possibility that this may not be a hallucination, rather quickly reaching a decision.

"Fill your boots," Sebastian said cheerfully.

"That's an order you would give a senior officer," Triven growled. "And with what shall I fill my boots? Shaa'ving cream?"

Shaa'ving cream is one of the few luxuries in abundance throughout the Callaxian Empire. No office, store or shop of any sort would ever be without it. The Callaxians themselves utilize its incredibly luxurious moisturizing properties to keep the blue or green hue of their skin as rich and vibrant as

Quickly, Sebastian realized he had not been translated properly.

"It's an old saying," he replied. "It means you have my permission."

Triven nodded at him and began to storm out of the room, clearly still irritated. He stopped at Sardok's now empty station and picked up the small pyramid, placing it in his pocket, before continuing to storm out of the room.

Sebastian however was wondering, if he was in charge and he ordered Triven to fill his boots with Shaa'ving cream, would he have to do it?

This thought cheered him up immensely.

He made a mental note to order Triven to fill his boots with it, if he was still in command when Triven came back. Sebastian sat back in his chair and allowed himself to smile, finally feeling he was starting to get a handle on the events in the room.

From the edge of the room, a junior officer closed his terminal, got up, and left through the door.

"This ends now." he muttered.

Once outside, he began running.

Chapter 35

Artun, Ertic and Bertlemas stood around a large desk which was being used for its large interactive screen showing reports with discrepancies. The reality distortion field had once more made Garrat a floating head by the portal as he struggled to examine the reports.

"Clear each as quickly as you can," Ertic said, "but be careful. We can't miss anything, and we have more information being provided by the Generals."

"Talk it through as it goes down," said Bertlemas, moving the information about the desk with an intense focus.

"Alright, put the odd decisions here," Artun said.

"These just seem like a lot of odd decisions," Bertlemas said. "A lot."

"Agreed," said Ertic.

They looked at the collection of odd decisions that had been made and reported, these were things that had been ordered that didn't add to the running of the system.

Bertlemas paused and looked at Artun.

"You're a Head of Security," the Emperor said as it occurred to him that Artun may have a level of oversight, at least for his sector, that would enable him to produce a shortlist. "What decisions have you seen that have just been 'off'?" he asked.

Artun looked up at him. "Carpets," he spat.

"What do you mean?" asked Bertlemas, wondering if he should have asked someone else instead.

"About a year ago they started installing carpets in the mezzanine observation decks across all the launch bays over the entire Empire. Took a while, but they finally finished about three months back," Artun said.

"Is that odd?" he asked.

"Why would you want expensive luxury carpet where you're going to have soldiers standing, when they've just come in out of the mud? It's just the shortcut to the launching bays and the officer's operating rooms," he replied, "but it's worse than that," Artun continued, "the carpet is laced with fur from an Aptakking Wombat."

"And that's a bad thing?" The Emperor queried.

"Not much good for the wombat," Garrat said, continuing to bounce around in an ethereal, headless manner.

The others ignored the comment.

"About twenty percent of the soldiers with fur get quite severe shocks from it," Artun continued. "For myself, they are dangerous, but not just for me but for anybody nearby. When they were first installed, I sat on the stairs and the doctor sat next to me. I reached out to her, and she ended up in hospital," he said quietly, his voice trailing off, "we just sat down to talk."

He paused for a moment.

"We've lost quite a few soldiers because of it. They're just not interested in working in an environment where the carpet might be more dangerous than the war zone they get sent to," he finished.

"If it's that dangerous then why did we get the carpet?" the Emperor asked.

"Beyond my pay grade," Artun responded.

"Not today," the Emperor replied, working to pull up all the information on the carpet ordering.

"I'm getting paid more?" Artun said hopefully, as he continued sorting reports.

"No," said the Emperor, "your duties are expanding."

Bertlemas tried to pull up the purchase order for the carpet, but the screen remained blank. He input his pass code and called up all hidden files and the order appeared. "That's odd," he muttered, "it's been sealed."

"Why's that odd?" Artun asked.

"Orders and commands are only sealed if they're highly secret. Why would this one need to be sealed at all? Purchase orders for military materials should be sealed, but carpets?"

He used his override to open the purchase order.

Bertlemas stared at the purchase order for the carpets. It was enormous. He whistled, "That's a lot of money for carpets. Who'd be an Emperor? I should be a carpet salesman," he said quietly.

At the bottom of the purchase order was a single name. Lieutenant Dana'Krt.

He called up the file for Lieutenant Dana'Krt. "She's been promoted multiple times, she's already a Sub-Commander," he said under his breath. "Right now, she's leading a team of fifty, and all in just a few years."

He hit a button on the corner of the table.

"Open communications to Sub-Commander Dana'Krt, high priority," he said.

Almost immediately, Sub-Commander Dana'Krt picked up.

"Yes, Sir," she answered formally.

"Sub-Commander," the Emperor said, "I'm just reviewing files at the moment, and your name came up. What are you doing right now?"

"We've just finished painting the top of the highest skyscrapers checkerboard pink and green," she declared proudly.

The Emperor paused, trying to think about it.

"Why?" he asked carefully.

"It's part of my plan to communicate with the creature," she responded. "As pink and green check doesn't appear naturally, there's a good chance that the creature will see the top of the buildings and turn back."

The Emperor rubbed his hand on the side of his head as if in pain.

"I thought we couldn't find any eyes on the creature," he said carefully.

"But it probably has them," she replied confidently.

The Emperor breathed in deeply.

"So, you've had a team of fifty soldiers painting the tops of buildings checkerboard pink and green as the creature is almost upon us? For how many days?" he asked.

"That's right, for the past thirty days, Sir," she said proudly. "They've done a great job."

The Emperor paused and composed himself.

"I'm calling to ask about the carpets that you ordered installed in all the observation bays," the Emperor began.

"One of my proudest achievements," she replied instantly. "In fact, after I suggested it, I got a message from my Number One stating I was being promoted."

"Your Number One?" the Emperor asked.

"Yes, Sir," she replied.

"The First Officer of which sector?"

"The Veltrid Sector, Sir."

"Stop any remaining tasks and evacuate your team to safety immediately," Bertlemas said.

"Yes Sir,"

The Emperor ended the communication.

"We have a suspect."

"That's the Number One we've been working with for a few years. He's not well liked, he'd probably lose a popularity contest to a flesh-eating fungus, but I can't imagine him betraying the Empire. He's as loyal as he is annoying." Artun stated.

The Emperor looked at him.

"Pull up an image of the First in Command of the Veltrid Sector. Let's see who we're dealing with."

An image of Triven appeared on the screen.

"Call up all personnel files regarding people promoted by or recommended by our Number One," Bertlemas ordered.

Immediately, hundreds of personnel files filled the screen, all of them sealed.

The Emperor picked one at random and unsealed it. "This

one was promoted rapidly. Where did he start?" He flew down the information on the screen. "He was on the Fliteling five years ago."

"That was the ship that encountered the robots attacking the carrier. One of the crew came up with a plan to counterattack and saved the carrier," Ertic said.

The Emperor scrolled down "That wasn't him, he opposed the plan and tried to mutiny. It says here that Number One commended him on his independence. Hence the promotion," he said, his eyes wide.

"Who suggested the plan, then?" asked Artun.

The Emperor pulled up another file "that was a Second Lieutenant called 'Sh'ockley', she's now a Communications Officer. Seems there were a lot of demerits for questioning the First in Command. I think you met her. She was the Communications Officer on the ship that brought you in. Her record before last five years was," he paused a second, "surprisingly unimpressive. It looks like she's tried to transfer several times, but Number One keeps refusing."

"Surprisingly unimpressive?" Artun asked, "she's good, very good."

"Oh," the Emperor said, surprised. "She's currently in ..." His voice trailed off as he looked at her file, "the main command room, best place for her then," he said, pleased.

"So, the good people are being passed over for promotion. It could be worse," said Artun.

"Once that happens a few hundred times, you only have useless people making decisions and the useful people in the system just age out or are disenfranchised by it. They either avoid it or begin working to undermine it. It creates a system that's rotten from the inside and attacked from without," Bertlemas said quietly. "The people that he put in the roles are now promoting new people into new roles. We could be looking at thousands of people starting to make and enforce poor decisions. We're in trouble, but this is something we can deal with after we face the more pressing matter."

"At least we've got the human in the middle of all the decisions," Artun said.

Suddenly, the door was thrown open. And a young lieutenant dripping with sweat and clearly out of breath made his way into the room before partially collapsing just a few steps from the door.

A shocked Artun and Ertic immediately took up position in front of the Emperor. Ready to attack the intruder, Garrat growled.

"It's all right," called the Emperor. "He's one of my people on the inside, a distant cousin."

The officer was completely out of breath and struggling to speak.

Artun went over to him. "Just take a moment and catch your breath. Whatever it is can wait for a few seconds."

The officer shook his head to imply that it really couldn't wait.

Eventually, he managed to get a few words out.

"The human," he said, breathing heavily.

"Go on," said the Emperor, observing him.

"The human has ordered an attack on the creature," He managed.

"Ah," said the Emperor, "An inspired choice putting him in charge," he said, puffing out his chest. "But that action is really quite expected."

The officer breathed deep, trying to get the sentence out.

"He ordered the marines to pleasure the creature into submission," he blurted.

For a moment, everything in the room stopped. The very air moved by a fly's wings would have been deafening.

"Come again?" Artun said.

"That would seem to be the plan," chuckled Garrat as he bounced from side to side.

A wail coming from the Emperor broke the silence in the room.

"Well, this is new," said the grinning floating head.

Chapter 36

"Artun, find Triven. Let's see if we can figure out what else he's been up to," Ertic shouted to Artun as they ran down the stairs into Garrat's lair.

They ran through the beautiful marble room. "Garrat, can you fly?" Ertic asked.

"Indeed," replied Garrat, who appeared to be having a wonderful time.

"Get outside with Artun, take to the skies, and try to see if you can find him as well. Don't get spotted," Ertic continued. "We'll try to see if we can fix whatever is happening in the control room."

Garrat ran next to the Emperor. "So you left him in charge with all the powers of an Emperor," Garrat teased. "I'd like to see your field reports–any good words from Triven in there?" He asked.

"Stop enjoying this," the Emperor puffed, unused to the exertion. "Focus on your task and see if we can save what's left of this place."

They continued through the room.

"I'll head outside. I need a bigger exit," Garrat stated.

"I can't get anything on my locator," Ertic shouted.

"This is a pocket universe," Garrat responded, moving away in the other direction, "wait till you're outside."

Ertic, Artun and the Emperor ran to the base of the stairs and rushed up through the stool. They ran as hard as they could, not pausing for breath. The guards jumped as they burst out of the residence doors. The Emperor motioned for them to follow him as he continued.

Artun stopped and consulted the interface on his wrist.

"Locate The First in Command of the Veltrid Sector," he said into it, trying to get his breath back.

"Unable to locate The First in Command of the Veltrid Sector. Location services have been turned off," the machine responded in a calm and soothing voice, almost as if it was an attempt to offset the effect of the answer.

"Dammit!" he said aloud, clearly frustrated.

Triven entered the hangar through the side entrance, checking carefully to see if anybody was following him.

He quickly made his way up to and across the carpeted mezzanine floor, down the other side and into the hangar itself. The soft carpet of the mezzanine and stairs giving way to the cold hard floor. The hangar was still half full of attack craft covered in meteoroid marks. Clearly, they had started to use the remainder of the hangar to hold the craft to be repaired or that were out of service.

The troops had taken the last of the working craft out. Everything left was useless, with one exception. He had read the report that a working ship in the unit had been grounded. There was one usable attack class transport left.

Many of the hangars from the Veltrid Sector had arrived nearby, but the hangar docking requests had been altered so that this particular one would be the one landing nearest main command.

He walked rapidly and quietly through the hangar to the ship. There was nothing of use here. The hangar was empty of personnel and his footsteps echoed softly on the floor. He found the ship he was looking for among the battered remnants of a dozen others. He pulled out a small stun pistol, before entering through the rear ramp.

As he entered the craft, he could clearly see Sardok, the Second in Command of the Veltrid Sector, under the console. He was cutting the navigational wiring, a large metal box beside him.

"I had my suspicions," he said loudly as Sardok jumped out

from under the console and stood to face him, an odd-looking weapon in his hand. Triven kept his stun pistol trained on Sardok, and Sardok kept his weapon pointed at the ground.

"Once I found that the hangar docking requests had been altered, there were really only two people who would have any reason to do that." He said. "Imagine my surprise when I found out I was the one who had ordered it."

"I can only guess why you would have done that." Sardok said.

"I didn't." Triven barked. "You did and then you sealed the orders so that they wouldn't show up in the console."

"I cannot lie." Sardok responded. "You are correct."

"Why did you betray the Empire?" Triven demanded.

"The Empire betrayed me first, I'm just re–balancing." He said.

"It doesn't matter. You can explain yourself to the General's Council when you're tried. I will not have this mark against my name" Triven said shrilly.

"I don't think that's what's going to happen." Sardok said. "Tell me, have you ever heard of a damping field?"

The two stood facing each other.

"Your silence speaks volumes." Sardok said.

Triven raised his stun pistol, still pointed at Sardok, and fired. The energy blast exploded towards Sardok and just seemed to dissipate as it got closer, eventually vanishing to nothing.

Sardok watched Triven. "A damping field, expensive piece of equipment. I was able to pick it up from the Kevorans."

Triven looked at him. "Why would the Kevorans trade their military weapons?"

"For enough money, even the Kevorans trade. You might want to check your budget though." Sardok smiled and raised his odd-looking weapon. "Now this will give you a headache, but you'll be mostly unharmed. Although I imagine your pride will take a beating."

He fired his weapon, and an energy ball flew out of it

moving rapidly towards Triven. It hit him and he flew backward onto the ground, unconscious.

Sardok dragged Triven back out of the ship and left him safely on the hangar floor, beyond the reach of the shields. He turned and passed his hand over a large, rounded sensor at the ships entrance and the craft locked down. Moving quickly, he crawled back under the console and finished cutting the remote navigation controls.

Nobody from command could change his direction now. Unfortunately, at this point neither could he. Once the ship was off the planet, he could patch in an interface and alter the flight coordinates himself. As long as the last flight coordinates the computer had received were blank, or just somewhere else off this rock, he'd be home free, and his task would be complete.

The odds were in his favor.

He looked about. For some reason, the toilet was out of order. He looked at it and shook his head slightly, what an absurd reason to ground a ship.

He started the process of rewiring the ship for basic takeoff.

Garrat landed near Artun and tried to hide by the side of the building. "I just saw him going into hangar VS3."

Artun thought for a second. "Are you sure it was VS3? That's from the outpost," he queried. After all, the Newt may not have left his little universe for an eternity.

"It's whichever one has VS3 written in fifteen-foot-tall letters along its side," Garrat responded.

Artun suspected he could hear the sarcasm in his voice.

"It's two buildings over that way." Garrat gestured.

Artun started to run. The hangar being here meant that Triven had intentionally moved it from the Veltrid base to this location. The salvaged buildings were arranged at random about the flying city. To move it this close to the control room meant he must be planning on using it.

"Get up to the skies. I'll need you to keep a lookout in case he leaves." Artun shouted quickly and continued to run toward the hangar.

He quickened his pace. He was running at full tilt, but Triven had a head start.

Artun ran as fast as he could. He rounded the final building and before him was the hangar. It sat in front of him on the lawn, battle scarred.

His heart sank. In front of him, the closest and fastest entrance was the most decorative. It only led to the mezzanine floor and Triven was already inside. Artun kept running. He knew what this meant. He could catch Triven, but only if he took the mezzanine. To stop Triven, he would need to risk killing himself.

The exterior walls of the hangar were covered in dents from collisions with small meteoroids as it travelled here from the moon base. Artun reached the large decorated outer door of the building. This was the ceremonial entrance, the entrance for dignitaries. There was no access to the lower level here, but it was the fastest route. He yanked the door open hard, and the hinges groaned.

In front of him lay the carpeted steps, the lower level could only be accessed through other entrances, and he would lose too much valuable time trying to reach them.

Triven had to be stopped, now.

From the moment he touched the carpeted stairs he could feel the electricity building in his fur. By the time he was two steps in, his fur was standing on end. Artun kept moving forward, running up the stairs. Electricity was now arcing from his fur and a glow surrounded him. The more he ran, the more electrically charged he became.

By the time he reached the mezzanine he knew if he touched anything, there was no coming back. He moved onward, charges building in his body. The electricity tried to discharge, arcing about him and creating an aura a foot wide. A small dragonfly like creature exploded as it got too close.

Artun continued to push through, ignoring the danger. He was running towards the edge of the observation deck.

Chapter 37

Sardok flipped a switch on his box and brought down the interpersonal communication about the hanger. He started the takeoff sequence, sat back in the chair, and put his feet up on the navigation console. The ship gently rose into the air as he continued to work with the wires on his lap, connecting them with wires from the box on the floor next to him. There was a gentle creaking in the pipes, which was unexpected, but otherwise the ship seemed perfect.

He toggled one of the switches on his metal box to start raising the shields about the hangar. Once raised it would add to the confusion and buy him a little more time.

As the ship reached the height of the mezzanine level and began turning to leave, Sardok looked up to see a terrifying sight from the very edge of the viewscreen. It was wearing a Chief Security Officer's stripes, and was covered in streaming blue lightning, looking like some kind of angry, hairy god. It almost appeared as though someone had reanimated the zombie corpse of a bearskin rug and given it supernatural powers and a bad attitude.

The creature pointed its finger at the ship and seemed to shout something, but the sheer act of pointing a finger caused a huge arc of lightning to form before melting away.

The hair of the creature had spread out so much due to the static charge that it resembled an angry striped pom–pom.

Sardok watched, shocked, as the creature ran towards his ship and gathered speed. Part of his shock came from the god-like appearance of the creature, surrounded by a blue glow with lightning arcing out and vanishing. Part of the shock also came from the fact that this was not the type of behavior that one would expect of a pom–pom, angry or otherwise.

Artun raced along the carpet, every step increasing the charge stored in his body, lightning coming from his fur, searching for something to ground on. The communicator on his chest had started to 'beep' so he knew that his communications were down. He saw the ship starting to appear right in front of him, some ten feet past the edge of the mezzanine.

He roared in defiance as he saw it rising and turning, his anger growing as he thought of the communications, which were down, the locators, which were down, the relocating of the hangar, the sabotage of the Decimator, the sabotage of the Diplomatic Gateway Program, all of it happened under his watch. Most of all though he thought about how much he wanted to repay his debt for the carpets and for hurting Selim. He kept running, picking up his pace as he did so. He ran as fast as he could screaming all manner of obscenities. If this was how he was going to die, then he was taking this ship down with him.

He ran towards it, reaching the edge of the mezzanine, moving fast, surrounded by a blue light. His fur now charged to millions of volts. The carpet beneath his feet was immensely thick, its luxurious nature keeping his charge contained. He aimed for the craft rising before him. It was ten feet to the edge of the ship. He could land at the edge of the viewport and rip anything off it he could. He focused his anger at it and jumped, howling in rage as he did so. Looking down at the hangar floor he was shocked to see Triven lying unconscious on the floor. When he landed on the ship and saw Sardok through the edge of the viewport, he understood.

As the angry god reached the edge of the mezzanine, it threw itself, flying, into the air and landed, grabbing hold of the outside of the viewport. It was literally only feet from Sardok. Electricity arcing off of it in all directions. Sardok could see that it was Artun. Angry god–like Artun, but Artun none the less.

It occurred to Sardok that if he'd still been on the ground, the sheer act of touching the ship would have grounded the charge and killed him, but in the air, he was relatively safe. He admired that level of dedication. There was no way to ground the lightning that seemed to surround Artun.

Sardok started to find himself rather more concerned with the relative safety of the ship. This was especially true now Artun, who had become a giant fur-based death battery fueled by anger and static, was banging with all of his considerable strength on the outside of the ship. There were too many smaller pieces that he could damage.

"I really think it's about time we parted ways," said Sardok, looking directly at Artun, who seemed to be in some kind of rage. His anger only seemed to increase as he saw Sardok reach over and turn on the shield generator.

Artun was still hitting the window when Sardok turned the shield generators on.

The effect was instantaneous. Artun was in the space where the shield bubble would manifest. All of his fur and clothing were separated from him, and he was thrown outward, back onto the mezzanine floor with immense force as the shield activated.

He lay there naked on the carpet, panting, his rage dissipating, replaced only by an icy hatred.

Artun watched as the ship continued to turn. Sardok give him a little wave and the ship slowly pulled away, his fur and clothing stationary, stuck in the chrono-bubble. Blue light and occasional sparks flew slowly between some of the pieces indicating their immense charge.

Artun continued to watch the ship as he passed into unconsciousness.

Sardok took one last look at Artun on the ground and paused.

He paused a little longer.

"Dammit," he muttered, he only had about twenty seconds before the shields would finish raising up around the building. He reached across the console and fired a distress beacon next to Artun. Nobody was going to die today; he'd be found soon enough.

Sardok finished turning the ship until it pointed out of the hangar and left through the launch window.

Garrat flew high above the hangar, watching below to see if Triven would leave the building, occasionally casting his eye over other areas to ensure nobody one the ground was able to see a thirty-foot Newt flying in the sky. As he watched, a ship exited the building, lightning sparking in slow motion about its surface. Slowly, the security shields that covered the hangar started to rise.

He saw a large amount of black and white fur, as well as the remains of a shredded uniform on the shield of the ship and felt a surge of anger.

He dove towards the ship, his claws outstretched, but the ship rose into the air too quickly, reaching the edge of the atmosphere in seconds.

He cursed under his breath and flew quickly down to check on Artun as the shields about the hangar started to seal. He dove in through the main launch window, flying into the hangar as the shields closed behind him.

He saw Triven unconscious on the hangar floor and Artun, unconscious and furless, naked atop the mezzanine.

He flew down and picked up Triven in one of his large paws before flying up and over and carefully picking up Artun. He could feel Artun's internal injuries.

Garrat looked protectively at Artun, there was only one way he could get him to the medical bay quickly. "Better to live as a Newt than a Dragon," he muttered, and manifested a portal in the wall that led into his lair. He beat his large wings hard, lifting himself, Artun and Triven high into the air, and dove downward to get as much speed as he could. He flew through the portal, barely pausing, the wind whistled through the scales along his head and body, his wings folded back to allow him to fit.

He moved through his lair rapidly, the massive room rushed past him as he raced through it aiming for a portal he had made to the hospital in case the Emperor needed help.

He flew to the base of the stairs, poked his head through to check the placement of the room, and, reaching up with one paw, gently placed Artun onto the only bed.

He shuffled his position a little, reached up with his other paw and placed Triven through the portal and into the sink.

He jammed his head and neck through the portal and called out loudly, "casualties."

A few moments later the door burst open, and a doctor ran inside.

Selim stopped and stared at Garrat as she entered the room. "What the...?" she began.

Garrat cleared his throat. "I am a floating head," he began grandiosely attempting to wave his head eerily from side to side, unaware the reality distortion field was inactive.

Selim stared at the giant scaled head and neck of a near mythical creature stretching some eight feet through a hole where a picture of the Emperor had been hanging. At this point, the near mythical creature was pretending, rather unconvincingly, to be a floating head.

"You're a Newt," she whispered.

Garrat paused, realizing his mistake.

"Bugger," he muttered and tried to pull himself backward using his rear legs. It was at this point that he realized he had jammed his head and neck into the portal with such gusto that he was now stuck like a giant scaly wine cork. He tried to pull himself backward, putting ever more effort into the action.

He finally pulled himself through with such force that he hit his head on the top of the portal to his lair as he disappeared awkwardly, backward down the stairs, and back into his pocket dimension. When the two nurses arrived, they were just in time to see a swinging painting of the Emperor on a wall, behind which the portal was well hidden, Triven had been placed haphazardly in a sink and a perfectly smooth, hairless Artun was lying on a hospital bed.

"Artun?" said the doctor, surprised, as she looked a little closer at her new patient.

Selim pulled up a scanner from the edge of the bed and immediately began scanning him as the nurses checked for any external signs of trauma. She relieved the swelling in his brain and stymied the internal bleeding. She smiled as he seemed to flirt with consciousness. He would be fine.

"He looks quite banged up," one of the nurses commented.

"He's had worse," said the doctor with a little smile, her worries relieved. "Check on the other one and get another hospital bed and a gown."

She looked softly at Artun. "I imagine that this will take some getting used to," she continued. She reached down and held his hand. "You're going to wake up with quite the bruising," she smiled, relieved that he was safe.

"Move the beds to the shuttle and prepare to evacuate the patients." Selim commanded.

"Yes, doctor," they replied, wheeling Artun's bed towards the door as another bed was being wheeled in for Triven.

Selim walked towards the ground underneath the picture and picked up a scale of blue and gold. She flipped it over in her hand, placed it in her pocket, and went to join her patients in the medical transport.

Chapter 38

The Emperor barged through the door to the command center, followed rapidly by Ertic, the two ceremonial guards, who had been more than a little surprised to see so many people appear from a residence which nobody had entered, and the Emperor's cousin, who had now run himself out and collapsed in a sweating heap.

"What the hell is happening?" the Emperor demanded, exhausted as he unsteadily made his way towards the platform in the center of the room.

Sebastian was a little surprised by this as he had been expecting some sort of 'good job', or even an 'atta boy' so a 'what the hell' had left him rather taken aback.

He decided that this entire thing was probably just a misunderstanding.

"Just following orders, attacking the space creature and ensuring task separation," he replied cheerfully.

"Did you send a team of highly trained attack troops to pleasure the creature into submission?" the Emperor demanded forcefully.

"No," said Sebastian with certainty.

"Yes, he did," came a female voice from the navigation center.

"Pretty sure I didn't" said Sebastian feeling that if everything he knew about his existence in the Universe was shaken, the one thing he knew, maybe even the only thing he knew with absolute certainty, was that he didn't send a group of highly trained military pilots to pleasure some sort of giant space slug into submission.

The logistics alone would be terrifying.

"Yes, you did," came a voice from another part of the room.

"Nope," said Sebastian.

"What exactly did you say, Earth–man?" Ertic asked gruffly.

"I just asked if they thought they could win," Sebastian replied.

"That's not what you asked," came the female voice from navigation once more.

"Oh, go fill your boots with Shaa'ving cream," Sebastian muttered, feeling a little irate.

"What exactly did he ask?" the Emperor demanded through clenched teeth.

"He asked them if they thought they could pull it off," said the female voice again.

"Thank you for your clarification," said the Emperor, glaring at Sebastian.

"You're welcome, Sir," said the voice, standing up and smiling at Sebastian. He recognized her as the woman whose workstation he had defiled as a toilet. She seemed to be enjoying this.

"Stupid language," muttered Ertic.

"Do you think you could call them back?" the Emperor asked, his teeth still clenched.

"Certainly," said Sebastian, feeling rather uneasy at the mistake.

He pushed a button on the arm of the chair. "Attack team: Pull back."

The Emperor's jaw dropped, and his eyes widened.

"Engaging tractor beams now," came the reply.

"Dammit, why are they engaging the tractor beams?" Sebastian muttered as the Emperor began to shake. He hit the button again. "Pull back," he shouted into the arm of the chair.

"There's no change, nothing's moving," came the response.

"What's wrong with you?" muttered the Emperor, clearly shaken.

Sebastian suddenly realized his mistake and tried to word it differently. "Turn around," he said, his voice starting to halter, as his own eyes widened.

"Do you think that'll help?" he asked.

"What?" said Sebastian.

The Emperor was now in shock.

"Whatever it takes," came the response once more. "Exposing the rear of the spaceship to the creature, attempting erotic movements."

Everything stopped. The Emperor was shaking his head, his mouth open in disbelief. Ertic was watching Sebastian in shocked horror and Sebastian was just looking between the two.

Sh'ockley jumped onto her desk, Shaa'ving cream coming from the top of one of her boots. With a leap, she jumped from the top of her desk and over the partition. She ran up to the command seat, pushed one of the buttons on the arm of the chair and called out, "return to base on the orders of the Emperor."

She held Sebastian's eye.

"Stupid language," Ertic kept muttering and shaking his head.

"You're in my seat," she whispered.

"You're not my boss," Sebastian retorted quietly.

"Not yet," she said firmly, continuing to hold his gaze.

After a few seconds, the Emperor regained some composure.

"Are they returning?" he asked, a tinge of desperation in his voice.

"Yes Sir," replied Sh'ockley.

He breathed a sigh of relief.

"Human, I don't doubt your motives, but I think your time in the chair is at an end." He turned to the Communications Officer. "I think we would do well to have you replace him, for the time being, at least."

"Your Excellence," she responded.

Sebastian felt a flood of relief that he was finally able to relinquish the command.

The Emperor approached Sebastian, reached up and

removed the band from around his head.

Sebastian got up from the chair and the Communications Officer sat down.

"What is your name?" the Emperor asked her.

"Second Lieutenant Sh'ockley, Sir," she replied.

"I've heard good things about you, Sub-Commander Sh'ockley," the Emperor said as he placed the band on her head.

"I'll try to live up to your expectations, Sir," she said confidently, beaming with pride at her new title.

"We're getting a distress beacon from a hangar," said a voice from communications.

"Send security to investigate," replied Sub-Commander Shockley as she adjusted the chair to her preference.

"One of the ships has just taken off and I can't establish a link with it," said one of the remaining navigations officers.

"Who is on the ship?" Ertic demanded.

"Unable to tell, Sir. All the monitoring systems have been disabled. There also seems to be a localized communications blackout around that hanger," he replied.

"Triven," Ertic said, looking at the Emperor.

"He asked if he could go up and attack the creature with his squadron," Sebastian said helpfully.

"Seems that Triven may be the person who's been sabotaging our efforts, possibly for years," Ertic said.

"Can't you just pilot the ship back?" Sebastian asked helpfully.

"There's no response. He must have manually disabled the remote uplink as well," said the Navigation Officer.

"If he's disabled the uplink, then the ship will be locked on course to its last programmed destination. It will take him time to override that internally," Sub-Commander Sh'ockley said thoughtfully. "Where was the last course set to?" she asked, looking over at the navigation team.

One of the lieutenants was looking back at her, his eyes wide.

Chapter 39

Sardok sat in the pilot seat as the planet below him gradually faded away. He pulled up the metal box, checking connection points. He couldn't shake the feeling that he'd seen a Newt flash past him as the ship rose. He knew they were real. He'd seen one once as a child. His father had said he wanted to show him something special, and they had gone to an isolated planet somewhere in the Vega system. They'd concealed themselves behind a tree and watched as it glided effortlessly about the sky. It had been glorious as it swooped and spun in the air.

It would explain why the Emperor was able to move so quickly about the citadel, something which he had been trying to figure out for years. It didn't explain where he'd found one though. He finished checking the connection points.

"This should do it," he muttered.

He started to unfurl some of the wires when he looked out of the window again and saw that the stars were gone. Sardok stared a little longer trying to get a sense of his proximity to the creature. He was almost upon it.

"Dammit," he muttered, "What course did they set? This is way too close for an attack vector."

He rushed to remove the wires and refinish them. Between him and the creature, making it more difficult to see, was Artun's clothing and fur, still shooting lightning in slow motion.

The sounds from the piping had moved far beyond gentle now and were starting to screech.

"What the hell?" he said, as he started to hear parts of the pipes buckling from the straining in an effort to maintain their structure.

He tried to work faster, the noise was increasing, as was his proximity to the creature.

The creature, for its part, was at the beginning of a rare cycle where it would shed back outer layers of its body armor and neutron shielding, leaving itself exposed, and allowing it to relieve itself.

This was such a rare event that no person had ever witnessed it before.

It was, however, currently being witnessed on the long–range scanners by the crew in the command room.

"Where did you send it?" Sh'ockley demanded.

A seasoned Navigation Officer sat looking rather uncomfortable under this current scrutiny. He appeared to be hoping to gain the skill to teleport instantly somewhere else.

"I was aiming approximately at where the creature's lower abdomen.... should be," he sounded unsure as his voice tailed off. "To er..." He cleared his throat. "To help pull it off," he finished.

"So that's where it is now?" she asked.

"It's a living thing, so it was a best guess for position, and it seems to have moved a little from its projected path," he said.

"The creature's armor seems to be parting," said the Science Officer.

"What's happening?" Ertic asked.

"It's definitely parting its external armor," came the response.

"Why?" Ertic asked.

"Absolutely no idea," the officer responded.

"So, where is the ship?" Sh'ockley demanded once more.

"It seems to be approaching the newly exposed region."

"What do you think it is?" asked Sh'ockley.

The Science Officer paused, thinking as hard as he could about all the species he'd studied. There were, as far as he could think, two possibilities, the unpleasant and the unthinkable.

He decided to go with the unpleasant, as he *really* didn't want to think about the other one.

"I think it's readying itself. Preparing to get rid of waste," he responded. "If that's what I think it is, then any second the ship could enter the urethra," he replied, horrified.

"That thing has a urethra?" the Emperor asked.

"And you can fit a spaceship in it?" Ertic continued.

"Maybe. It looks to have multiple urethra," the officer answered, "If he has the shields up, he'll likely make it through any obstructions by being bounced about. If not, I guess we'll see if it has a pain response."

Sub-Commander Sh'ockley sat with a look of distaste on her face. "Keep monitoring," she said.

Sardok looked up again at the window. He was much closer to that creature than he wanted to be. He was working furiously. He quickly attached a safety belt to himself before carefully slicing through the main power supply wire that powered the artificial gravity, the lights and the consoles.

Everything in the craft, that was not fixed down, began to rise. The lights started to flicker and then turned off as most of the internal functions of the craft powered down.

It was at this point that the recycling system on the craft, which had been pushed beyond all engineering tolerances, gave up with an almighty screech and a pop. The main containment lines exploded under the pressure, emptying all of their contents into the same room as Sardok.

The bodily excretions of twenty-three Callaxian marines and one human exploded under high pressure into the cabin.

Sardok could barely breathe because of the stench of the waste now drifting, weightless, everywhere about the craft. He let go of the wires and they floated off.

He composed himself as best he could, but he couldn't see anything. He undid the safety belt and floated towards the main viewport, wiping it down with his sleeve.

Eventually, he cleared enough of a space on the viewport that he could use the glow from outside to illuminate the cockpit.

He floated towards the wires once more and connected the box turning the power back on and bringing back the artificial gravity. This caused all the excrement and bodily waste to plop onto the floor, making a sound like marsh gas bubbling through a mud vent.

The lights came back on, exposing a scene of horror that no public toilet has thankfully ever seen.

A damp, rancid, coupon sat on the floor offering a two for one deal.

"The human did this?" he said, his eyes wide.

He turned and looked out of the viewport past the frozen lightning. "Is that some kind of tunnel in space?" he asked himself aloud.

The ship was violently buffeted about and, for twenty seconds, Sardok found himself unable to even stand, as he was thrown about the cockpit. Eventually it stopped, and he pulled himself unsteadily back to his feet, now completely covered in the excrement that surrounded him. He looked outside once more.

Out of the viewport he could see a vast system, lit by an eerie glow in the center. It contained hundreds of pulsating luminous blue structures that looked like a series of interconnected giant brains.

He was still choking on the smell, "Where the hell am I?" he asked of nobody in particular, which was probably for the best, as he really wouldn't have liked the answer had somebody been there to give it.

He finished connecting the remaining wires.

A small message on the box flashed, 'Ready to integrate control.'

He hit a button, and the control box began integration with the entire ship.

"Finally," he muttered, relieved but still reeling from the
stench.

"Plot a course to the nearest Ventrian base," he commanded.
The Ventrians were neutral. That meant they'd happily trade
for his safe passage, and he could finish dealing with this
mess.

'Course plotted,' flashed the box. 'Reboot the system to
consolidate control.'

"Sub-Commander, we're receiving a message from the
medical evacuation team, the First Officer from the Veltrid
Sector Command and Chief Security Officer Artun also from
the Veltrid Sector are being evacuated." Came a voice from
one of the remaining Communications Officers.

"Then who's in the ship?" asked the Emperor.

A silence descended for a moment.

"It can't be," said Ertic. "Number Two - Sardok?"

"That would explain the sealing of the files." Said the
Emperor. "If Sardok had Triven's access, then Triven would
never see the files, unless he specifically looked for them.
They'd be almost invisible, and everything would lead back to
the First in Command."

Sardok reached down and pushed a small button to begin
the system wide reboot.

Gradually the lights, air recycling and the shields powered
down, before powering back up again.

Unfortunately for Sardok, while this action did indeed
provide the capacity for the metal box controller to gain
control of the ship's main systems, it also released about
thirty-five pounds of black and white hairs, each at several
million volts into the multitudinous testicular sacs of a giant
space slug.

The hairs rapidly separated, forced apart by their enormous
electrical charge and quickly spread throughout the creature's
testicle sacs before embedding themselves in near unison.

Until this point in history, it was always assumed that it was impossible to propel a craft faster than the speed of light through some sort of pushing, or propulsion action.

This is no longer regarded as a hard and fast rule.

While some rules of physics can be bent and some broken, this one was warped.

The slug seemed almost to crumple into itself as tens of millions of highly charged hairs, each at several million volts simultaneously discharged in multiple locations about its gonads.

The ship, along with Sardok, was ejected from the slug's urethra at a speed so fast that it gave out a blue glow just before vanishing, as if it was never there.

On a curious note, for the bystanders watching, it appeared as if a fast–moving object actually flew towards the slug's urethra. It was only the blue cone of light that rapidly emanated out that told the story of the speed and direction of the craft.

The slug slowly started to change course, beginning its journey onward to a different star system in search of a small moon to fall asleep on. The creature, however, remembered Sardok and his ship, and would think of them fondly for some time to come.

Chapter 40

"What's happening up there?" the Emperor demanded.

"Report," said Sub-Commander Sh'ockley.

"The creature looks like it's convulsing," the officer replied. "It seems to have emitted something. That's not possible," he said, looking confused.

"What's not possible?" Ertic asked.

"An object was just emitted at superluminal speeds," the officer said.

"What?" asked the Communications Officer.

"It was emitted at superluminal speeds and then it just… vanished," replied the officer, clearly stunned.

"What about the creature?" demanded the Emperor.

"It's still convulsing, but the readings are different," he paused, uncertain, "it might be changing course." Everything in the control room stopped as the Communications Officer watched the screen closely. There were inputs coming in from the science officers as well as engineering as they worked to chart its course.

He watched the monitor as the minutes continued onward. Silence filled the room as the Communications Officer continued to review the feedback he was receiving. It was being updated every few seconds with constant calculations for the creature's trajectory. A hundred satellites passed data, giving accuracy to within centimeters of its position.

The silence continued to fill the room as everybody held their collective breath.

After five minutes, an analysis for the changing positional data came in from the science desk and they passed it to engineering, awaiting confirmation.

They confirmed the analysis and passed it to communications.

"It is!" he said, euphorically, continuing to examine the information.

"Keep watching the creature," said the Emperor, excitement audible in his voice and his eyes wide. "Hold all evacuations unless it changes back to an intercept course. Remain on high alert."

As the hours began to pass, the slug moved ever farther from the planet. Slowly the ships that had left started to return.

In the pocket of an unconscious Triven, a small pyramid sat and smiled to itself.

Now things were getting interesting.

Chapter 41

The ship appeared in a flash as the craft slowed to a sub luminal speed, waves of blue light emanating from the space about the hull.

The viewport window at the front of the ship held a view of an unfamiliar star system.

Sardok found himself on the rear wall of the ship, half–way up and surrounded by filth. He seemed to be affixed to the surface. The stench of the room filled his nostrils and covered him from head to foot.

Sardok fought to maintain his thoughts. He needed to prioritize and repair any damage. Parts of the ship that weren't supposed to fizzle were definitely beginning to fizzle, and one part even popped. A small blinking light on the control panel went out. That was never supposed to happen.

"Is there a habitable planet nearby?" he asked struggling to maintain his composure with the smell.

A small message flashed on the metal control box.

It said 'Yes.'

"Take us to the planet, scan it thoroughly, land and find out where we are," he said, trying to contain himself while dealing with an odor so horrendous that he could barely hold ideas in his head.

Sardok pushed himself away from the edge of the wall. Parts of his clothing and some of his hair seemed to have fused with the rear wall of the ship. Tragically, for him, the jump to faster than light travel had somehow forced all the waste that had been ejected onto that same rear wall with him.

The ship circled the planet, gathering information.

Eventually, it finished. Sardok looked around, concerned, as more of the lights on the control desk seemed to turn off, one at a time.

The metal box flashed a message 'planetary scans complete'.

"Triangulate our position from the stars. Take us in to land," Sardok commanded.

The ship descended with the grace of a bowl of jelly, unwillingly going down some stairs. It came to rest on a beach at the edge of a lush forest, the water lapping quietly along the shore.

Sardok lowered the ramp and rushed into the fresh air. He ran down to the water, tested it tentatively, and then began furiously cleaning himself off.

After a while, he stopped and stormed back to the ship to retrieve his box. He pulled the cables off with less care than he could have, desperate to escape the overwhelming smell of the ship.

He removed the box and quickly made his way outside once more into the fresh air and returned to the shoreline to continue cleaning himself off.

"Where are we?" he demanded of the box.

'Processing data, attempting triangulation,' the message flashed on the box.

After a few moments, the box flashed another message.

'Stars triangulated, accounting for chronal displacement,'.

Sardok had returned to desperately cleaning the stench from himself and completely failed to read the message.

'Location identified, loading all known information on the planet.' The box flashed once more.

Sardok continued cleaning himself off, suddenly aware that there was every possibility his objective had been achieved. The Callaxians had abandoned their home planet, at least temporarily, and he was done. Suddenly he felt a vast wave of relief. This was masked slightly by the smell, but it was definitely there.

"Suggest a course of action to ensure the objective has been completed," Sardok demanded, slowly feeling like the stench was starting to fade.

The box flashed again, this time he read it.

'Temporal adjustments, care required, no deviation allowed.'

"What does that mean?" he asked, clearly annoyed.

The box flashed a message.

"Oh God, no." he muttered, a deeply haunted look crossing his face as he sank to his knees.

On the box, two little red words continued to flash.

"Build wall."

Chapter 42

Six thousand years ago, around lunchtime, in the Anatolian region of Turkey, a group of humans were huddled around a fire. They were telling each other stories when their peaceful relaxation was rudely interrupted by an ungodly roar.

Carefully, they snuck up to where they heard the noise and peered through the bushes.

They saw a creature, the stench of which had already reached them. He seemed to be possessed of a rage and had brought his cave with him. His cave was a huge latrine.

They watched him a while until their curiosity gave way to wariness, eventually deciding that they didn't want anything to do with a creature who used a perfectly good cave as a toilet.

They threw some rocks at him and ran away.

If you are interested in updates to see how the next book is coming along then please check at:

www.MikeAlread.com

If you are interested in seeing how my wrestling with building a website that doesn't want to play ball is going, or more specifically, what the end result of a hairy primate bashing random keys on space age technology might be, then please check at:

www.MikeAlread.com

It will probably be going badly.

However, if you enjoyed this book and wish to tell others then please feel free to jump onto whichever website doesn't move fast enough and tell someone. But only if you want to, please don't feel obliged.

As an interesting side-note, in order to fully realize the book I had to create a new word, cistine - of or related to cisterns. "Pristine, cistine, monument to stonework."

I cannot imagine it will ever catch on, or perhaps even ever be used again, but it just seemed to fit beautifully.

Have a wonderful day, and stay awesome!
Best wishes - Mike.

Made in the USA
Coppell, TX
11 March 2025